WRECKED INTEL (IMMORTAL OUTCASTS®)

An Immortal Ops® World Novel

MANDY M. ROTH

Wrecked Intel (Immortal Outcasts) © Copyright August, 2019, Mandy M. Roth

ALL RIGHTS RESERVED.

All books copyrighted to the author and may not be resold or given away without written permission from the author, Mandy M. Roth®.

Mandy M. Roth®, Immortal Ops ®, PSI-Ops®, Immortal Outcasts®, and Paranormal Security and Intelligence Ops Shadow Agents® are registered trademarks of Raven Happy Hour, LLC

Paranormal Security and Intelligence (TM)

This novel is a work of fiction. Any and all characters, events, and places are of the author's imagination and should not be confused with fact. Any resemblance to persons, living or dead, or events or places is merely coincidence. The book is fictional and not a how-to. As always, in real life practice good judgment in all situations. Novel intended for adults only. Must be 18 years or older to read.

Published by Raven Happy Hour, LLC

Oxford, MS 38655

www.ravenhappyhour.com

Raven Books and all affiliate sites and projects are © Copyrighted 2004—2019

"Mandy M Roth is a true master of her craft! Her breathtaking stories sweep me up, mesmerize and leave me desperate for more. She is my drug of choice!"

- Gena Showalter, *New York Times* bestselling author

"Roth has the kind of characters and books that leave you hungry for more and stay with you long after the last page is read. One word sums up her writing style-addictive!"

- Shannon Mayer, USA TODAY bestselling author

"Roth writes from the heart, and her characters and worlds are guaranteed to suck the reader in and hold them hostage until the very last page!"

NYT Bestselling Author, Yasmine Galenorn

"The perfect mix of sizzling romance and heart-pounding action. If you like your heroes smoking hot…and not quite human, you can't go wrong with a Mandy M. Roth book." – **Laurie**

London, NYT and USA Today bestselling author

Suggested Reading Order of Books Released to Date in the Immortal Ops Series World

Immortal Ops
Critical Intelligence
Radar Deception
Strategic Vulnerability
Tactical Magik
Act of Mercy
Administrative Control
Act of Surrender
Broken Communication
Separation Zone
Act of Submission
Damage Report
Act of Command
Wolf's Surrender
The Dragon Shifter's Duty

Midnight Echoes
Isolated Maneuver
Expecting Darkness
Area of Influence
Act of Passion
Act of Brotherhood
Healing the Wolf
Wrecked Intel
Bound by Midnight
And more…

This list is NOT up to date. Please check MandyRoth.com for the most current release list.

More to come (check www.mandyroth.com for new releases)

Books in each series within the Immortal Ops World.
This list is NOT up to date. To see an updated list of the books within each series under the umbrella of the Immortal Ops World please visit MandyRoth.com. Mandy is always releasing new books within the series world. Sign up for her

newsletter at MandyRoth.com to never miss a new release.

You can read each individual series within the world, in whatever order you want…

PSI-Ops: Paranormal Security and Intelligence

Act of Mercy
Act of Surrender
Act of Submission
Act of Command
Act of Passion
Act of Brotherhood
And more…
(see Mandy's website & sign up for her newsletter for notification of releases)

Immortal Ops:

Immortal Ops
Critical Intelligence
Radar Deception

Strategic Vulnerability
Tactical Magik
Administrative Control
Separation Zone
Area of Influence
And more…
(see Mandy's website & sign up for her newsletter for notification of releases)

Immortal Outcasts:

Broken Communication
Damage Report
Isolated Maneuver
Wrecked Intel
And more…
(see Mandy's website & sign up for her newsletter for notification of releases)

Paranormal Security and Intelligence Ops: Shadow Agents

Wolf's Surrender
The Dragon Shifter's Duty

Healing the Wolf
And more…
(see Mandy's website & sign up for her newsletter for notification of releases)

Paranormal Security and Intelligence Ops: Crimson Ops Series

Midnight Echoes
Expecting Darkness
Bound by Midnight
And more…
(see Mandy's website & sign up for her newsletter for notification of releases)

Paranormal Regulators Series and Clear Sight Division Operatives (Part of the Immortal Ops World) Coming Soon!

Immortal Ops Series Helper

Immortal Ops (I-Ops) Team Members

Lukian Vlakhusha: Alpha-Dog-One. Team captain, werewolf, King of the Lycans. Book: Immortal Ops (Immortal Ops)

Geoffroi (Roi) Majors: Alpha-Dog-Two. Second-in-command, werewolf, blood-bound brother to Lukian. Book: Critical Intelligence (Immortal Ops)

Doctor Thaddeus Green: Bravo-Dog-One. Scientist, tech guru, werepanther. Book: Radar Deception (Immortal Ops)

Jonathon (Jon) Reynell: Bravo-Dog-Two. Sniper, weretiger. Book: Separation Zone (Immortal Ops)

Wilson Rousseau: Bravo-Dog-Three. Resident

smart-ass, wererat. Book: Strategic Vulnerability (Immortal Ops)

Eadan Daly: Alpha-Dog-Three. PSI-Op and handler on loan to the I-Ops to round out the team, Fae. Book: Tactical Magik (Immortal Ops)

Lance Toov: Werepanther and vampire hybrid. Book: Area of Influence (Immortal Ops)

Colonel Asher Brooks: Chief of Operations and point person for the Immortal Ops Team. Book: Administrative Control (Immortal Ops)

Paranormal Security and Intelligence (PSI) Operatives

General Jack C. Newman: Director of Operations for PSI North American Division, werelion. Adoptive father of Missy Carter-Majors

Duke Marlow: PSI-Operative, werewolf. Book: Act of Mercy (PSI-Ops)

Doctor James (Jimmy) Hagen: PSI-Operative, werewolf. Took a ten-year hiatus from PSI. Book: Act of Surrender (PSI-Ops)

Striker (Dougal) McCracken: PSI-Operative, werewolf

Carbrey (Car) McCracken: PSI-Operative, werewolf

Macbeth (Mac) McCracken: PSI-Operative, werewolf

Theodoar (Teddy) Beckert: PSI-Operative, werebear

Miles (Boomer) Walsh: PSI-Operative, werepanther. Book: Act of Submission (PSI-Ops)

Captain Corbin Jones: Operations coordinator and captain for PSI-Ops Team Five, werelion. Book: Act of Command (PSI-Ops)

Malik (Tut) Nasser: PSI-Operative, werelion. Book: Act of Passion (PSI-Ops)

Colonel Ulric Lovett: Director of Operations, PSI-London Division

Dr. Sambora: PSI-Operative, (PSI-Ops)

Garth Ingersson: PSI-Operative, werewolf. Book: Act of Brotherhood

Rurik Romanov: PSI-Operative, werebear

Johannes "Hans" Bach: PSI-Operative

Jannick Bach: PSI-Operative

Immortal Outcasts

Casey Black: I-Ops test subject, werewolf. Book: Broken Communication

Weston Carol: I-Ops test subject, werebear. Book: Damage Report

Bane Antonov: I-Ops test subject, weregorilla. Book: Isolated Maneuver

Cody Livingston: I-Ops test subject, wereshark. Book: Wrecked Intel

Wheeler Summerbee: I-Ops test subject, vampire hybrid

Ace Hargraves: I-Ops test subject, werehorse

Paranormal Security and Intelligence Ops: Shadow Agents

Bradley Durant: PSI-Ops: Shadow Agent Division, werewolf. Book: Wolf's Surrender

Ezra: PSI-Ops: Shadow Agent Division, dragon-shifter

Caesar: PSI-Ops: Shadow Agent Division, werewolf

Gram Campbell: Shadow Agent Division, werewolf and magik. Book: Healing the Wolf

Armand Faucher: Shadow Agent Division, vampire

Seth: Shadow Agent Division, vampire. One of the founders of the Crimson Ops Division.

Paranormal Security and Intelligence Ops: Crimson Ops Division

Bhaltair: Crimson-Ops: Fang Gang, vampire. Book: Midnight Echoes

Labrainn: Crimson-Ops: Fang Gang, vampire

Auberi Bouchard: Crimson-Ops: Fang Gang, vampire

Searc Macleod: Crimson-Ops: Fang Gang, vampire. Book: Expecting Darkness

Daniel Townsend: Crimson-Ops: Fang Gang, vampire

Blaise Regnier: Crimson-Ops: Fang Gang, vampire

Philandros "Landros" Mires: Crimson-Ops: Fang Gang, vampire

Paranormal Regulators

Stamatis Emathia: Paranormal Regulator, vampire

Whitney: Paranormal Regulator, werewolf

Cormag Buchanan: Paranormal Regulator, master vampire

Erik: Paranormal Regulator, shifter

Shane: Paranormal Regulator, shifter

Blurb

Wrecked Intel (Immortal Outcasts)
by
Mandy M. Roth

Operative: Cody Livingston (Shark-Shifter)

Wereshark and former Immortal Op Cody Livingston has spent decades keeping his head down and staying off the grid. Ever since he volunteered to be part of a test group when the government attempted to create super soldiers, he's been in a fight for his life and those of the men he sees as brothers—fellow Outcasts. You see, his own government turned against him when the DNA manipulation attempts didn't go as planned.

Now Cody spends his days trying to right the wrongs left in the wake of the experiments and protecting any innocents caught in the crossfire. This is easier said than done when he's had to escape the clutches of a madman hell-bent on possessing Cody's healing gifts and longevity. As old foes resurface, the stakes get even higher when Cody realizes he not only has a mate but that she's in the crosshairs of the enemy as well.

To Jenn, Shane, and Kelli for setting aside everything to help make this book a reality. I couldn't have done it without you. You are an amazing support team!
To the fans of the Immortal Ops Series World for letting me do what I love to do in each and every story. Thank you!

Note from Author:
_____

While this book is a stand-alone title, I highly recommend reading *Isolated Maneuver, Act of Passion,* and *Healing the World* first for maximum reading enjoyment.

I hope you enjoy the fruits of my labor. I spent many hours and much brain power taking courses about sharks and marine life as well as researching it all in hopes of making Cody's story the best it could possibly be. Any errors are my own and not that of the professors, instructors, and so on. I ask that you give me a bit of leeway, especially considering I'm asking you to believe a man can turn into a great white shark. LOL

To see a full list of the recommended reading

order the Ops Series World please visit Mandy's website. You can find it on the Immortal Ops Series page. Be sure you're signed up for newsletter updates for information about the next book's release.

Chapter One

SEVENTEEN YEARS AGO...OFF THE COAST OF COSTA RICA

CODY LIVINGSTON STARED at the bonfire before him, his beer in one hand, and a guitar propped near him in the sand as he sat on a beach blanket. The night air had a slight chill to it, which wasn't exactly normal for that time of year in Costa Rica, so the bonfire was a welcome addition. Next to him was a sexy brunette (whose name he didn't bother to catch or ask) who was downing yet another beer while she wore a bikini that covered next to nothing.

Not that he was complaining. Looking at her was no hardship by any means.

But he was pretty sure she should have stopped drinking several beers back. She and her girlfriends were in Costa Rica celebrating the upcoming marriage of one of them and had all flown from California to spend a week letting their hair down and apparently their panties as well.

If Cody was right, the bride-to-be was currently down the beach a way, having sex with two surfers she'd been hitting on earlier at the bar that was a short walk from the bonfire. What he did know for a fact was that neither of the surfers the woman was boning was her soon-to-be husband.

Cody didn't care one way or the other about the morality of what was going on. If the people involved were all consenting adults and having a good time, it wasn't his business. Sticking his nose in their affairs wasn't something he planned to do. It wasn't as if the woman was *his* soon-to-be wife or anything.

He snorted.

Not that he'd ever had one of those.

A wife. Soon-to-be or otherwise.

Hell, he didn't even have someone who could be labeled a girlfriend, let alone a steady one. He slept with a different woman each time the need for sex hit him, which was often, with his condition as an alpha male shifter. He didn't bother with things as trivial as names of the women he slept with or whether they were married. He wasn't exactly proud of that but since it was his truth, he didn't much care. He didn't need to know their names or relationship status. It wasn't as if he'd see them again. They were aware he wasn't in it for anything more than sex. He was never shy about stating as much upfront.

No need to promise something he'd never deliver—commitment.

To date, no woman had turned him down. Hell, he rarely, if ever, needed to ask. They just offered themselves up to him. The woman beside him had more than hinted at wanting sex from him already.

Any other time he'd have been all about banging a hot chick, but he'd been off his game the last few nights. The urge for sex wasn't there. And if it was, he hadn't noticed it over the unease and anxiety that had been at the forefront as of late.

The woman giggled and tugged on his arm, nearly making him spill his beer. She had one of those laughs that was off…forced. As if she didn't really find whatever it was that had prompted the laughing funny. Maybe she thought she was being cute. Or that her laugh was sexy.

He could assure her. It wasn't.

The hiccup that followed made him wonder just how far in the bag she was.

While Cody had made sure she and her friends weren't driving, he'd had no luck convincing any of them to slow down on the drinking. While he may not give two shits about their marital status, he did care about drunk driving. Innocents could end up hurt.

He was no role model, as he took another drink of his own beer. Then again, he wasn't driving anywhere. The small beach bungalow he was renting temporarily was just up the beach a short walking distance. It didn't matter that with his shifter metabolism, he would have to drink ten to twenty times more than a human just to feel the effects. It wasn't in him to put other people's lives on the line, and that was what someone did when they got behind the wheel impaired.

Since he wasn't driving, he was doing his best to make that ten to twenty times more drinking thing a reality. He wanted to numb himself. Specifically, his overactive brain. While it wasn't impossible for him to get drunk, it took some doing.

He needed something to take the edge off his current tense state. He didn't like feeling this way. Feeling worked up for no reason. Saying he'd been agitated was putting it mildly.

He glanced over at his longtime friend, Wheeler Summerbee, to find the man was kissing a sexy blonde who was also in a barely there string bikini. Evidently, the group of women shopped together at a store that was all about conserving fabric.

And bless that store for that fact.

Wheeler's current make-out partner was a member of the wedding party too, as noted by the sash she wore proclaiming her to be the maid of honor. Ironically, the sash had far more fabric to it than her bikini. She'd also been the one to encourage the bride to take off and have as much fun as she could before she got married.

Wheeler had picked a real winner.

The woman next to Cody ran her hand up his back and leaned in closer. She trailed a finger over the tribal tattoo on his upper arm. It was of a shark.

"Tiger shark?" she asked. "Or bull?"

Cody nearly took offense at the fact she'd guessed the wrong shark, two times in a row. "Uh, no. Great white."

She shuddered. "They scare me. I wish they'd gather up all the sharks and kill them. Make the waters safe for us."

Cody's jaw set. He did not share her opinion.

Then again, he was biased.

Even if he wouldn't have been able to change fully into a great white shark, he'd have taken exception with her comment and way of thinking. Sharks were vital to the ecosystem. Only dumbasses thought otherwise. Since it was clear her attributes didn't extend to brain power, he kept his mouth shut.

It would have been easy to launch into a diatribe on the decimation of a species, but he had a feeling the entire talk would go right over the woman's head. She didn't seem the type to have deep talks about anything other than the latest gossip about what celebrity was dating who and why. She'd also spent a good thirty minutes updating another of the women on what had happened on a television show she was obsessed with. Cody had never heard of it, but that wasn't a huge shock. He didn't watch much television or

Chapter Two
_____

AS CODY SWAM in full shark mode, he reflected on his loss of control on the beach hours ago and what had prompted it. He still wasn't entirely sure what the catalyst had been, but he did know it wasn't a great sign that he was struggling as hard as he was with his shark. Even remaining in shark form, swimming for hours, past the point of dawn and now well into the morning light, had done nothing to help take the edge off what he'd been feeling.

The beast was still restless. It was as if it were hunting for something or someone.

Not hunting, he thought.

Searching.

Yes, that was it. The shark was searching for

something or someone but felt no real need to clue Cody in on more details. Instantly, he was hit with visions from his dreams. Impressions of someone needing him. Of mortal danger.

Of death.

A tugging started deep in the pit of his stomach. It was as if he'd been caught on a fishing line, but without a hook or any tangible item. The feeling of being needed washed over him, filling every inch of him as he increased the speed with which he swam. He shot forward with purpose, despite the end goal being a mystery. Deep within, he knew it had something to do with the recurring dreams. The ones of someone he cared deeply for being in mortal danger.

The shark was still on a mission. Still searching for whoever or whatever it was on the hunt for.

Before long, he was near the waters of a protected area. The spot had been given protected status some time ago to help with the marine wildlife there. But that did nothing to stop the illegal poaching that occurred all the time.

More than once he'd heard talk of fishing vessels chumming the waters there to draw in as many sharks as they could. Shark fins were a hot commodity in certain countries. Shark fin soup was something of a delicacy, said to be beneficial to the health. In reality, it was something the elite treated themselves to at the expense of an entire species.

Finning was the practice of catching sharks, cutting off their fins to sell for shark fin soups, Eastern medicines, and whatnot, and then dumping the gravely injured shark back into the ocean to die. Shark populations were suffering because of the massacres, and if finning was left unchecked, sharks would die out.

People who feared sharks would think that was a good thing—like the hot chick who had wanted to do him back on the beach. Until they realized how vital sharks were to the ecosystem. Not that the woman would have grasped that concept.

The act of finning was disgusting, and if given a chance, he'd totally allow his shark side to munch on as many of the men partaking in the act as it saw fit.

He had half a mind to take the lead from his shark side and steer away from the fishing area, near a small island, but the shark seemed adamant they continue onward. Wanting to see how it played out, Cody didn't protest.

It was then he sensed something was off.

Danger.

Serious fucking danger.

But the inner alarm wasn't sounding for himself—no, it was for someone else.

The very same panicked feeling that he'd felt when waking from the nightmare came back to him tenfold. The shark did its version of acting out by moving like a torpedo through the water, right at the fishing vessels that lay ahead.

For a split second, Cody thought the shark would ram one of the vessels.

The beast wasn't fond of steel cages or certain metals used in the hulls of some boats. It disrupted its system of sense organs along its lateral line—the ampullae of Lorenzini. The shark had been known to charge more than one steel diving cage in its time. Thankfully, more and more cages were being constructed out of aluminum, which was all around better, as it didn't rust either.

He'd come up against things that overloaded his sensors and senses in the past, but this was different.

This wasn't confusion and sensory overload.

This was calculated yet frantic.

Help.

Someone needed his help.

It was then he picked up on the telltale sounds of splashing and the faint beating of a heart. He knew without being told the heartbeat was human. For a fraction of a second, his heartbeat fell into sync with the one he was hearing, as if the two hearts were beating as one.

The feeling passed and when it did, he heard the other heartbeat beginning to fade, to slow, and everything in him went on high alert.

No!

The shark veered off in the direction the sound of distress was coming from, and for a moment, the morning sunlight that was piercing through the water near the surface made it hard for Cody to make out what he was seeing. Then, it took his mind even longer to process it all.

It was a child.

A little girl, to be exact.

And she was sinking in the water, on her rapid descent, as blood floated around her.

She was hurt, and if what he was hearing was correct, she was dying.

Like hell!

Cody shut off, his mind a blur of panic and

rage. Why was a little girl out in the middle of the ocean, sinking like a rock, with no one around to help her?

His senses told him he wasn't the only predator in the area. That all the blood from the finning, combined with that of the child, was attracting other species of sharks. If one of them thought of harming the child, Cody would bite clean through them.

The little girl went limp in the water, her small arms floating up and above her head as she continued downward. Her long black hair swayed and danced around her face and head. As it lifted higher, he spotted a large gash at the base of her neck. Blood flowed from the open wound freely, swirling in the water, leaving a surreal pattern in its wake.

She was in a pair of white shorts and a blue top, both of which had blood on them. When he saw she was in sandals, and not barefoot or in a swimsuit, he wondered if she'd come from one of the fishing vessels.

Even if she had, he wasn't going to let her die.

It wasn't in him to let a child suffer, even if she had been with assholes who thought cutting the fins off his kind was a good idea. That was hardly her fault. Beyond that, there was something about this child that made him intent on saving her.

No matter the cost.

Cody reached her and tried to shift back into human form to be able to grab her with his hands, but the shark wasn't having any part of that. It was as worried about her as he was. And clearly, it wasn't going to chance the human part fucking this up.

He got the distinct impression it thought he'd take the situation as seriously as he took most things in life—not very much.

But that wasn't the case. Cody was dead serious about saving the child.

Not that the shark cared about his opinions on it all.

The shark took matters into its own hands, positioning itself under the little girl and thrusting its head up. The action forced the child upward. Unfortunately, it also left his razor-sharp teeth catching the delicate skin of her right forearm in the process. Instantly the taste of her blood filled his mouth. It didn't ignite hunger in the shark, as Cody feared it might. Rather, it made the shark's burning need to see the child safe intensify to a level that made it hard for Cody to concentrate.

The shark tried to be more gentle with her as he nudged her toward the surface. Once there, it backed off to some extent, detecting what Cody did.

Other sharks were in the area, attracted by the blood and noises. To make matters worse (not that it wasn't bad enough), the sharks he was sensing were ones with reputations for attacking humans.

Bull and tiger sharks.

A lot of people thought tiger sharks weren't in the waters around Costa Rica anymore.

They were wrong.

They were still there, just not in the numbers they had been. And right now, all the ones that were seemed to have converged on the area.

Just fucking great.

Most were pushing fourteen feet, which was large for their kind. And while he was much bigger, there were far more of them than there were of him. Not to mention, more sharks were appearing left and right. Already he was grossly outnumbered. But that did nothing to dissuade him.

He heard the faint sounds of someone yelling frantically from the island not far from where they were. If memory served, there was a rocky cliff face nearby. Had the child tumbled over it and into the chumming and finning area?

Cody struggled with his shark, wanting to return to human form to get the child to safety—to land. The shark's senses were in overdrive and it was as panicked as he was. Maybe more. Which was saying something because his shark side didn't get nervous or freak out.

Ever.

But something had unnerved it more than once.

Not something, thought Cody.

Someone.

The little girl.

He and the shark worked together to keep the little girl's head above water, the sound of her heartbeat waning more and more. The very thought of her expiring then and there sent Cody into a state of abject terror that he couldn't even begin to explain. There was simply no way in hell he was letting her die.

None.

Not happening.

He thrashed and went at a large tiger shark who had come in too close to the child.

The tiger wisely retreated but didn't go far.

No.

It, along with countless others, circled the perimeter, stalking their prey. They didn't seem to understand that if the finning crew didn't get them, Cody would. In truth, they stood a better chance of survival with the finning ships than they did with Cody should they make a move to attack the child.

Gathering as much control as he could, he pushed out with his mind, sending a signal to the marine life around him. No harm was to befall the child. Period. The signal was similar to how he could communicate to other men like him— other Outcasts. They had a shared mental pathway they'd all been taught to use.

For now, he could only hope the very way he'd reach out to his brethren when they were in shifted form would reach the non-supernatural marine life. That his warning would be understood and respected. He didn't want to take any of their lives if he could help it. Already the finning vessel had slaughtered so many sharks. Ending more wasn't in Cody's plan but he would if given no choice. He'd kill them *all* if it meant the little girl was safe.

Cody heard shouting in a foreign language.

Then the sounds of a motorboat reached him. The engine was small, meaning it didn't belong to the fishing vessels. Deep down, he knew that whoever was coming would assist the child. That didn't mean he was leaving her just yet.

He circled under her, and she sank once more.

This time, her eyes opened. Her hair lifted again, showing him the gash on the back of her neck once more. It was severe.

Her tiny body twisted in the water, turning with the force of the current pushing around her. Her gaze locked on him. Still, no fear showed in her.

She couldn't have been more than nine or maybe even ten years old, and scarcely weighed anything.

He expected fear to show in her dark brown eyes. Grown men would have been terrified given the circumstances. She was drowning, was injured, and a giant shark was next to her.

That wasn't the case.

Curiosity was there…and a strange calmness.

No signs of terror at all.

Was she in shock?

Maybe she was too young to fully grasp the danger she was in.

He went toward her, his intent to push her to the surface for air again.

Her tiny hand darted out—and she did the strangest of things when he was close enough.

She ran her hand over his head, petting him as if he were a dog, not a nearly three-ton predator.

As her fingers connected with his skin, the fierce need to protect her and keep her safe intensified to the point it was maddening. It became hard to hold on to anything close to his focus. The shark took hold of the momentary lapse and ripped away any small thread of control Cody had from him.

He roared from within, fearing the shark's nature would leave it harming the little girl.

When the shark nudged her up to the surface before darting wide to circle and come at her again, he calmed slightly. It repeated the act several more times, each time pushing her with as much care as it could to the surface for air.

The sound of the approaching small craft intensified.

Cody went wide again, needing to tip sideways slightly to maintain a visual on the child, his intent to remain close to the girl until help arrived.

He was almost to her again when something pierced his back, sending pain shooting through him. He'd been tagged once before, by well-meaning scientists, but it hadn't felt like this. He'd barely felt anything when they'd done it. But the act had left him having to dig a tracker out of his back when he'd returned to human form.

It had also given Wheeler one hell of a good laugh because Cody had needed the man's assistance.

Getting tagged was nothing like what he'd just felt.

Nothing at all.

In the next second, netting was under him, closing him in, yanking him toward the surface in the direction of the fishing vessel.

He was hardly a small shark.

His species alone was massive. Cody, being supernatural and not a normal shark, was even bigger than others.

Lifting him out of the ocean in full shifted form wasn't something that should have been possible with the ease in which it was occurring, yet that was exactly what was happening.

He thrashed, trying to free himself, to no avail.

As he broke the surface, he saw men leaning over the side of a vessel that was positioned near the fishing boats. He'd not noticed it before. The markings on the side weren't ones he'd ever seen. The shark couldn't make any sense of them, but Cody could. The logo read Donavon Dynamics Corp Research Vessel.

Great. I'm getting tagged again. Never going to live this down.

He waited for the men huddled near the rail of the ship to set about tagging and releasing him. The researchers in the past had always been very quick about taking their measurements, applying their equipment, and getting him back in the water. It was why he'd never shifted back into human form to get away.

There was no need to reveal the secret that supernaturals were real.

But there was a need now.

The little girl required his assistance. He didn't have time to play the dutiful part of the research shark for eggheads. They'd have to get their data elsewhere. He tried again to take control and shift, but the shark was stunned, its sensors off more than normal around large metal vessels.

Something was wrong.

Cody saw one of the men on the research vessel holding a small box. When he realized the box was emanating a sound wave that was interfering with his shark side, he took serious note of the men there, all watching him with nothing short of glee in their eyes. Not the excitement typically seen in biologists elated to be close to one of the biggest white sharks they'd ever seen. No. This was far different.

Disturbing even.

One of the men put his hand on a taller man's shoulder, patting it as he did. "Well done, Jasper. Looks as if the witch was right. *He* would be summoned here with the right bait. Get him in the holding tank and be sure to begin administering the drugs to keep him from shifting back. The acoustic disruptor won't keep him sedated long. See to it the vessels around us are paid to look the other way. And handle the small boat that came from the island."

"Yes, Helmuth," said Jasper. "Can I watch when the nerds cut him open to see what's inside? What makes him tick?"

Helmuth's gaze swept to Cody as the netting was brought up and over the deck. "I plan to keep him alive as long as possible. A dead wereshark is no good to me. He'll give samples and what I need for centuries. Perfect."

Wereshark?

They knew what he was?

Reason said Cody should have been worried about himself, since it was clear he was in jeopardy and these men were no ordinary boatful of eggheads. That they were more than likely supernaturals themselves, and Cody was in a world of shit.

But Cody's only concern was for the little girl. He'd lost sight of her in the chaos.

"David!" yelled a woman, her voice shrill, loaded with fear. It sounded as if it were coming from the direction he'd first heard the small craft approaching from. "Do you see her?"

"Cut the engine!" shouted a male before Cody heard the distinct sound of a boat slicing through the water.

Had help reached the little girl?

Was she going to be okay?

As he was lifted fully from the water, he realized he wasn't going to be okay. In fact, he was about as far from okay as he could get.

Chapter Three

PRESENT DAY, SAVANNAH, GEORGIA...

GENA ALEXIADIS LOOKED over the data she'd logged from the Baited Remote Underwater Video Systems (BRUVS) she and her team of researchers and scientists had taken to using to help document vital information about marine life, specifically sharks. While she loved everything to do with the ocean and its inhabitants, she was partial to sharks.

More to the point, she had a soft spot specifically for *Carcharodon carcharias*, or in layman's terms, the great white shark.

Freediving with them was her favorite thing to do. There was nothing like being able to reach out and stroke one as it glided past her in the water. The sharks came back, again and again, rubbing against her hand, liking the feel of being touched. It probably had something to do with the fact the act of touching them helped to knock off the parasites that no doubt caused them discomfort, but still.

Countless hours had been spent underwater, exploring, soaking in the sights and sounds around her in what felt like another world. An alien planet under the sea. A planet that felt like home.

She could hold her breath a freakishly long time under water and was often told she swam like a fish—fast and with fluid ease. She loved the water, and getting to dive with sharks was simply the cherry on top. There was a certain peace to be found out in the ocean. And while she'd had it drilled into her head again and again that she should never dive alone, she always did. It was something she'd done since she was younger, and even then, it upset her parents.

While she'd never recommend others go it alone, there was a certain tranquility found only when she was under the water by herself. Plus, she could *be* herself then. No need to hide the fact she could go almost thirty minutes without taking a breath. Maybe longer, but she'd never tried. It was bizarre enough, the fact she could last so long without coming up for air. Then there was the speed with which she could swim, both underwater and above. Phelps had nothing on her. Not that she'd advertised as much.

Her parents had noticed the oddities when she was small and had stressed that she not discuss them outside of the family. She wasn't the only one of her siblings who could do things termed outside the normal. All the things they could do were certainly strange and unheard of, but it wasn't as if anyone was shooting fire out of their eyes or anything. They were simply stronger and faster than most others.

Deep down, Gena knew there was more to the story. That was part of the reason she'd decided to take DNA samples and blood from herself and send it all through one of the labs used by the facility she worked for. That had been several weeks back. The results hadn't come in yet, which was unusual. Normally the lab was speedy, but on this, they'd been moving at a snail's pace. She'd even gone so far as to reach out asking about the status of the samples, only to be told a number of different and conflicting stories.

They'd also been very curious as to the samples' origins. Wisely, she'd only put Subject-X on the paperwork, and she had no intention of telling them more. If something was off, she didn't want the company she worked for to know.

"My luck, it will come back I'm part fish or something," she said with a chuckle. "Area-51 thinking for sure."

Not that she believed in aliens or anything.

No matter the reason the lab gave, the samples weren't in yet, so she had nothing to work from. Only a hunch. And that hunch said she might be presenting markers that indicate a new step in human evolution. Then again, she was a scientist and tended to look for answers to everyday mysteries within the field of science.

There was more to it all than being able to swim fast and hold her breath a long time, but Gena wasn't sure she was ready to face it all fully, let alone acknowledge it out loud—even if just to herself.

No.

There was a certain satisfaction that came from not knowing or understanding. Even though such a thing went against her natural curiosity. For now, she'd wait on the results of her tests and continue to seek out time to free-dive with sharks.

The stigma surrounding them still left many

afraid to get in the water with them. The brave who did often did so in a cage rather than face-to-face. Not that she could blame them. Everything Hollywood showed of the great white was scary. Fear sold. Curious beasts with brains didn't. It was easier to see them as mindless killers. Sold more tickets and got more ratings.

To hell with what it did to the shark populations because fear led to the needless and senseless killing of the creatures.

She teared up just thinking about it.

She'd recently gotten her PhD in marine biology and was doing a privately funded postdoctoral fellowship with an amazing team of researchers specializing in shark conservation. It was the opportunity of a lifetime for her, and she was thankful for it each and every day.

Gena intended to devote the rest of her days to the study and conservation of sharks—great whites on the forefront. Some might think that odd, but she didn't care. She wanted her life to mean something. Wanted to leave a positive lasting mark on the earth long after she was gone. And shark conservation was a very important mission.

She looked at the screen once more. "Good girl. What else can you tell me?"

The data from the BRUVS had been coming in at a steady pace since the team had deployed the devices, and already the researchers had been able to analyze the preliminary findings. Each time additional information came in, it felt like Christmas to her and everyone else involved.

Geeking out over data was just one of the reasons she loved being a scientist and had spent so much time and hard work in school. It was also part of the reason why she didn't have much in the way of a social life outside of work.

That, and no man had ever really appealed to her enough to want to go on a date. Of course, it had to be pointed out to her more than once that she was, in fact, being asked out at all. Those types of things tended to fly right by her.

Romantically stunted.

It's what Clara, a childhood friend, often referred to her as.

That summed her up nicely.

She'd have taken offense but, in all honesty, the assessment was accurate.

Case in point, she was here on her morning off to see what, if any, new data had come in.

Sleep had been elusive at best for her as of late. When she was able to nod off, bizarre dreams came to her. The common theme had been dreaming of an incident that had happened when she was ten, but in the dream, she wasn't a little girl. No. She was a fully grown woman.

That wasn't all that kept changing in the dreams.

They managed to get X-rated very quickly.

Her upper chest heated just thinking of it all.

"You're still at it?" asked Dr. Bonnie Fowler, the senior scientist and director of research at the facility, as she entered the laboratory. Her dark curly hair was pulled up into a thick ponytail, which was pulled through the back of a baseball cap. She was dressed in clothing that had the logo of their primary benefactor on it. Their research facility had been named after the corporation for the longest time as well, but had recently undergone a name change. But everyone who knew them still referred to them as Donavon Dynamics Marine Research Institute.

Bonnie began setting down everything that she'd brought in with her, which was two backpacks, a messenger bag, and a laptop. The woman was always weighted down with countless items.

Gena had once tried to lend a hand and ease the load, only to realize Bonnie had a system and messing with it threw Bonnie into a tailspin. So now Gena only helped when she was asked, which was very rare.

Bonnie's light brown skin had a tinge of pink to it.

"You didn't use the sunscreen I got you, did you?" asked Gena with a shake of her head.

"I did. I just forgot to put it everywhere. I got distracted after I did my shoulders and one leg." The woman stepped out from behind the partial wall that was the same height as the desk, with a small ledge on it. The thing was hardly functional and screamed old, but it was there all the same.

As Bonnie stood there, Gena saw how unevenly burned her friend had gotten.

Gena tried but failed to keep from laughing. "I once had too much in one spot on my forehead and too little elsewhere. I ended up with a big white spot circled in red. The tan line later was awesome."

Bonnie chuckled. "I bet. But seriously, thank you again for finding me ocean-life-safe sunscreen. I refuse to pollute the water with the crap they peddle to the public. The number of reefs dying is at an all-time high and the chemicals in everyday normal sunscreen are dangerous, plus... Wait, I'm preaching to the choir. Sorry."

"No worries," said Gena with a smile. "I feel the same way. We can soapbox it together."

"Sweet," said Bonnie as she opened her laptop and set it on the ledge. A paperback spy novel fell from the bag. It skidded to a rest on the ledge as well. Bonnie nudged it back with the laptop, paying it little mind.

The woman had a serious weakness for thrillers and spy novels.

Her laptop woke and on the screen was a blog Gena had seen Bonnie reading more than once. From what Gena could tell, the blog was dedicated to government conspiracy theories. The topics got downright insane, as noted by the current image shown on the blog—it was a drawing of a wolf morphing into a man.

Gena lifted a brow but didn't comment. For as science-minded as Bonnie was, she had a love of the weird and wacky.

Bonnie logged into the research center's private system, or at least tried to log in. When it didn't work, she slapped her laptop. "I don't know what is with our system here, but it's been so temperamental lately."

That was putting it mildly. The computers and the entire database had been off. Gena dreaded having to tell Bonnie that the problem they'd thought they'd gotten fixed as far as their computer systems were concerned had started up again.

Bonnie gave up on her laptop and checked the box on the counter where incoming mail was placed. As she did, Gena got a better look at everything the woman was wearing.

She couldn't hold back her laugh at the sight of Bonnie. Logos were on everything that Gena could see and probably places that weren't visible either. "Is there anything on you that doesn't have Donavon Dynamics stamped all over it? Shouldn't you have gone with our new logo and name change?"

"I'm giving a nod to the big guys footing the bill," said Bonnie with a smile. Putting her arms out wide, she turned in a circle, modeling the outfit. She tugged on the shirt front. "Too much?"

Gena raised her hand and made a small pinching gesture with her thumb and forefinger. "Just a little."

Bonnie frowned. "They've saved our bacon more than once this year alone. I really want to make a good first impression on the bigwig they're sending to talk with us. They've been funding our research for years now without ever setting foot near us or meeting any of us in person. At least no one from the new team. I found a few notes from the older teams—Ray's days and before. The place was active then. Now they just toss money at us. Now that they've requested face time, I want things to go right. I'm kind of scared they're requesting a meeting in person to tell me they're shutting us down or slicing our funding."

"I'm sure it will be fine. You can probably pare down to maybe just the shirt. Ohmygods, is their logo on your sandals?"

Sure enough, it was tiny but there.

Gena shook her head. "Way overkill. Tell me you're not wearing undergarments with their logo on it too."

Bonnie laughed. "Hey, I got a sale on custom items. When I went to check out, the online cart offered me huge discounts on *more* items. I have a bottle opener and a calendar in my car. Want one?"

Gena's eyes widened. "Uh, no. I'm good. Thanks though."

Bonnie shrugged. "Suit yourself. But when you're in the middle of nowhere and need to open a bottle, you'll be sorry."

"That has happened so many times in my past, I'm unsure how I've survived this long without one," returned Gena with a wink.

Bonnie laughed. "Smart-ass."

"Thanks. Hey, I was checking over the new data this morning and everything looks good, but there are a few discrepancies that I think you might want to look at before we take all this to our meeting," said Gena, nodding to the laptop in front of her.

"Are they like the others?" asked Bonnie, referencing what had happened over the past month. Their system had been glitchy at best. To the point they were sure they'd had a virus or that one of the new pieces of equipment was malfunctioning. For a brief period, they'd feared one of the BRUVS had shorted out. But that didn't seem to be the case.

Gena nodded. "Yes. Same."

"I'm going to change and then I'll put in a call to

Colin. He swore to me he had that all figured out the last time, and the time before that, and the time before that," said Bonnie, looking frazzled. She and the IT guy—who was twenty if he was a day and didn't roll out of bed until close to noon, only to show up in his pajamas—never really saw eye to eye.

His work ethic was nearly nonexistent.

Bonnie's was go, go, go.

The two tended to clash.

Gena lifted a brow. "Want me to call in Colin for you? You get annoyed with him two words into a conversation. I, on the other hand, speak fluent socially awkward."

Bonnie set a hand on the counter as a tired look came over her face. "Yes. I guess. If we *have to*. I should really learn how to code and repair computers."

"Add that to your laundry list of degrees," said Gena, amused at how much Bonnie dreaded dealing with the tech guy.

"If he starts talking nonstop about the newest video game that he's into, I can't promise not to maim him," warned Bonnie as she removed her sunglasses, setting them next to the box on the counter.

"Understood," said Gena, giving in and laughing at her friend.

Bonnie's attention returned to the box of mail. She pulled out an envelope that screamed "government issued." She tore it open and read the contents. "Damn," she said in a hushed whisper, a forlorn look on her face. "We really needed that."

Gena tensed.

Bonnie had been hoping to get a grant for additional funding, but apparently, the government wasn't much into helping save sharks. No real surprise there.

"We can apply for other grants," said Gena, trying to be optimistic.

"I bet Ray got funded," she said snidely, her dislike of the man she liked to refer to as a pseudo-scientist abundantly clear. "He's probably greasing palms again. Jackass."

Gena remained quiet, knowing Bonnie needed a second to come to terms with the news they'd not gotten the grant she'd been hoping for. Gena hadn't been part of the program when Dr. Ray Roberts had been on staff. But she'd heard talk of what the man had been like to work with.

A total creeper.

He made lewd remarks to the women on staff, talked to them in demeaning ways, and assumed they were nothing more than tits and ass—no brains.

Gena also heard he'd been forced out on questionable terms, but that he was tight with the company that handled the lion's share of the financial needs of the research team. Her guess was, it was simply a matter of time before some higher-up got the bright idea to put him back on the team. Maybe that's what the meeting they'd been prepping all week for was about.

Bonnie would be livid if that was the case.

While Colin may rub her the wrong way because of how different his approach was to most things in life, he was a nice young man. Not a creeper at all. Just really into gaming and vintage T-shirts.

Bonnie stared at the rejection and righted herself, pressing a smile to her face. She then lifted a brow. "Wait a second. Didn't we agree that you'd take the morning off and then come in to go to the meeting?"

Gena shook her head. "No. You told me I was working too much and needed to take the morning off. *We* never agreed to anything."

"Gena, you have to take a little time for yourself every once in a while," warned Bonnie. "You remind me of myself when I was starting out. Careful, or you'll blink and realize this job is all you have in the world."

Gena bit her lower lip and nodded. The job was already pretty much all she had in her life. While she did have her parents and her brothers and a sister, they were all spread around the globe, each doing their own thing. They always said they'd make time to get together in one location, but that, as of yet, had not happened. Everyone was just too busy. And her childhood friends in the area had been well-meaning by reaching out to her, but Gena's job kept strange hours, so it wasn't always easy to find the time for those who were outside of the field.

Bonnie sat on the edge of the worn desk, glancing at the monitor and the data displayed on it. "Seriously, Gena. I don't want to see you burn out. It happens more than you'd think. You should find a balance now."

"I'm fine. I swear," countered Gena. "I love what I do."

"I love what I do too, but I wish I'd have taken

a little time for myself," said Bonnie. "I have regrets."

She'd heard Bonnie mention once before that she'd been engaged at one point in time, but that she'd dragged her feet on picking a date and making the marriage happen. Her fiancée, who, if memory served, was a geologist, wasn't in the picture anymore that Gena was aware of. Gena had liked Ruby. She'd been nice and funny. It had been hard to watch Bonnie go through the breakup and even harder to be unable to offer any sage words of wisdom on how to move on with her life.

Gena had no relationships in her past to have life experience with. All she'd been able to do was take Bonnie out for ice cream. The two had bought more while at the ice cream shop and taken it back to Gena's houseboat, where they'd proceeded to gorge themselves to the point that they'd ended up with sugar overload. They'd woken up on the deck with spoons by their heads and a partially melted tub of ice cream near them.

Bonnie tapped the top of the open laptop. "You spend all your time here. Don't get me wrong. I love a dedicated associate as much as the next person, but I've lived through what this job can do."

"We're doing important work," said Gena.

"Yes, but *we're* important too. Never forget that."

Gena thought more on it and nodded. "I get it. I do. But I don't have anyone in my life to worry about."

"What about those girls I saw you having lunch with a few weeks back?" asked Bonnie. "They seemed nice."

"Nicolette and Clara?" asked Gena before smiling, thinking of her friends in the area. "I've known them since I was little. Our parents are all friends. They're all part of the same support group for parents of adopted children. I think they all might have even adopted around the same time. Not sure. I just know they're some of the few people my parents stay in contact with."

"Ah, the *famed* parents," said Bonnie, laughing slightly.

Gena groaned. Her parents were scientists and die-hard conservationists who were well known in the scientific community, publishing often, and even going rounds with poachers and other illegal animal traders. They were fantastic, loving, passionate people who'd opened their home to four orphaned children all at the same time, but they did have very different views on child-rearing. Gena's first and pretty much only toys were all educational ones meant to help develop and increase intelligence. Not really for fun or anything.

Her family never had a television growing up, and the first time she'd ever played a video game was in college, when someone living on the same floor of her dorm hosted a gaming night.

It was then she'd found herself the center of attention, when she'd casually mentioned all the places she'd lived while growing up, and how she'd not seen any of the movies or television shows the others referenced often.

Her family didn't have a home base, so to speak. They were always on the move, always part of this research team or that one. Wherever the research or cause took them was where they hung their hat for the time being. That meant the world had been Gena's backyard. Everywhere had been her home—at least it felt that way.

She'd spent time in the rain forest in her early years, been on numerous African safaris, chased down poachers, and her favorite by far had been when her parents became active in ocean-related conservation—whitetip and tiger sharks. That had given Gena a front row seat to the vast wonders of the sea and exposed her to regions the sharks were known to frequent.

Costa Rica was probably the closest thing to a real home she'd ever had, as they'd spent a full year there when she was younger. That had been record-breaking for her family. Sadly, it had been her fault that they'd had to leave when they did.

Had she only listened when her father told her to stay close as he and her mother worked on one of the small islands, in an area that was now protected, they'd have probably lived there another five years. Maybe longer. But her curiosity and natural-born pull to the ocean had left Gena wandering away from the watchful eye of her father and far from the rest of the group working there. She'd ended up on a rocky cliff edge and had just wanted to peek over the side to see the waves lapping against the rocks below.

It was then she'd seen finning for the first time. It was a grotesque practice that haunted her to this very day. Watching helplessly as countless sharks were pulled up before having their fins sliced off and their bodies tossed back in the sea had been too much for her at that impressionable age.

As it would have been at any age, really.

The sight of it all had startled her to the point she'd lost her footing on the cliff's edge, slipped, and fallen over, straight onto the rocky base below, then right into the open ocean. Gena could still remember seeing the water coming upon her quickly, and then the next thing she remembered was being deep in the ocean, the current pulling her away as the water turned red from her blood. The pain in her head had been great. Too much so to think or do anything but be ripped under the water.

During the fall, she'd struck the back of her neck on the rocky cliff face and ended up with a nasty scar that she still had to this day—along with one on her right forearm that had come from events in the water. The scar on the back of her neck was in a spot no one saw unless her unruly long hair was pulled up tight. Whenever it was up loosely, with tendrils hanging down at the nape of her neck, the scar was basically covered. The one on her arm wasn't angry and purple anymore as it once had been. It was now taut, white but still visible with ease from the sheer size of it.

Others liked to tease her for her account of events from that day seventeen years ago, saying she had a vivid imagination as a child. That she'd been too young to properly remember what had occurred. But Gena knew she hadn't imagined what had happened to her. That as she'd been sinking downward into the ocean's depths, out of the darkness below her came the most magnificent creature she'd ever seen.

A white shark.

The biggest great white she'd ever seen, and had ever seen since. It had also been the most beautiful creature she'd ever laid eyes upon.

The great white had zeroed in and come at her like a torpedo. Yet not an ounce of fear had come over her. Deep down, even then, she'd known its intent wasn't to harm her, it was to help her.

And help it had.

It pushed her upward, to the surface of the water, catching her arm with its teeth in the process before it stayed near, circling her, pushing her back up as she sank under time and time again. While she'd been able to swim at that age, the blow to the head she'd taken in the fall, and the fact she'd been sure she'd broken her leg, had made it nearly impossible for her to tread water with any sort of proficiency or for any length of time.

The white had stayed close, keeping all the other types of sharks at bay. She felt as if it had been silently telling the others that they could look at her, out of curiosity, but they weren't to touch her.

The ordeal had single-handedly set her on her life's path of shark conservation.

It was also closely tied to the dreams she'd been having as of late. Though, in addition to Gena being fully grown in them, the shark wasn't just a great white. One second it was the same majestic beast that had saved her life and in the next breath, it was changing into a hot blond guy with a body to die for. And in the dreams, the mystery man did way more than save her. He rocked her world in the biblical sense—in the water and out of it.

She nearly moaned thinking about it.

"So what do you say?" asked Bonnie.

Gena blinked and stared at her friend, wondering what it was she'd missed while she'd been deep in thought.

Bonnie laughed. "You didn't hear a word I said, did you?"

"No. Sorry."

"Daydreaming about your dream lover again?" asked Bonnie with a knowing smirk.

Gena groaned. "I'm really sorry I ever told you about the dreams."

"No, you're not. You love me and my witty repartee," said Bonnie with a wink, making Gena laugh. "Spill it. Were you in here at the crack of dawn because you had more dreams of the hot shark-dude?"

Gena bit her lower lip and considered lying to avoid discussing the topic. "Um, yes. Can we maybe call him something other than shark-dude? It's weird enough I keep having the dream at all, let alone that a shark changes into a man. I really do not want to dwell on what my mind is trying to tell me."

Bonnie licked her lips and waggled her brows. "I think your inner self is telling you the same thing I did—you need more in your life than just this job. Or you need a shark to turn into a hot guy and rock your world."

"Okay, since option two isn't plausible, I guess I'll work on getting a life," said Gena before she pointed at her friend. "But I refuse to let Rene set me up on a blind date or sign me up for any of those dating apps she's always on."

"Smart," said Bonnie. "We should grab her after our meeting with the Donavon Dynamics fancy pants and have some drinks. You in? We can launch Operation Get Gena a Life or a Hot Guy Who Can Turn Into a Shark."

Gena would have usually passed. Her idea of a nice night was reading a book and staying home, away from crowds. But Bonnie had a point. She did need to learn to live a little for something other than work, and Rene, who was the senior biologist on the team, was fun and turning into a good friend, just like Bonnie. "Yes. I say yes."

Bonnie clapped and stood fast. "I'll text Rene."

"Want to see if she's up for hanging with me while you go in and meet with the bigwig from Donavon Dynamics?" asked Gena.

Bonnie put a hand on the counter and faced Gena fully. "Mr. Bigwig's assistant was very clear. He said you were to attend the meeting too. Just you and me."

"Really? I'm a no one," said Gena.

"Hardly," replied Bonnie. "I'm heading to my office to change my clothes."

"And not be a walking billboard? I'm almost disappointed," said Gena with a laugh as her boss headed down the hallway.

Her attention returned to her work. BRUVS had been a game changer, and Gena couldn't wait for the next invention that would take researching marine life even further.

When she'd first learned about all that the BRUVS could do and the wealth of information they had opened to those who study anything to do with underwater research, she'd moved heaven and earth to be sure she was part of a group open to the usage. She'd lucked out and was able to get in on a project whose goals aligned with hers.

Protecting the shark species as a whole.

That was part of how she'd ended up in Savannah to begin with. Another reason was because of Clara and Nicolette. They'd been childhood friends of hers, despite the fact she was a little bit older than them (not that anyone would have guessed, considering how tall Nicolette had always been), and that was something of a rarity for her and her family, considering the unorthodox upbringing she'd had.

The memory brought a smile to her face as she checked over the data before her. Once she was sure everything was not only listed in the report but also checked three times for good measure, Gena backed up a copy of the file to the cloud server before hitting print to make sure a hard copy was on hand should it be needed.

She didn't want to risk a technological error hampering any of the findings. They were proof of the importance of shark conservation and the need to put a stop to finning for good.

While finning was illegal, there were plenty of ways to get around the law, and enough money to be made by taking the risks. It was big business. The kind that attracted dangerous players.

It sickened her, the number of sharks that were killed each hour around the world. The numbers were staggering, and at the rate it was going, the species as a whole would be extinct. Something that had managed to survive over four hundred million years would be wiped out by fishing, if finning could really even be labeled as such.

When the sharks went, so would go the rest of the oceans' ecological systems, followed closely by the rest of the world's. It was a sobering truth. Getting that through to the finners and the black-market traders was like talking to a wall. They didn't care.

Just so long as their pockets were lined, they cared little for their effects on the ecosystem.

"If I could get my hands on one, I'd…"

The thought trailed off as she thought about the *last* time that she'd managed to get her hands on one. She'd put him in the hospital with one blow. That blow had also landed her in hot water with the law. Thankfully, the judge had been lenient, and a big supporter of shark preservation. She'd sentenced Gena to anger management courses.

When Bonnie had learned of the ordeal, she'd taken Gena out for drinks to celebrate. Bonnie was fine with putting finners in the hospital. It was part of why they got along so well.

Gena secured her long dark hair on the top of her head in a messy bun and thought no more of it as she focused on the printed materials before her. Reaching out, she grabbed for her apple that was sitting on the edge of the desk. Absently, she bumped the apple rather than grabbing it, causing it to fall from the desk.

Without thought or even looking, Gena's hand shot after the falling fruit. She caught it in midair with ease and brought it to her mouth, taking a bite while continuing to read through the data.

Her reflexes had always been that way. Greater than those of others around her, unless her family was being counted in. They too all had extraordinary reflexes. She had one sister and two brothers. The boys were the oldest, separated by only a few months in age. Then it was her and finally her sister, who was only a year younger than Gena. They were so close in age because they were all adopted at the same time, from the stories their parents told them.

Since the parental units were rather tight-lipped about the details of the adoption, Gena and her siblings had all assumed it might have been a little gray in the area of legal. Not a surprise, considering they'd been adopted overseas from a shady orphanage, during a questionable time in the country's past.

While their parents didn't discuss the specifics, the shared looks that passed between them said Gena and her siblings had been taken from a situation that had been less than optimal and brought back to live with them in the United States.

Gena had been pushing seven at the time and while she should have been plenty old enough to have memories from her past, she had none. Neither did her sister. Her brothers, who were two years older, had limited recollections but had stopped voicing them by the time they were teens.

For the best…since what they'd been sure had occurred was nothing short of insane.

They had been sure they were all in labs of some sort, being tested on in ways that no child should be. Not to mention, the boys had been positive that men in special ops uniforms had burst in on it all and freed them—before one of them shifted into an animal.

Yes. Insane was the word for it.

Gena hadn't used to be one to dwell on the past or even give much thought to it growing up. She saw her parents as just that—her parents. She loved them as though they'd given birth to her, and they, in turn, loved each of their children the same way. But recently, a nagging feeling had come over her, making her wonder about her extra abilities and her past. It left her wanting answers, but she didn't want to upset her parents by asking for their help seeking out her birth parents. Not when her adoptive parents had been nothing but amazing.

Chapter Four

JUST OUTSIDE OF DENVER, COLORADO...

CODY STOOD ALMOST statue-like with one arm high above his head as he held a grenade launcher in the air. He'd been doing so for just under an hour. Long ago, the lactic acid in his arm had built up. He'd already gotten used to the discomfort. A little unease was worth keeping the weapon out of the hands of the madman hell-bent on destruction.

Okay, the madman (otherwise known as Wild Bill, if you believed the rumors circulating that he'd once rode a mechanical elephant during the Vietnam War and managed to take it down) wasn't so much bent on destruction, as destruction just seemed to happen in his vicinity. That could have been a by-product of his idea of a toy—a grenade launcher.

The man had gotten into a heap of trouble the day before with the very same weapon. It had been taken from him then as well, but he'd somehow managed to either get it back or find another. With the serious weapons caches on the grounds, it wouldn't have surprised Cody any if Bill knew where a secret reserve of hundreds of launchers were located.

It would be just Cody's luck that the man would have access to anything dangerous, let alone in bulk.

Bill's wiry hair stuck out in all directions, only adding to the air of insanity that seemed to surround him. It wasn't as if Cody was new to dealing with eccentrics. The people he dealt with daily tended to have overreacting down to a science. That being said, Bill was putting him through the paces, testing all of Cody's willpower and ability to remain calm. Which was saying something, since Cody was known as an easygoing guy.

Ironic, since Cody's shifter side was one of the most feared predators alive.

"You're a killjoy!" whined Bill, managing to

increase the man's exasperation factor as he continued to jump up and down, his arms outstretched to gain additional height and reach.

It didn't quite work as planned.

Instead, Bill ended up tumbling to one side, bumping into the wall, grunting loudly before farting, and then continuing to hop up and down. The pattern had emerged (minus the farting) nearly an hour ago, and Bill hadn't varied far from it. His threats had grown more colorful as the time ticked on, which amused Cody greatly.

The vertically challenged male wasn't going to get the object of his desire. At least not by leaping for it, since the man at full height came to Cody's mid-chest. And Bill's jump was only about an inch off the ground. It wasn't as if Bill was a model of health or anything.

Far from it.

Cody was sure the man's diet consisted solely of junk food and illegal substances. Possibly with more drugs than food half of the time.

Even with his poor life choices, Bill showed no signs of tiring despite having invested nearly an hour in the fruitless endeavor. He was tenacious, Cody would give him that much.

Cody shook his head, wondering if Bill was as

deranged as he suspected he might be. When Cody had discovered him outside, preparing to test fire the grenade launcher in the parking lot of the resort the operatives had commandeered only days prior, Cody had disarmed Bill at once. The man still hadn't given up on his quest to get the weapon back.

There was no way Cody was letting Bill loose with that kind of firepower. Hell, a match was too much firepower for the eccentric small man. In the past seventy-two hours, countless weapons and sizable amounts of narcotics had been confiscated from him. He seemed to have recreational substances falling out of his ears. And he was damn proud of the fact.

Cody had only known Bill just over three days, and that was plenty of time to understand the man wasn't playing with a full deck. Part of that could be blamed on Bill's past, and the fact he'd been part of Project MKUltra. Bill had been tested on by the CIA, and Cody was positive the experiments went far beyond what the public thought they knew of the mind-control project. LSD and who knows what else had been used during the trials. Since the government was notorious for giving half-truths and outright lying,

Cody didn't doubt for a second that whatever they'd done to the man had been unpleasant and damaging. Not that any of those involved would ever fully admit culpability.

No.

They'd already spun a partial truth to cover their asses. They admitted to some wrongdoing but left out a whole heap of information. And the Freedom of Information Act was nothing more than a smokescreen to make the American people feel safer—like they were being told everything.

Hardly.

He'd seen his fair share of supposed declassified documents. They were full of nothing but bogus bullshit to appease those who bothered reading the fine print. The *real* truth and the *real* documents weren't shared with the public.

After all, Cody was walking proof of the government's lies and deception, which was one of the reasons he did his best to try to keep his cool when dealing with Bill's antics. The guy had lived through something most couldn't relate to.

But Cody could.

He knew what it was like to be a plaything for the government.

To be lied to.

Told one thing while another was done to him.

In many respects, Cody was lucky to have come out of the other side of his testing at the hands of the government as sane as he was (which was often debatable).

Bill hadn't been as fortunate.

The man was damaged, too broken ever to be permitted to live on his own again without supervision, yet there was a certain charm about him that even the grumpiest of operatives found hard to deny. Cody had seen numerous alpha males growl and flash teeth at Bill over the past three days, but in the end, they all kept an eye out for him, monitoring him as if he were a child.

In many ways, he was. Yet in others, he was downright dangerous.

Such was the case with the grenade launcher.

That he was still trying to jump to get, and still failing.

Bill and his ever-faithful best friend, Gus—who was a character unto himself—had managed to wrap themselves up in the affairs of supernaturals to the point Cody had to wonder if they didn't possess a superpower themselves. If they did, Bill's would be the power of annoyance.

He was a master of the craft.

Bill was currently wearing a T-shirt bearing the logo of the retreat they were at. The shirt was about three sizes too small for him, leaving a large portion of his hairy stomach exposed. The man was furry enough for someone to mistake him for a shifter. There was a rather large clump of lint gathered in Bill's bellybutton, sort of hanging there, threatening to fall at any moment.

He had on a pair of jeans that were too big and cinched with a belt. They were rolled at least three times. Cody had assumed Bill's attire meant he didn't have the money for clothing that fit. He'd tried to take the man into town to buy him some things, but Bill had stared at him like *he* was the crazy one. Evidently, Bill had spent a considerable amount of time shopping for the jeans that he deemed were *just right*.

Cody had stopped trying after that.

Probably for the best, since Bill had then insisted on getting a pair of used high-top trainers from a thrift store because they'd already been broken in, saving him the time.

"Give it to me," whined Bill.

"Nope."

"Gill-face," snapped Bill, taking a jab at Cody's shifted form.

Cody merely grinned.

"Keep smiling there, Aqua-douche," snapped Bill. "While you're at it, can you do like the rest of us do before bed and choke the chicken? I'm sick of being woken up by your grunting and groaning."

Cody stiffened. "Grunting and groaning?"

Bill looked him up and down. "Don't go pretending you're not having wet dreams. We can hear you yelling for some girl, and then we hear you grunting and making lots of sex noises. That or you're in the john taking a big-ass dump. My constipation grunts sound a lot like my orgasm ones. Makes sense. Either way, I'm expelling something, shit or—"

"Dear God, stop talking," said Cody. The last thing he wanted to hear about was Bill's bowel movements or sexual escapades.

He shuddered as a mental image of both hit him.

Bill patted his gut. "Took me a big one this morning. Wished I'd have taken a phone in with me. I could have taken a picture of it. Thing of beauty. Gus complained about the smell all morning. Said I should see a doctor or something. Nah. I ate a bunch of hummus. The hippies have a ton of it down in the kitchen. Gives me gas. Big time. Keeps me regular though. Gus ain't too happy about that. Says I stunk up our room. I told him to light a match."

Cody wrinkled his nose in disgust. "Dude. Too much information."

"If you can't talk about it, you shouldn't be doing it," said Bill.

Cody stared at him a second. "Pretty sure people say that when they're talking about sex. Not bowel movements."

Bill glanced away, looking deep in thought. "Huh. Makes a lot more sense for sex. Learn something new every day. Want to talk about your sex dreams? She hot?"

"I don't know what you're talking about."

That wasn't entirely true. The last few weeks had been odd at night, to say the least. Since arriving in Colorado, it had been even more so. He'd wake several times a night, slicked in sweat, his body feeling as if he'd had marathon sex sessions. But, for the life of him, he couldn't remember the dreams in any kind of detail. Which was ironic and kind of pathetic, since it had been too many years to count since he'd had sex. Dream sex would have been something, at least. He did have weak impressions of a woman with long dark hair, creamy skin, and huge brown eyes. But the flashes were quick and chaotic. He could only guess the flashes of her were residual leftovers from whatever it was that had been happening to him in the dreams.

The last time Cody could recall having dreams that interfered with his sleep and his ability to function properly while awake had been Costa Rica. That had been seventeen years prior.

"So you ain't dreaming about shagging a hot chick-shark?" asked Bill.

Cody's eyes widened. "No!"

"You got something against sharks?" questioned Bill. "You do know you are one, right? They didn't mess with your head like they did mine, did they? They didn't convince you that you were a weretiger or some shit, did they? I knew a guy who they made think he was a chicken. He clucked and everything." He snapped his fingers. "Wait. No. That wasn't them. It was a hypnotist me and Gus saw at a carnival. Gus said it was all an act. I don't believe him. We know people who can turn into animals. Anything is possible. Who's to say a werechicken isn't real? Back to you screwing girl sharks."

"I do not have sex with other sharks," said Cody, his words clipped.

"That mean you do have sex with, say, a hot girl whale, or a girl dolphin?" asked Bill.

Cody considered hitting the man with the weapon just to knock him out. "No. To all of them."

"Oh, you like boys then?" asked Bill, no judgment in his voice. "That's cool too. To each his own."

"I like girls. But I do not have sex with animals. Do you ever stop talking?"

"No. Not really," said Bill. "There was this one time I was dared to go out to a field with this group of cows and—"

"I'll pay you to stop talking and *never* finish that story," said Cody, meaning every word of it. If the tale was headed in the direction that he suspected it was, he did not want a blow-by-blow. He'd never be able to bleach the mental image of Bill in a field with cows from his mind.

Bill groaned. "I thought you were the fun operative. The easygoing one. You're as repressed and boring as the rest. Especially *that* vampire."

Armand Faucher was the vampire in question, and a member of Paranormal Security and Intelligence's (PSI) Shadow Agents Division. At one point he'd been part of the Crimson Ops, or Fang Gang, as most liked to call them. Armand had moved over to the Shadow Agent side of things years ago and was now a handler whose job was to keep the solo operatives who worked under him safe. He also went in and assisted on covert missions when need be. That was how Cody had first met him.

When Cody had been captured off the shores of Costa Rica all those years ago, he'd ended up under the thumb of a madman. Walter Helmuth had his finger in the pie of just about everything wrong in the world. So did his partners in crimes, The Corporation.

Unbeknownst to Cody back in Costa Rica, the vessel that had scooped him out of the sea, bearing the logo of Donavon Dynamics, was owned and operated by The Corporation. The same assholes who were wreaking havoc throughout the supernatural community.

Armand had been posing as a guard in one of the locations where Cody had been held as a test subject. At first, Cody had assumed the vampire was in league with the enemy. Part of the group of men who made torturing him and testing on him something of a game. During one of the countless beatings Cody had been subjected to, Armand had entered the holding cell and told the guards they were needed elsewhere, that he would finish handling the prisoner.

Instead of inflicting more pain, something Cody had learned to live with over the time he was held, Armand had helped him. He'd gotten him something for the pain and had cleaned Cody's wounds before locking gazes with him and speaking telepathically, letting him know he was a good guy who was undercover and that help had finally come.

While Cody had been relieved, never actually believing any help would arrive, his concern had been for the others being held and tested on. Not for himself. Such was often the case. It was simply his nature. And he'd have it no other way. He didn't want to exist in a world where everyone only thought of themselves.

Besides, he'd seen and lived through what The Corporation scientists and guards were willing to do to someone. Horrific didn't begin to cover it.

Cody had gone into it all as an Outcast, a

wereshark whose shifted side was uncontrollable and difficult to weaponize properly, but he'd come out the other side even more unstable. So much so that he'd found himself keeping it all a secret from those he trusted.

He didn't want them knowing just how over the top his shark side was now. How it had increased in size substantially and become volatile. Gone were the days of being able to give control over to his shark side and let it swim for a week or so unmonitored in open water.

Cody barely trusted his shark enough to let it out at all anymore, but he had no choice. If he went too long between shifts, bad things would happen. Each time he gave in to the need to shift forms and swim as a shark, he clung to every shred of control he could gather.

The saddest part of it all was that he strongly suspected his issues with control were still better than those of many men he knew. They'd all been subjected to so much crap. It was grossly unfair, but it was what it was. There was no changing the past.

The best he could do was try to help as many people as he could, supernatural or not. In addition to helping others, keeping himself surrounded by friends he trusted was important. The men he thought of as brothers gave him something else to focus on than his unstable shifter side.

Cody was fairly certain that Armand had begun to suspect not all was right in Cody's world as far as shifting went. The French vampire was simply too polite to point it out. That, or he didn't think the issue was as big of a problem as Cody did. Armand tended to remain calm in extreme situations, making Cody look like a worrier, which was saying a lot.

Bill had managed to test Armand's limits too though. The small man had that much skill.

Armand and Bill had had a number of run-ins over the past few days, and Cody was fairly sure Armand would break his long-running streak of not killing an innocent human if Bill kept up his antics. After all, Bill had nearly re-killed the vampire with his grenade launcher stunt the day before. The grenade had gone higher and wider than Bill had planned when aiming at a van owned by the retreat.

Unluckily for Armand, he'd been in the building just beyond said van. The grenade had left him banged up but not seriously injured.

Though it had caught Armand's hair on fire. Thankfully, the flames had been doused quickly.

Cody hid his laughter as he remembered the sounds of Armand stringing together new curse words in his native French as the fire was extinguished. It had then taken eight other operatives to drag Armand away from the area and keep him from killing Bill with his bare hands.

Since Armand was typically very passive and even-keeled, it spoke volumes to Bill's annoyance level.

As much as Cody wanted to laugh at the man, it was best he not. Doing so would only encourage Bill. Not that he needed much in the way of motivation. Though at the moment, even with as even-tempered as Cody usually was, he was grappling with the urge to slip Bill a tranquilizer to get a few hours of peace. Then again, Bill snored loud, so there would still be that.

Every man had a breaking point, and Bill was fast on his way to discovering Cody's.

With a long, slow breath, Cody looked across the impromptu command center that had been set up some seventy-two hours prior. The walls were institutional white, as was most everything in the entire facility, and the place smelled heavily of lavender, to the point it had been making Cody's eyes water. The lavender concoction had been used to confuse a supernatural's senses...and mask other things.

Mission accomplished.

The resort had been a front for some nefarious activities carried out by crazy doomsday-cult hippies who worshiped a false prophet. The man they followed, Caladrius "Cal" Fabius, had been certifiable, from what Cody had gathered from those who had met him and who'd had direct dealings with him.

All evidence pointed to that assessment being correct.

Every new rock they flipped over showed yet another tangled web the man had managed to weave.

Evil geniuses weren't anything new. They seemed to be a dime a dozen as of late. But Cody had to hand it to the Flock, as the cult had liked to be called: they had put up one hell of a fight. Since the evil hippie dudes had outnumbered the good guys by about ten to one, the odds had been in their favor.

Big time.

Still got their asses handed to them though.

Admittedly, it had been touch and go for a minute there, with the side of evil nearly winning, but the tides had turned in favor of the good guys with a little help from the most unlikely of sources—Bill, Gus, and the cult leader's daughter.

Didn't matter.

It was still a win for the side of good.

Not to mention it went to show wearing all white, holding hands, and singing songs to a self-proclaimed messiah didn't do shit to prep you for an apocalyptic battle. One would have assumed the evil hippies' enormous stockpiles of weapons and the fact they were all supernaturals would have helped.

Nope.

They still lost.

"Aussie," said one of the other operatives in the room. "You need to put your humans on a leash."

Cody cleared his throat and glanced at the man in question. Theodoar (Teddy) Beckert was across the room, near a drop screen that was displaying information being fed to the location by one of the Outcast safe houses that was about an hour away. The safe house was state-of-the-art, one of the best Cody had ever seen.

Teddy's long dark hair was secured at the nape of his neck by a leather strap, something Cody could remember the man doing for decades. He had on a pair of jeans and a T-shirt with an image of a cartoon bear who had come out of the US Forest Service's push to educate the public on the dangers of forest fires.

The shirt was very ironic, considering the fact Teddy was a werebear. Cody wasn't sure if the man's nickname was a coincidence because of his given name, or if it had been born out of what he was.

Teddy caught Cody staring at his shirt, and he lifted a dark brow. "Comment. I dare you," said the alpha male, the tiniest of German accents poking through.

"Come on. It's almost too easy," said Cody with a shrug. "Where's the fun in mocking the werebear for wearing that shirt? And they aren't *my* humans. If memory serves, Bill and Gus started with Casey. They're making the rounds. I'm *all* for shipping them back to him."

Casey Black had been part of the same type of testing that had left Cody what he was—more than human. The men were all close and stayed in contact as much as they could. More as of late, because of the bad guys. Cody had tried to get Casey to fly out to Colorado and retrieve Bill and Gus, but Casey had refused, mentioning some crap about Gus telling him it was destined that they remain near Denver for now—specifically, near Cody.

Just my luck.

Teddy's attention went to Bill, who was now swatting at Cody's abs in an attempt to get the grenade launcher. With another arched brow, Teddy stepped toward Bill and bent to be closer to his level. "Little Crazy Man, you're giving me a headache. Why don't you go outside and play or something?"

Bill ceased his attempts to arm himself and shot Teddy a hard look. "Listen here, *Smokey*, I didn't ask for your input, and I'll have you know I *was* trying to play outside. The Great-White-Pain-In-My-Ass took my toy."

Bill nodded his head and did a rather obvious movement with his eyes to indicate Cody was the pain-in-the-ass in question. Like Teddy wasn't capable of following along.

Cody sighed. "The launcher is not a toy. You already blew up a van yesterday with it and Armand is still pissed."

Bill touched his chin before rubbing it, looking puzzled. "Refresh my memory, which long-haired dude is that one? You're all starting to look alike. Anyone ever heard of a barber? The phrase high-and-tight mean anything to all you *soldiers*?"

Cody snorted. "Fine one to talk there, Bill. Your hair is going in every direction."

"But you can't put it in a ponytail," he said, side-eyeing the men in the room. All of whom had hair long enough to wear tied up. "Bunch of girls."

Teddy's jaw set. "Can I eat him?"

"You werebears are always threatening to eat me," said Bill. "Ain't one of you ever done it."

"Yet. None have eaten you *yet*," added Teddy before folding his arms over his chest and glaring down at the man. "I may not eat you, but I'm not above hog-tying you and taping your mouth shut."

"I'd like to see you try," said Bill, raising his hands and swinging them around in a crazed manner that Cody suspected was meant to look like martial arts. It was anything but. The grunts mixed with air-chops that Bill began to do only served to drive home Cody's assumptions.

Bruce Lee, Bill was not.

For a second, Cody was worried the wiry-haired man would put out his own eye with all the air-chops and partial kicks he was doing. His rather animated sound effects only made the scene all the more comical.

Even Teddy's hard façade began to crack slightly as the edges of his lips curved a bit upward. "I'm sufficiently terrified of you now."

Bill jutted out his chin. "As you should be."

Cody snorted.

Bill eyed him. "Which one of you ponytail-wearing freaky-deeks is Armand?"

"The one whose hair you caught on fire yesterday," said Cody.

Bill bit his lower lip. "Hmm. I set more than one guy's hair on fire yesterday. Be more specific."

Teddy laughed but hid it quickly under a cough. "Armand is the vampire."

Bill pointed at Teddy. "Aha! Wait, I'm getting blamed for nearly killing an already dead guy?"

Teddy looked over Bill's head at Cody. "Let's just hog-tie him and direct-ship him back to Casey. We don't even need to poke holes in the box for air or anything."

"Okay, but we're going to need to do the same to his buddy Gus," warned Cody. "And I'm not sure if you know this or not, but Gus is not a fan of being touched."

"*And* how," said Bill with a slow whistle through his teeth, in a childlike voice. He finally stopped trying to get the launcher and leaned, his gaze going to the doorway. "Anyone seen him? He was supposed to meet me back here once Mona was done with her facial."

"Mona?" asked Teddy.

Bill rolled his eyes. "His woman. Geesh, Smokey, pay attention."

Teddy groaned. "He's on my last nerve."

Cody understood where the man was coming from. "Don't eat him. I'll have to explain to Casey why I let you. Not a conversation I want to have."

"I'll tell him myself," said Teddy, making a move to go at Bill, who wisely darted out of the room.

Seizing the opportunity to rest his arm, Cody lowered it. He then handed the launcher to Teddy. "Hold that for me a second. I need to get the blood back to my extremities."

Teddy grinned but took the launcher all the same. He set it aside.

Cody went to work getting the feeling back in his arm. As the prickling sensation of pins and needles started, Bill darted back into the room, snatched the launcher, and tried to make a run for it.

Teddy caught Bill with one hand, lifting him off the ground, and then seized hold of the launcher with his other hand. The look he gave Cody said he was very much entertaining the idea of eating the human.

Cody did his best to avoid laughing.

He failed.

Horribly.

Bill kicked at Teddy, and when that didn't work, he resorted to sticking his thumbs in his ears and waving his hands as he stuck out his tongue.

Cody laughed harder then.

"Och, do I want to know what all the ruckus is about?" asked a deeply Scottish-accented voice as a tall man with shoulder-length, ink-black hair and a matching beard, which he'd recently taken to wearing slightly longer than normal, entered the room, holding a cell phone in his hand. Tattoos covered everywhere except his face. Numerous silver piercings were all over him as well. He was in a kilt, which Cody was learning was common for him and his twin brother, paired with biker boots and a T-shirt that had a cross, a vial of holy water and a stake with a wooden mallet. The shirt was taking a dig at the Crimson Ops Division of PSI, better known to everyone as the Fang Gang, which was composed of vampires.

The man took one look at Bill being held off the ground by Teddy and grinned. "What did the li'l hairy man do this time?"

"Little Bow-Mac," said Bill as he grinned at the newcomer and batted his lashes as if he was oh so innocent. "The German here was talking shit about Scotland and William Wallace. I was just trying to set him straight. If you give me back that launcher he took from me, I'll see to it he doesn't bad-mouth the Lycan legend again."

MacBeth (Mac) McCracken glanced at Teddy, who just so happened to be on Mac's team that was based out of the Denver branch of PSI. He lifted a dark brow. "Tis clear the wee man has been exposed to my cousin far too much. Is there a detox program that's Striker specific?"

Teddy smiled wide. "No. But there should be. Should be one for everyone having to deal with any of you Scots."

When it became evident to Bill that his plan to get free wasn't going as he'd hoped, he switched tactics. "Tell him to put me down, or I'm gonna post the video all over the internet of you getting your hair put in bows by a little girl."

Mac stiffened, and then ran a hand over his beard. His gaze hardened on Bill. "You do nae annoy me as you first did, but if you even think of outing wee Andie on the internet, I'll rip you in two here and now. The lass is nae to be posted anywhere of the sort. Her father is no longer a threat, now that he's been dealt with, but I'll nae have a new target put on her tiny head. Am I clear?"

Andie was the other daughter of Caladrius. She had formed a strange bond with the giant Scotsman, seeming to tame Mac at least slightly when he was around her.

Bill grunted. "I wasn't gonna show her face. I'm crazy, not stupid. But I'll show *yours*."

Mac snorted and went to Teddy, plucking Bill from the man's hold. He then set Bill on his feet and pointed at him. "Stay."

Bill saluted the man.

When Mac turned his back, Bill seized hold of the launcher from Teddy's other hand and wrenched it away.

As he did, it fired.

Cody had half a second to react as a grenade

came flying at him. He dove out of the way just as Armand was entering the room, deep in conversation with Mac's identical twin, Carbrey (Car).

Armand's gaze slid in Cody's direction, and then widened a moment before he spun and tackled Car, taking him to the ground, where they both just missed being struck as the grenade went over them and landed in the hallway.

Armand moved with a speed most didn't possess, a testament to just how old the vampire really was, despite looking no more than thirty. He grabbed the grenade, opened the door to the room across from them, lobbed the grenade in there, and then closed the door fast, getting only a few feet from it before there was a massive explosion that rocked the area and sent the door hurtling at Armand. It hit him in the back and knocked him forward.

Cody moved quickly and caught his friend, more out of the knowledge Armand was going to try to kill Bill than the worry Armand would be hurt. He was hardy stock. Bill wasn't.

Flames licked past everyone in the immediate area, and when it was all said and done, everyone except Bill was on the ground, looking a bit worse for wear.

Bill was standing there, giving Mac a stern look. "Look what you made me do. I almost killed the already-dead guy—*again*. Y'all better hope vampires are like cats and have nine lives. Hmm, would that be nine un-lives? What's the politically correct term for a bloodsucker? I can never keep up on that shit."

Armand growled, his demon nearing the surface.

Cody kept his friend pinned to the floor. "It's been how long since you killed an innocent human? Don't throw that hard-fought-for control away over Bill."

Armand stiffened, and then sat up slowly, shrugging Cody off him. "It is about to be zero days since I last killed an innocent human—if one can even call that maniac innocent."

Bill pursed his lips and tried to sidestep out of the room, still holding the launcher.

Teddy let out a slow, long moan. "Ouch. Who is going to clean this place up? Huh? I'm not explaining to General Newman how something blew up in here. I vote we make Cody do it. It's his human pet who caused it."

"For the hundredth time," said Cody, sitting

up as well. "He's not my human. He's Casey's. Blame *him*."

Teddy got to his feet. "Oh, I intend to."

Mac pushed off the floor and de-weaponized the small male. "Go to yer room, Bill. Yer grounded."

Bill eyed the werewolf up and then down. "You can't tell me what to do."

Car was next off the floor. He joined his brother. Standing side by side, they looked like two imposing towers no one was getting past until the men were good and ready to step aside. "Och, yer an insane little hairy man, Bill. I love it."

Mac rolled his eyes. "You would."

Armand rose with an effortless grace and dusted off the front of his designer shirt and pants. He then looked at Bill and flashed fang. A hiss was quick to follow.

Bill grinned. "Those are some big fangs there. Nice. Hey, did the government give you those? Oh, did they give you a big dick too? You an Outcast? They all got handed big willies. I just got LSD out of my deal. Fun, but not as good as a big dick."

Armand glanced at Cody. "Before Yosemite

Bill so rudely tried to kill me—*again*—I was coming to tell you we have news."

Cody got to his feet and rubbed his right ear, which had a slight ring in it from the explosion still. "What's up?"

Car tipped his head as he stared at Cody. "You just had a grenade go off near you and you still look like you're ready to go catch some waves. Anyone ever tell you that yer verra blond and verra tan? And yer teeth are unnaturally white. It's unnerving."

Ignoring him, Cody set his sights on his friend. "Armand, what did you need to talk to me about? What news do you have?"

"It's Walter Helmuth and The Corporation," said Armand, his voice clipped. "We're picking up chatter about him. About something big that might be going down soon in or around Savannah. Nothing concrete but enough that I thought you'd want to know."

Cody didn't hear anything else beyond that, as his shark surged upright, wanting out, wanting to find the man who had tortured him and make him pay.

Armand was suddenly directly in front of him, cupping his face. "Livingston, pull back on the anger or we will have bigger issues to contend with."

Mac snorted. "Aye, like where in the fuck do we put you if you shift into shark form fully? In case you've nae noticed, Aussie, there is nae an ocean close."

Car grinned. "But we've a pool here that is saltwater. We can throw in some fish and sit around poolside, working on our tans, trying to catch up to his, while he stays confined to the pool, pissed off over some douche named Walter."

His brother nodded. "Aye. Come to think of it, I've never known anyone named Walter who wasn't a douche. You?"

"Nope," added Bill. "Total douches. Wanna go outside and blow shit up with me?"

The twins shared a looked before they both nodded.

Armand sighed, still cupping Cody's face. "The twins make Gram and Striker seem easy to deal with, don't they?"

The statement, with all its truth, made Cody laugh softly, helping him to fight off a pending shift. They were all right. Losing control and shifting into shark form would be very bad. The last time he'd come close to doing such a thing had been years ago in Costa Rica when he'd found the little girl drowning and been captured by Helmuth. At least then he'd been on a beach, with open water within running distance. Unlike here. Here he'd just be good and truly fucked.

He took a deep breath to gather control of himself. It worked to a certain degree. "I need to go back to Savannah."

Armand nodded. "I thought you would say as much. I'm readying a jet for us now. But, Cody, you need to understand if the chatter is correct and he is there, it is likely a trap. One possibly set for you. After all, have you not been calling Savannah home as of late?"

Cody thought harder on it. "Yes."

"And you still want to charge in head first?" asked Armand, a knowing note to his French-accented voice.

"Yes," replied Cody with no room for interpretation. "He has to pay. What he did to me…to others. And the people he's in bed with—the things they've done. They have to be stopped. If that means running into a trap to do it, fine by me. But if he takes me, put a bullet between my eyes. Don't let me fall into his hands again. What

I am, what I have in me, it helped make him what he is now—nearly unstoppable. He can't be allowed to get even stronger. You know it, and so does everyone else here."

"Aussie is right," said Mac.

Teddy grunted. "Doesn't make the plan any less stupid. We can't just let him run off alone and do this."

The twins stepped forward. They shared a look and Mac took the lead. "We'll be going with him."

"As will I," said Armand. "Teddy, can you take point here?"

Teddy inclined his head. "But only if you take the humans. I cannot handle babysitting them. I'll eat them."

"I heard that," said Bill. He then looked off in the distance for a moment before speaking again. "Gus says we need to go with Cody too."

"Of course you do," said Cody, his ire growing. "We need to go now. No fucking around."

Armand patted his cheek. "Calm yourself. It has been set in motion, friend. The jet is being readied. In the meantime, grab a bag and try to stay in control of your beast."

Chapter Five

FORTY-FIVE MINUTES OUTSIDE OF SAVANNAH, GEORGIA...

WALTER HELMUTH SAT on the back patio, overlooking the ocean. As he stared out from beneath the safety of the shaded area at the sun's rays on the boarded path that went over the dunes to the beach, his anger grew, his father's curse limiting what he could and could not do. Each passing day, he found himself more and more sensitive to sunlight.

He could still be outside during daylight hours, unlike many of his kind, but direct sunlight was not his friend. That was why he wore copious amounts of a special concoction that acted like sunscreen, as well as did his best to stay in shady spots—like the patio.

He'd thought he'd beaten the issue after he'd

spent time at a friend's wellness resort out in Colorado. The resort provided nearly everything a supernatural could need for rest, relaxation, and healing, should they require it.

And Helmuth had required all those things and more.

The man who owned the resort, Caladrius Fabius, was something of an eccentric (which was putting it mildly) but wielded true power, and therefore was one of the few people Helmuth respected and feared. Only a fool wouldn't be afraid of what Cal was capable of.

Helmuth had been a witness to the man's abilities on more than one occasion and it had certainly left an impression. There was no denying the level of power Cal had, and that he was not a man to be crossed.

When Helmuth had found himself injured and in need of special recovery methods to assist in his healing, he'd known instantly who to go to for help. And he'd not been wrong. Cal's facility was far more than it appeared to be to the general public. For one, it catered to the supernatural. For another, Cal liked to feed from alpha males, leeching their powers and quite literally sucking the life from them.

Helmuth had known the truth about Cal and his exotic tastes in food for decades but never batted an eye. He'd kept Cal in a good supply of fit alpha males, to be drained of their powers and who knows what else, and in return, Cal assisted Helmuth when need be. And there had been a need recently.

Who was Helmuth to judge the man? There were times when nothing but the sweet taste of blood would satisfy what lived deep in Helmuth. Then there was the dark need he had to kill—to tear flesh apart with his clawed hands.

That too was part of his curse.

Closing his eyes momentarily, he dug deep to center himself in an attempt to keep from shifting forms then and there. His shifter side wasn't like most supernatural males'. In fact, his species was so rare, they were thought to be nothing more than myths.

Something dreamed up in storybooks.

Creatures that were birthed from legend.

Gargoyles.

Helmuth was a testament to their existence. Proof there was more out there.

He'd studied all the lore surrounding his kind. All the rumors. Some were based in truth, many were lies more than likely spun by the gargoyles themselves to throw others off their trail, and some were outright comical. But one was certainly true.

Turning to stone.

And it fucking sucked.

The loss of control over your own body. The immobility of being stuck in stone form, vulnerable even during daylight hours. Then there was the monster side of it all. Above turning to stone. The shift into something that was a strange combination of reptile, bat, demon, and vampire. Each of which came with its own set of issues. Then there was the addition of witch that Helmuth had within him from his mother's side.

She'd been an unwilling participant in his creation, and he'd killed her while she was giving birth to him.

"My first murder," he said, lacking any real remorse over a woman he'd never known. There may have been a time when he'd wept for her. If so, he couldn't remember it now. He couldn't connect to any point in his past when he'd had anything close to compassion. Life and circumstances had beat the caring out of him, leaving him what he was today: a man who did what he had to in order to survive. It was hard to imagine he'd ever cared one way or another for his mother.

After all, she was why he was cursed.

His mother's people had taken exception to her being stolen away and forced to birth a child. One they saw as evil. They'd lashed out the best way they could. They'd cursed Helmuth's father and, in turn, Helmuth. As if the gargoyle's weakness during daylight hours wasn't enough. No. The witches had seen to it that his father was turned to stone for good. Not just during the day.

And that would soon be Helmuth's fate as well if he didn't find a cure or something to hold off the pending changes. The serum he'd been using had lost its effectiveness. And he'd gone so long fighting to keep away the change that it had left the monster side of himself fighting for dominance. There was a very real chance that if he fully shifted forms again, he'd be locked in gargoyle state and, from there, turn to stone for good relatively quickly.

But all hope was not lost as he'd once feared.

Caladrius—a man who was as close to a friend as someone could be to him, since Helmuth had trust issues—had stepped in and helped Helmuth recently.

He'd spent time out near Denver recovering and healing from a battle he'd gotten into with a group of do-gooders. He'd not gone down easily. No. It had taken more than one of them working together to injure him as much as he had been.

Helmuth's jaw set as he thought about the succubus he'd had in his grips and had nearly fully molded into the perfect mate. It didn't matter that fate hadn't given her to him. He'd found a way to circumvent destiny—to create the perfect woman to complement him. A woman who could help him fight off the darkness and the curse threatening to take hold of him fully.

Gisbert Krauss, a man Helmuth had aligned himself with out of necessity, not loyalty, had assisted in creating a way to alter the succubus's genetic makeup. He'd even come to oversee some of the process himself before vanishing like he was so good at doing.

Since her kind drew upon the energy of others in order to survive, she'd been the perfect candidate for the trials. Her natural-born ability to siphon from a supernatural had been the ideal catalyst. And the trial had been working. She had been turning into a hybrid. A blend of succubus and Helmuth's species.

Everything had been seamless and on track when she'd somehow managed to gain her freedom—and ran straight into the arms of her true mate.

"Bastard."

Hissing at the memory, Helmuth tipped his head back, his fangs distending quickly as his anger flared.

The damn weregorilla, who was what most knew as an Outcast, had been gifted the succubus as his mate. The beast didn't deserve her—or all of the hard work Helmuth had put into her. So much time and resources wasted, and for what? To leave him, injured, in battle, needing to hide out while he recovered.

It was enough to make him want to go on a killing spree to simply wash his palate of the taste of defeat.

He checked the time and did the time zone conversion, knowing Cal was two hours behind him. If memory served, it was about the time Cal and his minions had their morning worship before they gathered to eat together.

Helmuth didn't miss that or group sing-alongs.

But he'd gone along with what The Flock did in most respects while he'd been a guest among them. Though he also did not miss Cal's long-winded inspirational speeches, which were thinly veiled as gospel. What he *did* miss was Cal's oldest daughter and her healing remedies.

His friend's eldest daughter was something of an herbalist, though Helmuth liked to refer to her as an alchemist. That was certainly more along the lines of her abilities. She'd made him a salve that had helped the patches of his skin that were reptile-like and given him protection while out in the sun.

There was a slight breeze coming off the water, but it did little to cut through the heat and humidity of the south. It wasn't even noon yet and already it was oppressively hot.

Disgustingly so.

He despised the heat.

While he'd had the home built several years back, his plan had been to use it during months when the humidity wasn't as high. When the temperature stayed around seventy degrees. Necessity and circumstances had changed that timeframe for him.

Irritation coursed through his veins—something that seemed to be a constant anymore. The rage that lived just below the surface was no longer easy to hide or control. It was yet one more road sign indicating his path to hell was nearly complete. That the transformation he'd been fighting for years was coming, regardless of how hard he tried to stop it.

A curse he'd inherited from his father.

Bastard.

One more thing he could despise the man for.

The scent of rotting fish reached him, and he knew the smell was coming from the same dead one he'd found on his predawn walk and had considered burying, only to leave it and continue onward.

His nostrils curled as the smell beat at him more. It probably wasn't even that strong, but the transition he'd been attempting to stave off left his senses in a constant state of overdrive. He was acutely aware of every single person within the beach house, on the premises, and on the neighboring lots, all from the sounds of their heartbeats. While it was hardly uncommon for a supernatural male to be able to pick up the telltale sound of a heart beating, it was out of the realm of normal to hear it from the distance he was, and as loudly as he could. Especially considering the distance between his home and the houses nearest to him.

The sound beat like twenty drums in his head, all of which were out of sync, thumping over and over again. It was nearly maddening, and it took everything in him to avoid simply slaughtering everyone to finally have some semblance of peace.

Of quiet.

Even that wouldn't help. All it would do was bring about the inevitable bloodlust that he was doing his best to ignore. It too was part of the curse bestowed upon him by his father. As much as he wanted to feed that darker side of himself with the sweet, coppery nectar of life it craved, he didn't dare. Not right now. Not with how on edge he was. Surrender would take him down a path of no return.

The other day, he'd been sitting poolside at the wellness resort, relaxing, when he'd caught the scent of a coyote-shifter who had been on the premises. The female's smell had sickened him, and he'd demanded she be dealt with accordingly.

And she had been.

He grinned slightly, thinking about how it had all played out.

Perfectly.

Except for the fact his time there had come to an end. Now he was here, in humidity hell with the foul smell filling his nostrils. Thankfully, the wind shifted once more and stopped bringing with it the odor of rotting fish.

"Master," said Ernest, one of the men in his employment, as he entered the patio area. "Can I get you anything?"

Ernest had been with Helmuth for nearly twenty years, holding several positions, all of which were in the service capacity. The man looked to be in his early forties, but he was closer to two hundred. Ernest had been employed by more than one powerful family in his immortally long life.

Helmuth had been awarded the man as partial payment from a debt owed by a man whose gambling habits had drained his coffers. He did his job and didn't annoy Helmuth. That was saying something.

Helmuth nodded. "Brandy."

"Of course, sir," said Ernest, scurrying off and past two other men who were stationed just inside the doorway.

They were trained killers, men who were

feared by others. One had even worked for PSI at one point in his life but had been subjected to conversion techniques that opened his eyes and his mind, his true nature shining through. Of course, the guard was unaware of his true, full past. He'd been given exactly what he needed as far as memories but nothing more.

And he'd been molded into the perfect weapon and guard dog.

Or in his case, a guard orca.

The man's job was simple.

Keep Helmuth guarded and oversee the completion of the research vessel that had been in the works for some time. For a while, Helmuth hadn't been sure the project would be able to move forward, since his standing within The Corporation had been on shaky ground, but that was all behind him.

In Seattle, he'd already taken unnecessary risks that had left him scrambling to clean up the fallout. He'd not make that mistake again.

His beach home and the freighter that was currently out to sea but within a quick boat ride's distance were heavily guarded.

Veritable fortresses.

They had to be. They needed to keep out a

well-trained enemy and, in the case of the freighter, keep in test subjects that he and the scientists who were on loan to him from The Corporation had been working on.

Try as he might, Helmuth found it hard to contain his growing excitement over how everything was progressing. Even with the minor setback he'd suffered recently, things were working out in his favor. And he'd gotten information and news from Cal that only sweetened the near future.

Cal had been one of the driving forces affiliated with The Corporation who had refused to turn his back on Helmuth in his hour of need. Cal had believed in him.

Helmuth adjusted the rolled cuff of his long-sleeved, lightweight white designer shirt and brought up a leg, putting his ankle on his thigh in a relaxing position as he continued to stare out at the water.

All around him was peaceful, yet it was a façade. A state of mind, because the reality was vastly different. He was being hunted like a fox with dogs nipping at his heels.

At least that was what he wanted people to think.

Especially those who were trying to bring him to their version of justice. Which was a joke. Who were they to decide what was right and what was wrong?

He knew where all the pieces on the chessboard were, and he was controlling them. It was working out as planned. And the information he'd been given by Cal had panned out and was so very close to bearing fruit.

While the succubus may be out of his reach for now, Caladrius had given him hope that another female might fill the open slot…and perhaps be an even better candidate for the testing. And Caladrius claimed this wasn't the first run-in Helmuth had had with the new woman. That he'd been in close proximity to her once before, years ago. And that, like years ago, where she was, the other would be—the male that still held value to Helmuth.

The wereshark.

He licked his lower lip in anticipation of what was to come.

"Kahale," said Helmuth to one of the guards near the door.

The man stepped out, his long, dark, curly hair pulled up and back from his face. He wore a dress shirt with the sleeves cuffed much like Helmuth's. The way he moved was fluid, silent almost, making him the perfect assassin when the need arose, which was more often than one would think. "Boss?"

Helmuth motioned to his den window. "Bring me the results of the testing on the scientist."

Kahale nodded and headed inside, reappearing shortly thereafter with a computer tablet. He handed it to Helmuth and took a step back.

"Stay," barked Helmuth, pulling up the file he wanted to look at, yet again. When the DNA results were on the screen, he held it up for the guard to see. "Work of art, don't you agree?"

Kahale showed no fear of Helmuth. He never did. He looked over the tablet at Helmuth. "I wouldn't know. I'm not sure what I'm looking at, boss."

Helmuth touched an area of the report. "Look here. It says she has some of your kind in her."

"Shifter?" asked Kahale with a slight nod, seeming unimpressed, as was often the case with the man. There was a certain lack of emotion that even Helmuth found off-putting, which was saying something.

"Orca," corrected Helmuth. "And see here, this says she has traces of three different types of sharks in her, as well as dolphin—and this is the best part."

Kahale bent to look closer at the tablet. "Still don't know what I'm looking at, boss."

Annoyed, Helmuth grunted. "This is the marker for a succubus. They're in the Fae family, you know."

He nodded. "That much I do know. Nothing like a good romp between the sheets with one."

Helmuth grinned. "Tell me about it."

"This scientist, she the one coming today to meet with you?" asked Kahale.

"One of them, yes."

"And the other?" questioned Kahale.

"Is more than she appears to be as well," replied Helmuth. "But not a candidate for what I have planned. That one has ties to the Para-Regs so while they're here, do nothing to tip our hand. I do not want another organization crawling up our asses, got it?"

"Got it." Kahale was quiet a moment. "These results have something to do with the freighter and the overhaul you had done on it recently?"

"They do," replied Helmuth. "How is everything? Does Dr. Roberts have everything in place that I told him to have prepared? Remind him again that I want both subjects kept alive. I know how much he likes to kill things—especially women. The moment my need of him is done, feel free to dispose of him any way you see fit. Do me a favor, make it painful."

"With pleasure. And as far as I know it's all set. I can take a boat out to check if you want."

"Can't you just swim out or something?" asked Helmuth snidely. "Isn't that what your kind do? Swim?"

Kahale never batted an eye at the comment. The way he looked at Helmuth said he'd kill him too if provoked.

"Why is it you're the only guard I have who doesn't fear me?" asked Helmuth.

"I fear you," said Kahale. "I'd be stupid not to. But I figure there is no real point in getting worked up about it. If you want me dead, I'm dead. But I'm guessing it would be one hell of a battle before I ended up dead, and who knows, I could get lucky and take you with me. Want to see if my theory on mutually assured destruction holds water?"

"No." Helmuth admired the man's honesty.

"Get on the radio and check on the ship's progress. I want to be sure everything is in order for our guests."

"You still sure that wereshark you've had your eye on is going to come to you?" asked Kahale.

"I am," replied Helmuth, his finger sliding over the screen on the tablet. "I'm told I'll have something he desires very soon."

Kahale stood there, blocking some of the sun with his massive frame. "The woman. You think he'll have an interest in her? Didn't I hear some of the guys who were with Krauss and his men over in Egypt say that this wereshark you're so wrapped up with was held there after being held by you. They said he escaped about five years ago. That right?"

"It is. It is where he managed to escape from," said Helmuth, still bitter about the matter. Had Krauss and those he did business with been better about screening their employees, two undercover agents with PSI would not have managed to make it through, posing as guards. Many a good test subject was lost that day, and the mad dash to recover them all had begun.

Unfortunately, only a select few had been recovered. Most scattered to the winds and were still out there, still being hunted. A small number had only just resurfaced after five years of staying hidden. With them was the wereshark Helmuth wanted back so desperately.

Soon, Helmuth would have the wereshark back in his grasp. And this time the bastard would not escape.

"Boss, the guys who worked details at the holding facility over there said the wereshark didn't take an interest in any of the women they tried to force on him. Guess they tried breeding him or something while he was held. From what I'm hearing, he was protective of the females, but had no real romantic or sexual interest in any of them. What makes you think this one will prove different? That he'll want to fuck this woman?"

"What makes *you* think *his* interest will be sexual?" questioned Helmuth, having never mentioned anything of the sort to the guard.

Kahale shrugged. "Just assumed that was what you were hinting at. Was I wrong?"

"No, according to Cal, you're not wrong."

At the mention of Cal, Kahale tensed.

"I know your thoughts on Cal," said Helmuth.

Kahale stiffened. "He's bad news."

"Yes, but he gets results," stated Helmuth.

"And he's sure this woman will draw the wereshark back into the fold and that she could be someone special to me."

"Your mate?" asked Kahale. "Really?"

"Mine? No. Not to start with," said Helmuth. "But from what Cal has told me and with these test results, she has every ingredient I'll require in her genetic makeup already to be compatible with me. The rest can be altered and forced."

Kahale said nothing more on the matter. He seemed almost bored with the conversation.

Helmuth tapped the tablet front. "Call out and check with Cal's right-hand man. Ask Taggert if Cal has had any more visions about me and my future."

"Will do," said Kahale, heading into the house.

If Caladrius was correct, one of Helmuth's pets who had managed to escape would be back in his clutches, assisting in holding off Helmuth's darkness—even if unwillingly. Oh, how Helmuth missed having the wereshark under his thumb. And the samples he'd been able to have constant access to while holding the wereshark captive had proven to be helpful in holding back the tidal wave of change happening to Helmuth.

At least to some degree.

Yes, they'd stopped working toward the end, but that had been years ago now. If memory served, just over four years. And in that time, advances had occurred in leaps and bounds in the black-market science area. So much so that Helmuth firmly believed that between the wereshark's DNA and the introduction of the new female, he could beat the curse once and for all.

Since Caladrius had a knack for simply knowing things that would come to pass, Helmuth had no reason to doubt the man. It took all of Helmuth's patience, which wasn't in abundance, to bide his time and get everything in order as it should be.

Looking back on the events that had left him sweltering in the southern heat, he realized he'd been impulsive and launched his attack plan too early the last time with the succu-bitch. Without adequately understanding all the players in the game. But that had been because desperation clung to him daily. He didn't want to succumb to his curse. He didn't want to become a monster for good, and then turn to stone close thereafter.

This time would be different. He'd do things the right way. He'd make sure all his proverbial ducks were in a row. That was what he was doing now—sweating his balls off in the southern heat.

Things had been different from the mistakes he'd made in the past. At least so far. Unlike Seattle and what had happened there, he'd kept his true nature a secret here. Those in the area thought he was just a wealthy venture capitalist. Not one of the principal heads of the paranormal underground, as was the case.

Caladrius had helped set up the false identity and paper trail as well, having owed Helmuth for gifting the man a never-ending supply of alpha males to draw power from before killing.

Supernaturals were something Helmuth had in excess. His underground fight clubs were notorious. If he wasn't pitting the males his people captured against one another, he was loaning them out for testing or to fill other needs of his business associates. And there were plenty of times he merely sold them to the highest bidder. The black market for special-order supernaturals was hot and extremely lucrative.

If everything went according to plan, the well-constructed trap would yield far more fruit than merely a wereshark and the female he sought. It would bring him additional alpha males to infuse into his fight club scene. They would fetch a pretty penny too when others heard they were captives and being forced to fight.

Nothing brought out paying customers more than the knowledge one or more of the men in the ring were special operatives of the enemy. Yes. The money would keep flooding in when that happened.

He could hardly wait.

Everything was lining up perfectly, and soon, all his hard work, all his struggles with remaining patient would be worth it. Hell, even being seriously injured and hunted would be worth it. He'd regain his position of respect within The Corporation and have his cure. The battle would be a hard one, but he was ready. So were his men.

Others might crumble from the pressure, but not him. No, Helmuth welcomed the challenge, finding sick pleasure in knowing precious man-hours and resources were being expended by the other side in an attempt to capture him.

The men hunting him were a tenacious bunch. The kind that championed causes. Those types were always the worst. So full of themselves as they sat upon their high horses, sneering down their noses at those they deemed beneath them.

As if any of the men currently searching for him were his betters or even his equals. They were not.

Very few were.

The heathens were simply coming in numbers greater than he could handle in his current state. But he wouldn't be this way forever. He'd regain his full strength, and they would regret making a play for him. Of that, he was sure.

It didn't help matters any that the men coming for him had started to set aside old differences to work together. He missed the days when they'd kept each of their divisions relatively separate, each dealing with their own set of issues.

More than once, he'd heard rumors that the vampires and shifters within the PSI organization had been doing more joint missions than ever. It was far easier to skate by undetected in the world of crime when one hand didn't know what the other was doing.

They were no doubt responding to the fact the side Helmuth played for—which was often referred to as bad, but he didn't exactly see it that way—had been pulling ahead in the larger war, while still losing some battles.

Labels were pointless.

No one person was merely black or white. They were all fifty shades of who the fuck knew what.

Helmuth didn't view his actions as evil. He was merely doing as he'd been born to do: be more than human.

He didn't see the point in forcing supernaturals to deny their nature, to forego hunting or hurting humans. They were a food source to many types of supernaturals, but the side that heralded themselves as good forced their own kind to live a lie. To deny their inner beasts and demons. Witches and Fae were obligated to hide their magiks from the watchful eyes of the humans, while the race as a whole acted as if supernaturals didn't exist.

Helmuth had seen the lengths PSI was going to in an attempt to walk back classified information that had been leaked to the public. He had to give credit where it was due: their public relations department had a true gift for spinning the truth to seem like nothing more than fiction, the rantings of a few crazed souls.

The truth was so much more interesting.

Humans' simple little minds couldn't possibly comprehend all that was really around them in the world. Just thinking about humans made his blood pressure increase. He had a great dislike of them.

Why should they bow down to a species that was lesser than them? A species they were born to rule?

The answer was simple.

They shouldn't.

At least not in his mind. Doing so made them look weak. They were anything but. They could rule the world with ease. If only I-Ops got out of their own way. Why they ever thought kowtowing to a bunch of ignorant humans was a smart idea was beyond him. They'd never taken a vote. If so, he'd have cast his in favor of making humans their pets. But no, the side of good had just up and decided the way of things, and all were expected to obey or risk their wrath.

Fuck them.

Helmuth's fingernails began to lengthen as his temper flared. It was a side effect of the control issues he'd been suffering from for decades. A sign that he was on borrowed time before he lost his human side totally to that of his supernatural one.

Chapter Six

"WE'RE HERE," said Bonnie, causing Gena to jerk awake in the passenger side of the white SUV.

Gena blinked several times, disoriented before she realized she must have dozed off during the drive to Hilton Head. It wasn't much of a shock, considering how elusive sleep had been for her as of late. But falling asleep on her way to a work meeting with her boss wasn't exactly how she'd wanted her day to go. It was a good thing Bonnie was more than just her boss; she was her friend as well.

"Sorry. I'm not getting anywhere close to enough sleep lately."

"Hard to do when your nights are being rocked by a hunky shark guy," said Bonnie with a playful expression as she killed the engine. "Wish I had that issue."

"You want to dream about drowning and a shark shifting into a man?" asked Gena.

Bonnie glanced at her. "You left out the part about you drowning. The only bits you mentioned to me were the racy ones. And no, what would I do with a *male* shark-shifter? I prefer my racy dreams to be about women. But I won't lie, I'm not opposed to looking my fill of a hunky man. But looking is as far as I go. Men are so full of drama and kind of pointless for pleasure. Nothing I can't handle myself. No thanks."

Gena ran her hands over her face to wake herself up fully as she laughed softly under her breath at her friend. "When I grow up, I want to be like you."

Bonnie blew on her knuckles and winked. "It's a gift."

Gena faced forward in the SUV and did a double take as she found herself staring at a twelve-foot-high ornate white gate with an intercom system and a keypad. Landscaping was done in a way to lessen the harshness of it all, but even the foliage couldn't totally take from the slight prison feel the entrance let off.

When Gena noticed several mounted cameras, all facing the SUV, she nodded to them. "Who is this guy again, and why does he need all of this?"

"Guess when you're loaded, you have a new set of problems to worry about beyond how to keep the lights on," answered Bonnie. "For the record, I'd rather have the need for security measures than a shut-off notice, but that might just be me. Plus, if I was independently wealthy, I'd make sure we had all the funding we needed at the center."

"Nope. Not just you. I'd pick security over shut-off notices too, and I'd help the center as well. I'm not rolling in money though. Probably why I live on the world's oldest boat. Have I thanked you again for letting me dock at the research center's marina?" asked Gena. Bonnie had taken pity on Gena, letting her use an empty slip the facility had.

It saved Gena a lot of money that she didn't really have. And while her parents had offered to help her out while she was getting started on her own, she wanted to do it herself, no matter how hard it was. Her boat, while old, was still seaworthy, and she tended to it with a loving hand. It would last many more years if she continued to take care of it.

Which was the plan.

Bonnie winked. "No need to thank me. I like having an ice-cream binging spot close to work. After dealing with Ray again last week, I nearly showed up and asked to come aboard for another night of eating nothing but sweets."

Gena tipped her head slightly. "Ray was back last week? Why?"

"I don't know," said Bonnie, looking forward a moment. "I came into the facility earlier than normal and I found him in my office. He says he left some personal effects in the storage closet in there."

"Uh, shouldn't he have waited until we were open to come and ask for them? And how did he get in?" asked Gena before gasping. "He has a key still? I thought you got the keys back from him."

"I did," said Bonnie. "Apparently, he'd had another made. I have a call in to a locksmith who has yet to call me back. Gotta love the South and laid-back Southern time."

Unease settled over Gena quickly. Unsure why she suddenly felt as if she wanted to have Bonnie turn the SUV around and leave, Gena ran her hand up and over the back of her neck as she attempted to wipe away the worry.

"You okay?" asked Bonnie.

Gena shivered slightly, and Bonnie was quick to turn down the air conditioning. Whenever they went anywhere, Bonnie tended to turn the air on to a setting that could keep food from spoiling. At least it felt that way to Gena, who preferred warmer temperatures than freezing.

"Sorry, I'm fairly certain I've started the dreaded change," said Bonnie. "I'm hotter than Hades at random anymore."

"*Dreaded* change?" echoed Gena. "Weren't you telling me how much you hated your period and wanted to donate your uterus to science and that you wished menopause would hurry up and get to you?"

"Yes, but everyone makes out menopause to be such a horrible thing. I felt I needed to play the part. Well, and the hot flashes do suck. If someone would have told me I'd be going through this in my early forties, I'd have laughed them out of the room. I'd like to add this to the column of stuff they don't tell you when you're born with a vagina."

Gena did her best to avoid laughing. "You're

always adding something to that list. What's it up to now? Has to be at least ten pages."

"Oh, easily." Bonnie nodded. "Men have it so easy."

Bonnie opened her window and pressed the call button on the keypad. No one responded, but the automatic gates began to open all the same. They drove through them, and Bonnie pulled the SUV to a stop on the large driveaway.

With a shake of her head, Gena exited the white SUV that had the research center's new logo on the side and stood in the ornate driveway, staring up at the mansion before her. She shoved the bottle opener that Bonnie had insisted she take into her front shorts pocket. The woman hadn't been joking. She really did get calendars and openers made with Donavon Dynamics' logo on them.

Should Gena ever find herself in need of a small metal bottle opener, she could rest assured, she was covered.

Because that happened often.

She walked forward a bit and looked across the hood of the SUV at Bonnie, who was staring at the home as well.

Bonnie let out a low whistle. "I feel like some

random guy with a hand towel will be waiting in the restroom should we need to use it," said Bonnie, looking at the house. "Think he'll spritz us with scented fragrances too while he wears white gloves?"

"I really hope not," replied Gena as she soaked in the sight of the home. There was a huge fountain out front that had a bronze mermaid, who was more than blessed in the cleavage area and topless, holding a large conch shell that was spitting water directly up and into the air. She was sitting on the back of a sea turtle with small dolphins leaping in the air around her.

Tipping her head, Gena soaked in the sight of the artwork. The time put into it was evident, and she could only guess at how much it had to cost to have done. More than she made in a year, for sure.

The mermaid's long hair cascaded over its narrow shoulders, only just managing to cover where nipples would be on its way down past the mermaid's slender waist. Its tail had intricate scale patterns that had started to green somewhat from oxidation, making Gena wonder how long the fountain had been installed, as it wasn't totally overtaken by the naturally occurring event.

Bonnie stepped to the left and then to the right. "That turtle is giving me the stink eye."

With a roll of her eyes, Gena snorted. "You are so weird."

"Thanks," said Bonnie with a smirk. She then righted herself, pushing at her hair to be sure it was all back before facing Gena fully. "Do I look like a well-respected professional whom you would trust with your money and expensive toys?"

Gena nodded. "Yes, but maybe avoid calling the equipment toys in front of him."

Bonnie pointed at her and snapped her fingers. "Good call. Shall we do this?"

"If we're getting a vote, I'm going to go with no." Gena couldn't help but look at the fountain again, getting lost as she stared at the mermaid. She noticed something strange and eased closer to it, leaning in a bit to get a better look. She pointed to a small dragon-like creature tucked in behind the fluke of the mermaid's tail. "What is that?"

Bonnie examined it as well and then touched her chin. "Hmm, water dragon maybe?"

"I guess. Can't say I've ever seen a mermaid depicted with one before," said Gena, having seen her fair share of mermaid art in her travels all over the world. She stared harder at the creature the sculptor had added. "It kind of reminds me of a statue of a gargoyle. You?"

Bonnie put her hand in the water of the fountain and lifted it, allowing water to cascade through her fingers. "It does. It's creepy."

Gena agreed. There was something off-putting about the expression on its face.

"Did you see the inlay in the tile near the front door up there?" asked Bonnie.

Gena looked in the direction of the door and noticed what Bonnie was talking about. The tiles were all monochromatic but formed the shape of a gold mermaid with sharks on both sides of her.

"It would appear our benefactor has a thing for chicks with fish tails," said Bonnie. "Rules me out. By chance do you have a secret fish tail? It could so land us more funding."

"Sorry. We're out of luck there," said Gena as she looked around more from her spot near the SUV. The whole place was huge and eerie, yet there wasn't any one thing Gena could point out as off-putting. It just was. While the day was sunny and warm, there was a certain coldness that settled over her as she stared at the mansion.

Bonnie tapped the hood of the SUV. "Is it me

or does this place have a weird vibe? Kind of like the Munsters meets the Kardashians?"

Gena glanced at her friend. "I don't know what half of that reference was to, but yes, it has a very weird vibe."

"My poor, sweet, pop-culture-challenged friend," stated Bonnie with a snort. "You told me your college roomie helped to expose you to a bunch of references."

"She must have missed that one," said Gena, still in awe of the home before her. "One man lives here, or does he have a family of, say, thirty or so?"

"Oddly, I couldn't find out much about him," said Bonnie. "I tried looking him up on the internet, but there isn't really anything there."

"How is that possible? Everyone is on the internet, especially people with a net worth like this guy," said Gena. "Even *I* know that."

With a shrug, Bonnie shook her head. "No clue. Hey, maybe he's really a secret spy or something and the identity is false, or he has people who scrub the internet for references to him."

Gena cast a worried gaze in her friend's direction. "I think we need to take away those spy novels I see you with all the time. Not to mention block you from the conspiracy theory blogs. Don't think I didn't notice those pulled up on your laptop this morning. Do I even want to know why they're featuring an illustration of a man turning into a wolf?"

"Total guilty pleasure. Like the Kardashians and old black-and-white television episodes. Don't even get me started on *I Love Lucy*," returned Bonnie. "And they had the illustration to show what the shifters look like."

"Shifters?" asked Gena.

Bonnie nodded. "Yeah. You know, guys who turn into animals."

Gena simply stared at her friend. "You've gone round the bend, haven't you?"

"Hon, I went around the bend years ago. You should join me," said Bonnie. "It's really fun over here on the dark side."

"Considering you have enough bottle openers for everyone on the dark side, it *should* be really fun. One heck of a party."

Bonnie laughed. "Damn straight. I like to dispel any misconceptions that smart, successful women over the age of thirty can't have a good time too."

The oversize front door opened, and a man

in an honest-to-God butler outfit was there. Gena blinked several times. Nope. She wasn't imagining it. He even had on white gloves. "No way."

Bonnie snorted and tried to hide her laugh. "I should have gone with formal attire. No logos needed. Think he's named Jeeves?"

"Jeeves?" asked Gena as they made their way up the front steps.

The man at the door gave a curt nod. "Ladies, Mr. Helmuth will be with you shortly. He's arranged for lunch to be served in the sunroom. What can I get you both to drink?"

Bonnie slid the man a sideways glance. "Too much to hope for something with vodka in it?"

The man's lips twitched. "Not at all. And for you?"

Gena bit her lower lip. "Water, please. No ice. Thank you."

He nodded and then pointed in the direction of the back right hall. "Please come in. The master will be with you shortly."

"Thank you," said Bonnie before glancing wide-eyed at Gena.

The master?

The man hurried off.

Gena tensed. "I know I'm not the only one thinking it."

"'The master'? He did say master, right?" asked Bonnie. "I've changed my vote from his name being Jeeves to it being Igor."

"I don't know what that means," confessed Gena.

"Dr. Frankenstein's assistant," said Bonnie with a shake of her head.

"Oh. Right. I knew that," offered Gena before licking her lips to hide a laugh. "Okay, I didn't know that. I knew there was a sidekick. I just didn't know his name."

"That's it, I'm going to rent a bunch of old movies and shows, and we're going to binge-watch them all until you're hip and cool," said Bonnie with a wink. "Like me."

Gena smiled. "Best of luck with that. I've been told more than once that I might be a hopeless case in the cool department."

"As much as I want to have your back and say that isn't so, you might be right," Bonnie said with a wide smile. "Shall we do this?"

The second Gena's foot crossed the threshold of the front entrance, she had the strangest urge to turn and hightail it out of there. Since running from the deep pockets that kept the research center operating was silly, she chalked it up to nerves.

Bonnie leaned toward Gena, bumping arms with her as the women walked side by side into the enormous foyer, which opened into a great room.

Gena's attention went directly to a massive painting on the far wall of the room. It stood out as it was done in color when everything else in the home thus far had been stark white. The painting called to her for a different reason as well.

It was of a massive great white shark in what looked to be an enormous tank inside a warehouse or something.

Since holding one in captivity simply wasn't possible for any length of time with any degree of success, the painting was odd. Finding it in the home of a man who claimed to be a champion for shark conservation was even odder. Protecting them and keeping one in a container were two very different end goals.

The more she looked at the painting, the more she felt as if she'd seen the exact shark that was depicted there.

When she realized where, she stiffened.

No.

That couldn't be.

Her mind was clearly playing tricks on her. There was simply no way the very great white that had saved her when she was ten was the one being shown in the oil painting. The odds of that were staggering.

Your mind is playing tricks on you, she thought. *It's the heat. That has to be it.*

Still, denying the similarities was difficult.

The shark depicted in the painting even had the same scars and markings as the one that had rescued her. The scars and markings were a way to identify sharks. Dorsal fins were another way to ID a shark, and the shark in the painting had the very same dorsal fin Gena remembered the one from her past having. Granted, she'd only been ten when she'd seen the shark, and she had suffered a traumatic head injury, so it was possible she was simply filling in the blanks with what she was currently seeing.

"Gena?" asked Bonnie, nudging her arm and drawing her away from her fixation with the painting.

Gena turned to look at her friend but paused as the hair on the back of her neck rose. Slowly, she turned the other way to find a tall man standing just inside the archway to the hall. His dark hair hung partially over one eye, and his head was tipped as he leaned, one arm resting against the archway.

It looked as if he'd been there for hours, almost statue-like, but he hadn't been there only minutes prior.

The man was handsome, like male-model kind of good-looking, but there was something about him that left Gena wanting to take several steps back. As if distance was needed.

She resisted, keeping her feet planted where they were.

It was hard.

The man's eyes, while very attractive, lacked warmth. The more she stared at him, the more she realized he hadn't so much as blinked. He was more statue-like than she'd first thought, and it was downright creepy.

Finally, he did a rather long, slow, clearly deliberate blink, as if sensing her unrest with the unnatural way he presented himself.

The blink did little to help her unease.

A smile touched his lips and he stood to his full, imposing height. "Dr. Fowler?"

"Me." Bonnie lifted her hand, staring blankly at the man.

The man gave a slight nod, smiling more, except it didn't quite reach his eyes. Yet another checkmark on the running list of unnerving things about him. At the rate Gena was going, she'd be running for the hills rather than staying for lunch.

He stepped forward, covering the short distance between them. He extended his hand to Bonnie. "Nice to finally meet you," he said. "I'm Walter Helmuth."

Bonnie took his hand and shook it with a bit too much enthusiasm, still staring at him funny. It took Gena a second to realize Bonnie was enamored by the man.

"It's a pleasure to meet you, Mr. Helmuth," said Bonnie quickly. "I can't thank you and your company enough for all you've done for our facility."

Helmuth had to practically pry Bonnie off him. His smile never broke. "Ah, my pleasure, but I have to confess. Donavon Dynamics isn't *my* company. I'm simply one of the board members. Think of it as a conglomerate, composed of many, many companies and backers. I'm one of those backers."

Nodding, Bonnie reached for his hand again, starting to shake it once more. "Got it. A cog in the wheel. Right."

Gena grabbed her friend's hand, artfully drawing it and Bonnie to her more. She gave a slight squeeze, and Bonnie blinked several times before clearing her throat, and a tidal wave of pink rushing over her cheeks. "Oh my. Is it hot in here?"

Helmuth grinned. "It's nearly unbearable outside, and it's evident you've had some sun recently."

Bonnie's hand went to her cheek. "Um, yes. Might have gotten distracted while applying my sunscreen."

Helmuth stared at Bonnie, unblinking once more, his smile still frozen. "Skincare and UV protection is something of a passion of mine."

"You have great skin," said Bonnie, her eyes wide.

Gena couldn't help but groan softly.

Bonnie cleared her throat and then rubbed the back of her neck. "Wow. That came out vastly different than I'd pictured it in my head. I'm sorry. I'm nervous. I'm afraid we're here for you to tell us you're pulling funding. And I looked you up on the internet but couldn't find out much about you. Not even a photo. Then you appear, and you're like a walking sculpture or something."

Gena elbowed her friend lightly.

Bonnie sighed. "That fell out too. I'm super nervous. Did I mention that already?"

"You did," said Helmuth, his smile widening more, finally reaching his eyes. "Dr. Fowler, I can assure you that I did not request this meeting to tell you that you're losing your funding. In fact, I called it because I'm very interested in the work you and your team are doing. I think sharks are invaluable."

"I couldn't agree more," said Bonnie, sounding relieved and a lot more like herself.

"I can't wait to talk more about the research you've been doing," said Helmuth, though the words didn't ring true to Gena.

She had to wonder why she was being so critical of the man.

The butler appeared once more.

Helmuth nodded at him. "Ernest, would you be so kind as to show Dr. Fowler to the sunroom and be sure she has some water? The heat is getting to her."

The way Helmuth said it all didn't hold the

warmth the words should. It was as if he was trying too hard to be respectful of Ernest. Like maybe, just maybe, when extra eyes weren't on him, Helmuth was anything but nice or respectful to the man.

That bothered Gena.

A lot.

Ernest cast a speculative glance over the women before coming to them. "Of course. Dr. Fowler?"

Bonnie touched her upper chest lightly. "I'm fine, really. No fuss is needed. And please call me Bonnie."

Ernest smiled softly. "Very well. Bonnie, please come with me. I'll get you some water."

Gena went to follow as Bonnie and Ernest headed away, but Helmuth stepped in her path, cutting her off.

Drawing up short, Gena tensed and then took a significant step back.

Helmuth stared down at her. "You must be Dr. Alexiadis."

"Yes," said Gena softly, wanting to back up more, but she wasn't sure why. The man had been nothing but pleasant so far. And he and Donavon Dynamics had been instrumental in making the research facility a reality, letting her live her dream. Still, there was something about him that was off. "Mr. Helmuth, I should check on Bonnie."

Helmuth remained in place, blocking her path. He adjusted the cuff of his dress shirt, looking nonchalant, yet she could almost taste his inner turmoil. The calm exterior was a façade. "Please, Dr. Alexiadis, call me Helmuth."

"You don't go by Walter?" blurted Gena, more out of nerves than genuine curiosity.

He chuckled. "Ah, no. Would you if you were named Walter?"

Some of the tension eased out of Gena at his attempt at humor. Maybe he was nervous too. Perhaps he was as socially awkward as she was at times, and she was simply judging him harshly. Like others probably did to her often. Feeling slightly guilty, Gena did her best to act normal. Whatever normal was.

"I don't know about that. Walter isn't a bad name. Beats Gena," she said. "People read it and think it's pronounced Jenna, not Gene-A like it is. Or my favorite is the time a girl in college asked if it was pronounced Gy-na. Like vagina."

As soon as she said the words, she wanted them back.

She was crap at small talk with strangers.

Clara and Nicolette would love hearing about how she managed to bungle the meeting. She made a mental note to remember to reach out to them both after the meeting was over. Bonnie was right. It was time she made a point to live for something more than work.

Helmuth laughed softly. "Can't say that has ever happened to me."

Gena bit her lower lip. "I should wait in the car. I'm not really the one you want to talk to. Bonnie runs everything and knows the ins and outs. It was nice meeting you, Helmuth."

He reached out, coming just shy of touching her. "Stay."

It wasn't phrased as a question, but rather a statement. The push behind the single word made it seem like she didn't have a choice.

He eased even closer. "Please. I've been looking forward to meeting you since a colleague brought you to my attention."

Gena lifted a brow. "Me? Why me?"

He never missed a beat. "You've become a valuable member of the research team in a short period of time. Bonnie has nothing but good things to say about you in her reports. She thinks you have it in you to run your own team sooner rather than later."

"She does?" asked Gena, in awe. She idolized Bonnie. If Bonnie thought that about her, it meant a lot.

He inclined his head. "And I read your thesis paper. You have some rather interesting theories on why it is sharks have been around as long as they have and what a world without them might look like."

"You read my paper?" asked Gena, surprised.

"I did," said Helmuth. "I have to admit I was curious to learn more about you, so I might have had my people dig up additional information. Well, as much as they could find."

She quirked a brow. "You looked into me?"

He offered what she had to guess he thought was a reassuring smile. "I did. I never make any investment without knowing who and what I'm investing in."

"Investment?"

"Ah, I buried the lede," he stated. "I'm interested in increasing the funding for the center and possibly expanding the research you're doing there."

"Shut up!" yelled Bonnie from the hallway. "I mean, really?"

Helmuth glanced over at her. He didn't seem pleased she was back. If anything, he appeared agitated.

Ernest was behind Bonnie with a nervous look on his face. "Sorry, sir. She wanted to rejoin her friend."

"So I see, Ernest," said Helmuth, his words as rigid as his posture.

Flinching, Ernest gave a quick nod.

Bonnie was all smiles, clearly unaware of the obvious tension in the room. "Thank you so much. We just found out today that a grant we were hoping for didn't come through. This means so much to us. To the center. To the work we're doing. Gena, can you believe it?"

Gena pressed a smile to her face. "It's amazing."

"Dr. Fowler, erm, Bonnie," corrected Helmuth. "If you don't mind speaking more with one of the men who work for me, I would appreciate it."

He snapped his fingers and a tall, built hunk

with long, dark, curly hair and bronzed skin came walking down the hall with a certain swagger about him. He smiled, but it seemed to lack sincerity as well. His gaze slid over Gena, and he faltered in his step slightly, as if she'd somehow put him off his game.

He recovered quickly.

Gena exhaled slowly, wondering if the lack of quality sleep was impairing her judgment. Maybe the men were totally nice, ordinary guys who really were interested in making a difference. Maybe she was simply reading too much into it all.

That had to be it.

And Bonnie didn't seem to have any issue with them, so it was more than likely a case of Gena overthinking everything.

"Kahale, I'd like you to meet Dr. Bonnie Fowler," said Helmuth to the newcomer.

Kahale focused on Bonnie. "Ah, I was reading over some of the research data you've submitted and can't wait to pick your brain. Would you like to join me for a walk around the grounds before lunch? We can discuss your work."

Bonnie rushed to him. "I would love to."

He put an arm out and Bonnie took it,

buddying up next to him as if they'd been friends for years. Bonnie wasted no time launching into talk about the research center and the work they'd been doing.

As Bonnie and Kahale left the room, Gena found herself wanting to run after them. She didn't. But it was hard to resist.

Gena once again found herself alone with Helmuth.

Trying to rise above her lack of sleep, and her misguided issues with the man, she bit her lower lip. Small talk wasn't really her thing, but the giant silence stretching between them was unnerving. She scrambled for something to fill the void. "You have a very interesting home. I mean big. I mean nice."

Pink stole over her cheeks.

He chuckled, and it sounded legit. The action helped to ease some of her worry. "The word you're looking for is gaudy. I'm aware. My other homes are not quite like this one. In fact, they aren't anywhere near this level of tacky. This one is dedicated to certain interests I've always had."

"Other homes?" asked Gena before thinking better.

He nodded. "I have a fair number of properties. This is one of many."

"Cool," she said, at a loss for what more she could offer to their small talk.

She hoped Bonnie's tour of the grounds and talk with Kahale would end quickly. The less time she was forced to stand there feeling every bit as socially awkward as she knew she could be, the better.

Her attention went to the shark painting. Slight nuances she'd missed before caught her attention. Like how the tank the shark was in looked to have chains hanging from the back wall of it. If she wasn't mistaken, there were shackles on the end of each chain. Ones that were made to fit a person.

There was a mix of rage and desperation in the shark's large blue gaze. The artist had painted it in such a way that her heart ached for the creature. Then there was the fact that no amount of rationalization was working to explain away the similarities between the shark that had saved her life seventeen years ago and the one depicted in the painting. They were nearly identical.

Helmuth was much closer than he had been only seconds before. She'd been so engrossed in the painting that she'd never noticed him moving. His arm brushed against her and cold spread through her, racing to her chest, making her breath catch. It felt like she'd just stepped outside in the dead of winter.

Unable to stop herself, she jerked away slightly, breaking contact with the man.

He stared at the painting with nothing short of rapture on his face. He looked almost turned on by the scene. That was absurd. No one would get off on the torture of an innocent creature, would they?

And if they did, what kind of sick monster were they?

He noticed her watching him and tilted his head a tad. "Magnificent, isn't it?"

She said nothing.

He lifted his hand, weaving it in the air as if he was the one doing the painting. "The way the artist's every stroke evokes such a visceral response. Just as art should be. Don't you think?"

"I don't call that art," she said quickly before biting her lower lip to keep from blurting out anything else.

"You don't like it?" The slightest hint of amusement hid behind his every word.

"I think the artist is very talented," she said. "It's just the subject matter is disturbing."

He shrugged. "To some, yes."

Some?

Everyone she counted as a friend would agree with her.

Helmuth stared at the painting harder and Gena could have sworn he smiled ever so slightly.

She took the smallest of steps away from him.

"You're wondering why someone such as myself would have a painting like this," he said, never tearing his gaze from the artwork.

"Actually, I'm wondering why anyone would have something like that."

"Something like what? A shark?" he questioned.

"A shark being held in a containment tank of some kind, clearly being harmed," she countered.

"As a reminder."

"Of?" she asked.

Another of the smiles that didn't reach his eyes appeared on his handsome face. "Of atrocities, of course. I'm sure you're aware that holding a great white in captivity has never been done with any degree of success. It's merely a painting to represent all the ugly in the world, and it touches on my interest in science fiction."

Some of the tension leaked from Gena at his explanation, but she wasn't entirely sure she believed him. "You like science fiction?"

"I do. And mythology. You?"

"I've always enjoyed learning about various cultures and their beliefs and mythos," said Gena.

"Did I read that you grew up traveling the world with your parents, who are also scientists?" he asked.

She nodded. "Yes."

"That had to be an interesting upbringing. Full of so much knowledge and culture," said Helmuth. "Tell me, what was your favorite place?"

"Costa Rica," she said without thought, her gaze returning to the painting of the shark that looked identical to the one she remembered saving her life.

"Costa Rica?" asked Helmuth. "What did you like most about it?"

"Well, I was young when I was there, but I remember it being beautiful," answered Gena, still focused on the painting. Absently, she reached up and began to rub the back of her neck. As her fingers brushed over the smooth skin of the scar she had there, her chest warmed with thoughts of being rescued by the most amazing shark she'd ever seen in her life.

When she looked back at Helmuth, she found him staring at her. He didn't stop. He just stood there boldly watching her, never even blinking. It felt like forever before he took a deep breath. "My apologies. It's just…"

She waited for him to finish what he was going to say. When it became clear he wasn't going to, she found herself stepping closer to him. "Just what?"

He returned to staring at her. "Forgive me for saying this, but you remind me of a mermaid. Or rather, what one would look like if they were real."

A nervous laugh escaped her as she thought of Bonnie's desire for her to have a fish tail to secure more funding. "Thanks?"

He grinned. "If you'll humor me a moment longer, I'll show you what I'm talking about."

He turned and led her down the hall but stopped at a room on the left. Each step she took behind him left her feeling a lot like she was being led to a spider's web, one she'd never be able to free herself from, and that the spider himself had escorted her.

He opened the door and waited.

Gena followed and drew up short as she entered the room.

It was filled with mermaid memorabilia. So full in fact, she wondered how someone had managed to not only amass such a collection but fit it into the space. Not that the space was small by any means. The collection was simply that large.

On the far wall hung another colossal painting. This one was of a mermaid. No surprise there, considering Gena was fast suspecting the guy really did have a thing for chicks with fish tails. The obsession seemed harmless enough.

What was surprising about the painting was how very much the woman in the painting resembled her.

"It's uncanny," said Helmuth, stealing the thought from her. He also invaded her space, easing up close behind her. "You wouldn't by chance be a mermaid who is merely pretending to be human, would you?"

She tensed and then pushed out a laugh,

hoping he was joking and not batshit crazy. "Not that I'm aware of."

"Interesting," said Helmuth.

"What's interesting?" asked Bonnie, entering the room with Ernest by her side.

Kahale was nowhere in sight.

Ernest cleared his throat. "Mr. Kahale received an urgent call regarding our friends in Colorado. He asked that I see Dr. Fowler back to you."

Helmuth's jaw set as a thin smile pressed to his face. "Thank you, Ernest. That will be all."

Ernest scurried away.

Bonnie entered the room more and her eyes widened as she spotted the large painting of the mermaid. "Gena, that's you!"

Gena's cheeks flushed. "Uh, no. It's not."

"Uh, yes, it is," countered Bonnie before walking closer to the painting. "Wow. The resemblance is uncanny."

"It is, isn't it," said Helmuth, watching Gena in a way that left her skin crawling.

Chapter Seven

"YOU JUST *HAD* to tell Cody there were leads on Helmuth," said Car as he shot a hard look over at the passenger seat of the SUV, where Armand sat.

"He deserved as much," stated Armand evenly, facing forward. "If you would be so kind as to keep the vehicle on the correct side of the road, that would be great."

"Eat me," Car retorted.

"Ever the mature one," mused Armand.

Car added a hand gesture for effect.

The pair had been going back and forth for the majority of the trip thus far. It had started on the plane and spilled over upon landing. At some point they'd either come to blows or lose interest in one another.

At this point, Cody didn't care who won out, only that the two shut up and cease their nonstop bickering.

Cody sat in the center row of the large vehicle in one of the captain's chairs. He was directly behind Car, who was driving. Mac was next to Cody, in the other captain's chair, while Bill and Gus sat in the back third row, close together, or as Cody liked to think of it—corralled.

If they were both pinned in to the smaller space, everyone knew where they were, and what they were and were not getting into. Since trouble seemed to follow the pair wherever they went, it was for the best.

Gus, who was as tall as he was skinny, stared out the side window while he held a football helmet on his lap. In the helmet was a female mannequin head that looked as if it was vintage and had seen better days. Cody suspected it wasn't actually that old but had already seen a lot in the way of action. It had scuff marks on it. The paint of the eyes was starting to chip away, and there was damage to the right ear area. It didn't seem to matter to Gus, who treated it as a prized possession.

Gus carried the head, which was named

Mona, as if it were a security blanket or, at the very least, a real person, rather than an inanimate object. Cody wasn't going to point out the difference to the man. For as out there as Gus seemed to be, he was incredibly intelligent.

If the smart man wanted a giant doll head around to comfort him, so be it. Whatever it took. Besides, Cody had seen weirder in his lifetime. But Gus did manage to give the strange in Cody's life a run for its money.

Gus, while harmless, was a touch on the unnerving side.

To lend credence to the fact, the man was currently wearing a wetsuit, complete with a snorkel mask, while fins that he'd had to be pried out of before getting in the vehicle sat propped next to him on the floor of the SUV. To add yet another layer to the oddity known as Gus, he wore a pair of bright orange arm floaties, inflated.

Upon landing at the airport, he'd insisted, by way of Bill, on changing into his current outfit. No amount of reasoning or pointing out they weren't going snorkeling had talked the man out of it. Finally, everyone involved had given in, but they'd drawn the line when Bill had tried to talk them into letting him break out his swim trunks.

Especially since Cody knew how small the trunks were on the guy.

Bill and Gus were a perfect match. The ying to the other's yang. But they were very, very odd men.

Gus's facemask was on too tight, but he wouldn't permit anyone to loosen it. Evidently, it was just the way he liked it. All it did was draw attention to the fact he didn't make eye contact.

He never appeared to be looking directly at anyone yet somehow managed to see everything. He could communicate via the mental pathways the operatives shared and came off as scarily intelligent, as well as prophetic. It was enough to put any alpha off his game.

Cody included.

Gus, who was a good deal younger than Bill, was rarely too far from the older man's side. When Cody had first been introduced to them several days back, he'd assumed Bill was Gus's keeper, for lack of a better term. The more time he spent around the men, the more he got the sense it was the other way around. That it was Gus who kept Bill in line as much as possible, all while having Bill act as his spokesperson when need be and a way to keep others at bay.

Whatever the dynamic between the men, it worked for them. It was very easy to see they were the best of friends, almost like brothers. And they cared greatly for each other.

That type of bond lasted a lifetime, and anyone who was lucky enough to have it needed to hold on to it with both hands.

Bill glanced up in Armand's direction and curled his lip. He and Armand had been trading jabs for hours. "If you'd stop walking in the way of my grenades, I wouldn't be in trouble right now. Stupid dead guy doesn't know how to stay out of the way of an explosive. Don't they teach you that in Vamp School?"

Armand began to growl, making Car laugh.

"Do nae try to eat him again, vampire," said Car. "I think three times on the flight here was more than enough."

Mac turned slightly, focusing on Bill. "Yer still in a no-talking time-out. Or do you nae remember how you behaved on the jet ride here?"

At the mention of the word jet, Gus began to rock in place and grow visibly agitated. Saying the man wasn't a fan of flying was an understatement. It had been so bad with Gus on the plane, the men had been left no choice but to restrain him for his own safety.

Cody had been eager to hear every detail that Armand and the others had discovered about Helmuth while on the plane, but even with as much as he wanted revenge, he didn't have it in him to leave Gus that upset. Cody had given up a chance at a full briefing, opting instead to sit in the seat nearest Gus and read to him. Cody had started with a magazine one of the twins had brought along, but it became clear rather quickly that Gus had no interest in anything the men's adult periodical had to say—or the pictures.

Cody traveled so much that he always had a bag packed, which he didn't ever really unpack fully. He also kept a book with him at all times. He'd packed *Walden*, by Thoreau. The second Cody had started to read it out loud, Gus had calmed before finally nodding off briefly.

That should have ended the flying drama, but Bill had managed to somehow sneak some of his special stashes onto the jet, despite Cody having basically shaken him from his toes prior to leaving. Bill dipped into enough of what he'd brought to leave him running up and down the center aisle of the plane, shouting instructions at the men as if they were all back in Nam and about to be ambushed.

It would have been sad if not for the fact the man then decided Armand was perfect to fill in for the part of the mechanical elephant that Bill was famed for having taken down. He'd charged the vampire, leaped on him, and then proceeded to scale him, which was comical for more than one reason. The fact Bill accomplished this while Armand was sitting was even more hysterical. In the height of it all, Bill knocked Armand from his chair, leaving the vampire on the floor and Bill sprawled out on top of him.

And that had been the first of three attempts Armand had made on Bill's life on the jet alone.

Bill looked over at Gus, and his brows met. "How come I gotta warn Shark-boy about your helmet?"

Gus continued to rock, still appearing worked up over the mention of the jet.

Bill tossed his hands up and let out an irritated grunt. "How was I supposed to know it wasn't *that* helmet? I ain't you. I don't just know. Hey, don't take that tone with me. Yes, I'll tell Sharkie about the Helmet-Head. Quit your bellyaching.

Someone here needs a nap and this time, it ain't me."

Mac eyed Cody then he did the same to Mona. "Aussie, you do nae have a thing for dolls, do you? If so, I do nae want to be the one to break it to you, but she's taken. You'll need to be findin' yer own head in a helmet. Mayhap it will get you through the long nights of wet dreams we've all heard ya havin'."

"Asshole," said Cody with a grin. He knew the back and forth was all in fun, to help lighten a tense situation. After all, they were in Savannah for reasons that were anything but sunshine and roses. Dwelling on as much at all times would get them nowhere, fast.

Mac laughed. "Aye. And thanks."

Bill locked gazes with Cody. "We have to drop you off, Sharkie. You ain't coming with us to the secret superhero base. You gotta meet a dead wheel at a park or something. He your dealer? Meeting at a park is amateur hour there, buddy. Meet under a bridge or on a rooftop. Take my word for it. I'm an expert."

Cody looked to Mac for clarification.

Mac shrugged. "Do nae look at me. I do nae speak crazy."

Everyone stared at him, begging to differ. If anyone in the vehicle spoke crazy fluently, it would be Mac.

Mac shrugged. "Okay, I do nae speak *that* brand of crazy."

Armand stiffened—and then turned all the way around in his seat slowly. He stared past Cody to Gus. The way his eyes glossed over briefly said he was doing his vampire-mind-reading thing. "And you're certain?"

Car did a dramatic show of rolling his eyes. "Oh guid. The dead douche's antenna is up and he's tuning in to Gus's brainwave channel *again*. That's nae the least bit troubling."

"Has anyone ever told you that you are a waste of space?" asked Armand, centering his heated gaze on the man.

"Aye," said Car, running a hand over his beard. "Twice today alone. Why?"

Armand sighed, his attention returning to Gus.

Gus kept rocking and said nothing that Cody could hear, but it was clear Gus was communicating with Armand telepathically.

Armand faced forward. "Carbrey, change of plans."

"We're nae going to the PSI office here, or as Bill likes to call it, the superhero secret base, are we?" asked Car, sounding tired. "Before you answer, I just need to know, is a crazy cult guy going to want to eat us on this new adventure? If you recall, that's what happened the last time. Father Hippie wanted to have us as a snack or something. I'm all for finding the asshat who hurt Aussie, but I'd rather nae be anyone's lunch. And I've a strict rule: only-be-a-potential-meal-for-a-bad-guy-once-a-week rule. I've met my quota this week already."

Mac snorted. "Hey, I'd taste great."

"Nah, you'd be less filling," argued his brother.

"Gus did not say one way or another on that," said Armand, cutting the twins off, his tone even. "But I will admit to having hope you are indeed devoured by a bad guy."

Car grunted. "Well, can you ask him?"

"*He* can hear you," said Armand.

Car glanced up at the rearview mirror, his expression saying he wasn't so sure.

Gus rocked more in his seat and began to make a strange low moan. The noise was muffled because he had the snorkel in his mouth. The entire thing seemed less and less strange to Cody the more he got to know Bill and Gus.

Bill patted the man's shoulder and Gus began to calm somewhat.

Nodding, Bill kept patting him. "I know it's important. You ain't gotta tell me twice. It's these dipshit alpha males who need to be told more than once. When the government was handing out big willies, they apparently had cutbacks when it came to brains. That or they made all these alpha males the day before a holiday. You know, when *them* scientists were in a hurry to get the hell out of the lab and to their cookouts. Wanna bet the scientists are in a union?"

The comment earned the small man several dirty looks from the alpha men present. No surprise they'd taken exception to his statement.

As Cody thought more on Bill's words, and the fact the doctors and scientists had indeed fucked up when making him, a small laugh came from him. "He's not entirely wrong. It would explain the Outcasts."

Mac rolled his eyes. "Dumbarse."

Bill continued to pat his friend's shoulder reassuringly even if the act seemed awkward, as if a toddler was trying to do the comforting. In a lot of ways, a toddler *was* doing it. "Calm down. It will be fine. I promise."

Gus got louder.

Mac glanced over his shoulder at Bill. "What's wrong with him *now*?"

"He thinks the Great-White-Pain-In-My-Ass is gonna ignore what he said and demand to be part of the search for info on that Helmet-Head dude," said Bill, as if what he'd just said was perfectly rational and required no further explanation.

"Of course I'm going to insist on being a part of the search for Helmuth," snapped Cody before taking a deep breath. They weren't the source of his agitation. Helmuth was. It was wrong to take it out on them. "I've waited a long time to find him and stop him. I plan to be the one who kills him."

Bill watched him. "He's who hurt you most?"

Cody glanced away.

"Yes," said Armand, answering for him. "Helmuth was either directly responsible for most of what Cody had to endure or he had a hand in it all. Regardless, he is the main reason Cody was forced to go through what he did."

Gus rocked faster, making a louder grunting noise. He then began to slap his hand against his thigh. As his agitation grew, so did the volume of the sounds emanating from him.

Cody wanted to console the man in some small way, but he knew the best person for the job was already seated next to Gus. Bill, for all his faults and oddities, had a way with Gus that no one else seemed to possess.

As if on cue, Bill caught his friend's hand and held it, slowing Gus's rocking almost instantly. As if the small act of making contact provided the lifeline the man needed to find comfort.

Gus kept his gaze averted from everyone in the SUV, including Bill. Instead, he stared out the window, almost trancelike. While it appeared that he wasn't really seeing anything, Cody suspected the man was soaking in everything. That he alone knew every single thing that was happening around them at all times.

Cody could still remember what it had been like to be locked away, denied human contact and interactions for so long that he often thought he'd go crazy alone with his thoughts. Then when he'd finally be taken back to a cell that had other prisoners nearby, he would feel as if all his senses were being overloaded all at once. That lights were too bright. Sounds were too loud. Touch was downright unbearable. He didn't want to think what that must be like to live with on a daily basis, never able to escape it.

And he strongly suspected that was what life was like for Gus.

Bill cleared his throat, still holding his friend's hand, his gaze on Cody the entire time. In that second, Bill seemed completely sound and rational, making Cody wonder if deep under all the insane ramblings and impulsive behavior lurked a mentally stable individual.

One the government had damaged beyond repair.

"Gus says Helmet-Head is the only reason you weren't killed when the bad dudes got the samples they wanted from you," said Bill, his voice low while his words were spaced evenly, as if he was going out of his way to be as relaxed as possible. Maybe he was, since he'd only just gotten Gus to settle. "Says you'd have been terminated within minutes of them getting what they wanted in Costa Rica. Then they'd have cut you up in pieces and studied you. You'd have been sushi. That sushi bit was me adding my two cents. Gus didn't say nothing about no sushi. He's not a big fan of it. We like grilled cheese sandwiches and peanut butter and jelly. And cheeseburgers. You know, the staples. That reminds me, I'm hungry."

"Aye, we'll feed you soon," said Mac with a nod. "I'll nae let you starve."

Cody focused on Gus, wanting desperately to understand how it was the man knew about Costa Rica and what had gone on there. Whatever it was that Gus could do, it was downright disconcerting at times.

This was one of those times.

Gus began to rock once more, his hand still in Bill's.

Cody thought about what he'd just been told. About how Helmuth was the only reason he'd not been killed right after he'd been captured. "So, I should be grateful to him? Be forever thankful he's the reason I was held as long as I was and put through everything they put me through because he kept me from being killed? I should let him live? Let him keep hurting others? You do realize I was taken seventeen years ago and have only been free just over five years now? Not sure I should be singing that asshole's praises."

Gus stopped rocking and fell silent.

Bill kept hold of his hand. "No. That ain't what he's saying at all, Sharkie. Don't go gettin' pissy with him or you're gonna have me to deal with. Gus is just the messenger. Helmut-Head has gotta die, but right now, you gotta let your friends worry about finding him. You gotta be somewhere else."

Cody drew in a long breath, his nostrils flaring as he fought to keep hold of a temper that he didn't like seeing manifest. "Pretty sure I'm exactly where I'm supposed to be and that I *do* need to be there, alongside everyone else, hunting for the prick."

"I do nae disagree with Aussie," said Mac right before belching loudly. "He's earned the right to hunt this bag of dicks. I'll admit I'm looking forward to hunting the asshat myself. I've never seen a gargoyle before. The last year has opened my eyes to a lot of shit I dinnae think was real. Next, I'll be forced to fight a spaghetti monster or the Easter Bunny."

"Aye," said Car from the driver's seat. "Christ, brother, what did you eat? Yer burp smells like rotten eggs."

Mac beamed with pride. "Because I had eggs for breakfast. Just be thankful the gas picked coming out the top and nae the bottom."

Bill laughed but didn't sound amused. "You

don't get it, do you? Gus ain't saying Fin-for-brains can't hunt for Helmet-Head. He's saying Sharkie's got somewhere else he's gotta be. That if he don't go, bad, bad things will happen. That someone else needs his help more than he needs his revenge right now."

"I'll bite," said Mac with a cocky grin. "Where does Aussie need to be instead and who is this he needs to help?"

"I already told him. He's gotta meet a dead wheel at a park," said Bill, annoyance evident in his every word.

"Och, crazy talk and riddles are nae helpful," said Mac. He looked at Cody. "He's insane. And I'm saying this as a card-carryin' member of the club."

The edges of Bill's mouth curved upward. "Thanks. And yeah, I'm crazy, but that don't mean Sharkie there doesn't gotta go to a park and see a dead wheel. He does it every week. That's what Gus says. Says Sharkie always meets the dead wheel there."

Armand exhaled loudly. "He's speaking of Wheeler, Cody. You meet Wheeler once a week in the park whenever you're both in Savannah, do you not?"

Cody stiffened as the pieces seemed to start to fall into place. "Yes. I do."

"The vampire Outcast?" asked Mac. "One the li'l crazy man would see as dead?"

"Dead wheel," said Cody in a hushed tone, finally following along. Confused as to why it was he'd need to be hanging with his buddy shooting the shit rather than hunting for an evil bastard, he stared back at Gus fully, which took some doing. "How is that going to keep bad things from happening? You're not saying Wheeler is in Helmuth's sights, are you? Is he the one in danger? The one who needs my help more than I need revenge?"

Worry for his friend rushed over him.

It was one thing to know he'd be going up against the likes of Helmuth again. It was something else entirely to think Helmuth might harm a man Cody saw as a brother.

Bill stared at his friend for a few seconds before he spoke. "Yes, the wheel is in danger, but it ain't from Helmet-Head. And it ain't gonna be a problem just yet. He ain't the one needing the help from you *right* now. You gotta go see the dead wheel in the park because *she* needs you."

Mac huffed. "I do nae think the skinny one is

getting his signals right. Wheeler is nae a girl. Well, he's a vampire and they're girlie."

Armand shook his head, mumbling in French about annoying Scotsmen.

That only served to make the twins laugh. Getting under Armand's skin was something the pair enjoyed greatly.

Bill rubbed his temple with his free hand. "Gus says you're all smart guys. I ain't seeing it. Bunch of morons if you ask me. Running around with your heads up your asses, puffing out your chests, growling and snarling."

Mac opened his mouth and started to protest only to stop and shrug. "Aye. We do that. Car more than most."

Car kept driving and facing forward as he lifted a hand and flipped off his brother.

"Sharkie, you gotta go see a dead wheel about a mermaid," said Bill.

"Well, that just managed to get weirder," said Cody, hoping for a laugh.

Armand stiffened before turning more in his seat. He stared past Cody once more at Gus and there was no doubt he was in deep conversation with the man mentally. He looked to Cody next.

"Go. Do as he says. Meet with Wheeler. Change nothing in your routine."

"Why? What's going on?" asked Cody, curious as to what Gus had told Armand.

"Cody, this is one of those times it's better you know the bare minimum to keep you from overthinking the steps that will need to occur," supplied Armand.

Mac grunted. "When I think of the beach bum, I do nae think of a worrier or an overthinker."

Armand never broke eye contact with Cody. "Looks can be deceiving."

Cody wasn't sure he liked the way the conversation was headed. "Can Gus just give me the rundown himself?"

"No," said Armand and Bill at the same time.

Bill tipped to one side, lifted a leg and proceeded to break wind for a full minute, sounding as if someone was letting the air from a balloon. He whistled. "Damn. That was a good one."

In an instant, the SUV was filled with a stench that made Cody wonder if the man had an underlying medical condition that needed to be addressed. For a second, it felt as if his nostrils were being singed by whatever it was that had come out of Bill's body. He could only hope another baggie full of Bill's goodies hadn't emerged with the passing of the gas.

Gagging, Cody tried to put the window down, only to find it didn't work. "Car, turn off the window safety locks."

Mac fumbled with the button on his door as well, to no avail. "Och, hurry! I can taste it. That is foul and nae right."

Car coughed and fumbled with one hand while he continued to drive. He released the window locks. Cody and Mac were quick to lower their windows, letting in fresh air.

Armand kept his window closed, for good reason.

The windows of the SUV were treated with UV protectants. Rolling down said protection would be incredibly unwise for anyone with a serious sun allergy.

Such was the case with Armand.

He simply suffered in silence as Bill's fart lingered, clinging to everything and everyone in the vehicle.

Mac twisted around to face the small man. "I think yer dying. Smells like it."

Bill smacked his lips and took a huge breath in. "Nah. Smells like tuna fish."

"You dinnae have tuna for breakfast this morning," said Mac. "I know. I've been keeping an eye on you both."

That was news to Cody. He'd thought he'd been the one left holding the babysitting bag. He had to wonder if Casey had asked Mac to help as well, or if the wolf-shifter had simply assumed the responsibility out of an affinity for the two men.

It felt as if the latter was the right answer.

Bill waggled his brows. "I know. I said it smelled like tuna. I didn't say it was *caused* by tuna. Admit it, you're jealous of it. Your burp looks weak compared to my fart."

Mac shook his head and chuckled before rolling up his window.

Cody's attention returned to Armand. "Can we get back to me needing to meet Wheeler because of a mermaid? Gus does know those aren't real, right?"

Bill snorted. "You do get that most everyone out there doesn't think tree huggers who can turn into sharks are real, yet there you sit. There is a lot of shit out there that no one thought was real until they learned it was."

Mac shrugged. "He has a point, Aussie."

"Don't help," advised Cody.

Bill released Gus's hand and leaned forward slightly, patting Mac's shoulder over the top of the seat as best he could, considering the fact he wasn't exactly a tall man with a long reach. "Thanks, Braveheart."

A droll look fell over the Scotsman's face. "Does he make you tired too? Or am I just showing my age?"

"He makes me want to sleep for a decade," returned Cody, meaning every word of it.

Three days with Bill and Gus were going to be his undoing. If Casey didn't take his little friends back soon, Cody might be the first op to actually break down and eat them.

Bill huffed. "Gus says you'd spit us out, Rip Van Sharkie. That your shark side wouldn't want us for lunch. We're not as yummy as a sea turtle."

Slowly, Cody slid his gaze to Gus once more, wondering just how good the man's mind-reading gig was.

So far, it seemed spot on.

Armand stared back at Gus for another few tense seconds, saying nothing. When next he spoke, his attention moved to Cody. "Meet with

Wheeler. If you don't trust Gus, at least trust me."

Cody didn't like it, but he nodded all the same. "Fine. But first light tomorrow morning, I'm hunting for Helmuth, like it or not."

"Understood," added Armand.

Bill let out a long, exasperated breath. "Here we go again, Gus. Can't there be one of them who listens when we tell him something? Why do they always gotta go running around swinging their dicks and shouting about how alpha they are?"

Cody couldn't help but laugh. "I hardly call wanting to find an asshole who gets off on torturing people swinging my dick around."

Bill raised his shoulders and let them fall quickly. "You say tomato… I say dick swinging."

It was painfully clear to Cody that the drama would not stop until he agreed to meet with Wheeler. "I'll reach out to Wheeler about meeting tonight. But I draw the line at telling him it's about a mermaid."

"Don't ya want him to have all the facts?" asked Bill. "What kind of soldier are you? Can't even brief your fellow operatives fully. Geesh. You're kind of shit at this. It's amazing anything gets done without me and Gus helping. Elite units my ass."

Cody's fingers curled and his hands burned with the need to shift shapes and choke the man. Ever since his time in captivity, he'd been able to do partial shifts with far more ease than before. That didn't mean he ran around doing it whenever he got the urge. Giving the shark too many freedoms wasn't wise. Especially on land. If it thought it could get away with forcing a change, even a partial one, whenever it felt like, Cody would walk around stuck in between forms.

Mac reached out and put a hand on Cody's shoulder. "No sharkin' out and eatin' the li'l hairy man."

Cody fidgeted in his seat, unable to get comfortable. He bounced a foot, hoping to burn off the buildup of energy that had come out of nowhere. He'd need to shift forms and swim it off soon if it continued. It was painfully clear that talk of Helmuth was a trigger that he needed to learn to cope with. If he lost his head, bad things would happen. He'd learned as much in Costa Rica.

Images of the little girl sinking like a stone in the water beset him. The mental picture was as fresh in his head today as it had been the day it had happened. He could still vividly see her wide brown eyes looking up at him, lacking any fear as blood floated around her from her wounds. He could still taste her blood. The same blind rage and abject terror that had gripped him concerning her being in the water, and her safety, filled him quickly and his hands began to burn with the pending change.

Cody tried to hide them from the line of sight of the others, but he wasn't fast enough. Not that there was anywhere to really go.

Mac snatched Cody's hand and lifted it higher, examining it with wide-eyed wonderment. "How in the hell do you have claws, Aussie? Yer a shark-shifter and sharks do nae have claws."

Armand exhaled loudly and shot Cody a look that said he wasn't thrilled with the loss of control. "Much changed with him while under Helmuth's thumb."

"So yer saying he's nae a shark-shifter anymore?" asked Mac, earning him a worried glance in the rearview mirror from his twin.

Armand faced forward. "He is."

"Gus says that ain't all Sharkie is now. Says Helmet-Head and the Nazi wannabes messed him up real good. Like them things that are popping out of the woodwork all the time anymore that are smelly and rotting," said Bill.

The twins gasped at the same time.

"No," said Car, swerving slightly before gaining control of the vehicle once more. "He's nae sayin' yer a hybrid, is he?"

"Cody is not what you know a hybrid to be, no," said Armand, coming to Cody's rescue. "But he's not as he once was. Then again, he's never been as you are—a natural-born shifter. If you'll recall, his shifter side was brought about from testing. While held by Helmuth, Cody was subjected to more experiments. The kind that even the I-Ops scientists wouldn't have dreamed of doing to a person. So to answer you, yes, he's still a sharkshifter, but when fully shifted now, he's much larger than he once was and there are other side effects."

Mac held Cody's clawed hand up higher, turning it, showing off the grayish color that it now was and the long, dagger-like claws that had emerged where his fingernails once were. "I'd say so. Note to self, do nae be gettin' captured and tested on by anyone from The Corporation. You do nae know what will pop out the other side."

His comment made Cody laugh slightly, helping him gather his control once more. His hand re-formed to human. "Don't I know it."

Mac released his hand. "You've my word that if we get any leads on this Hel-butt-munch, I'll reach out to you. And if I cannae reach you, I'll rip his head off myself. He'll nae be allowed to do this to anyone else, Aussie."

Cody nodded but said nothing more on the matter.

Mac snorted. "Now, you've got to see a wheel about a mermaid. I cannae wait to see where that leads."

"I'm almost afraid to find out," said Cody, meaning it.

"Rightly so," exclaimed Mac. "We saw the two stooges with Gram. Gus knew things. Things he should nae know. And I'm guessin' yer other Outcast buddies who have mated recently have whispered of this lot as well, no? Did they nae help some of yer Outcast friends with their mates recently?"

With a hard swallow, Cody nodded. "Y-yes."

"Yer lookin' a little pale," said Mac. "If you pass out, do you change into a shark? Or a megalodon now that you've been amped up? That would be really somethin' to see. I've got some whiskey in a flask in my suitcase. I can pour it on you or somethin' to keep you wet."

Cody barely registered what Mac was saying. He was stuck on the fact Gus seemed sure he needed to meet with Wheeler about a mermaid. Even with all Cody had seen and lived through in his life, that was a stretch. But it was clearly important to Gus that Cody carry on with his normal meeting. And Armand seemed to agree.

"Gus says you're overthinking it all again, Sharkie," said Bill. "Gus ain't never told anyone to do nothing that wasn't for a good reason."

Mac blinked several times. "That was clear as mud."

Armand sighed. "Cody, go. Meet with Wheeler. Allow us to search for additional leads on Helmuth while you are there. We will reach out if we find anything. Gus believes you have to carry on as you normally would for events to line up accordingly. You have to ask yourself if you trust in what he can do or not. If so, go. Meet with Wheeler. Talk as you always do and go for drinks like normal. Gus believes the answers will make themselves known to you."

"Can't he just tell me why? If he knows so

much, why not come right out and say it?" demanded Cody. "Why frame it with abstracts?"

"Because that is how the information is presented to him," said Armand. "He isn't shown things in their entirety. He mentally opened fully to me for a fraction of a second and I saw what he does, Cody. I saw you on a park bench with Wheeler and felt it deep down that it was imperative you be there. That you not worry about anything other than that for now."

"He tells me I can't hunt a madman who tortured me and that I have to instead go shoot the shit with a buddy in a park?" asked Cody. "That is one hell of a big ask."

"Not if you trust in him and what he can do," said Armand.

"Yeah, listen to the dead guy," said Bill, earning him a growl from Armand.

"Fine, let the record state I'm not happy about this," said Cody.

Mac nodded. "Noted. Now, let's stop and feed these two knuckleheads."

Chapter Eight

THE LAST THING Cody wanted to do was delay searching for Helmuth, but it was clear his friends, while well-meaning, weren't planning to give him any peace until he did what Gus wanted him to do—continue with his regular scheduled programming.

Easier said than done when it came to Helmuth and the atrocities the monster had committed. The man was probably still causing someone pain and finding great joy in it all.

Cody needed to track down the man and end him. He couldn't be permitted to continue carrying out his madness. It had to stop, and Cody wanted to be the man who made that happen.

He'd earned the right.

More than earned it.

And his shark needed it.

So did the human side of Cody.

He had half a mind to turn around and head into the Paranormal Regulators (Para-Regs) office in the heart of Savannah to use their resources, rather than the "superheroes secret base" where the twins and Armand would be.

He refrained.

For now.

Cody had been meeting Wheeler for their Thursday night ritual since first coming to Savannah. In that time, talk of a mermaid had never come up and he highly doubted it suddenly would. This was a waste of precious time.

Time that would be better spent hunting down new leads on Helmuth.

Wheeler would understand. Hell, he'd help search for the bastard.

"This is asinine."

His cell rang.

He fished it from his pocket, and when he spotted Armand's number, a smile touched his lips. Good. They'd come to their senses and found something more on Helmuth. "Yeah?"

Armand sighed. "I'm to tell you that it is most certainly *not* asinine and for you to stay the course. To discuss the mermaid that you have not spoken of before with Wheeler. A life depends on it."

Cody froze and stared at his phone as if Armand might actually pop out of it.

"Livingston?" asked Armand. "Are you still there?"

"He can read us from a distance too?" questioned Cody in a voice so low it would be hard for even a supernatural to hear.

"Gus? The fact I was instructed to make this call should answer that question," said Armand. "Be a good boy and do as you're told."

Cody flipped him off.

Armand chuckled. "Nice. Is that an offer, Aussie?"

"He can see what I'm doing too?" asked Cody, stunned at Gus's ability. Whatever the government had done to him left him one hell of an asset, or weapon, depending on how one was looking at it.

"No, he did not tell me what you were just doing. I merely know you well enough to know you are expressing your thoughts on my comments with hand gestures," said Armand before cursing in French. His voice was muffled a moment before it became apparent that he was speaking to someone other than Cody. "Little hairy man, I will drain you of every last drop of your blood if you do not stop. Now, go sit at the table or I will take your bowl of ice cream away and send you to bed early."

"I ain't scared of nobody who sparkles when the sun shines!" shouted Bill from the background.

"I do not sparkle. *Ever.* In the sun or not. Where is it you get your information on vampires? From reading the newspaper's Sunday funnies?" Armand groaned.

"Bullshit," said Bill. "I saw a doco about vampires sparkling when the light hits them. Hey, how is it you're not blond? The doco showed a lot of blond vampires. Except for the bad guys. You a bad guy? We all already know you got the angsty part down pat. Rest true too? And for your info, Dead-Dude, no one reads a paper anymore. They get their news online. Get a pulse and with the times."

"For the hundredth time, documentary would be shortened to doc-u, not *o*. And I will be considered a bad guy *very* soon if you keep testing the limits of my patience," replied Armand, sounding exasperated.

Cody couldn't blame the man. Dealing with Bill was draining.

"That a threat, Frenchie?" asked Bill snidely. "You better check that tone before I shine a flashlight on you and blind you with your own sparkling."

Armand let out a long line of curses and hexes in French, all of which were aimed at Bill. After several seconds of continued back-and-forth between the men, Armand grunted loudly into the phone. "Cody, express my condolences to Casey on the soon-to-be loss of his friend. I am going to kill William."

"I go by Bill, Count Dick-u-la!" yelled Bill from the background. "The only reason I haven't staked ya is because Gus likes you. I don't know what he sees in you. Plain to see his character judgment is flawed."

Laughing, Cody hung up. Hearing Armand trying to deal with Bill was just what Cody needed to help curb his yearning to hunt down Helmuth.

At least for now.

He'd give his friends a chance to do whatever it was they were planning to do, and he'd carry on with his normal routine, even if it meant talking about mermaids. But the second he got wind of where Helmuth might be, all bets were off. He'd resume his hunt for the bastard.

Sliding his phone back into his pocket, Cody made his way to the park bench in Johnson Square that seemed reserved only for him and Wheeler. He knew better. Knew the reason the bench was being given a wide berth was because of his friend's vampire traits. Ones the man was drawing on to keep others at bay and provide them with some semblance of privacy, despite being out in the open.

Wheeler, who was in a dark blue T-shirt with a faded record cover image from a folk artist who had achieved great fame back in the '70s, stared out at the people walking by. The area attracted a mix of humans from young to old.

That was part of the charm.

Part of what Cody liked about Savannah.

Cody reached the bench with Wheeler on it in seconds. He took a seat as well.

A group of males who had apparently hit the local Savannah bar scene early walked toward them. One of the men tried jumping over the small black-chained landscaping fencing that only stood about a foot high. That twelve inches was all it took to send him toppling over it, into the bushes, taking two other men with him in the process.

"Been a while since we drunk-walked anywhere," said Wheeler, the smallest of laughs coming from him.

Cody smirked. "Thank the gods. I don't miss that."

They watched the men getting up, each razzing the other about having had too much to drink. They thankfully made the sound decision to call for a ride home, ending the night early.

"When is the last time we drank anywhere close to that much? Was it Costa Rica?" questioned Wheeler.

At the mention of Costa Rica, Cody tensed. It had been seventeen years since he'd set foot there. While it had once been a favorite stopping point on his surfing circuit, the events of long ago had soured him on it all. His last time there had been when his shark had been acting up, and he'd been forced to swim it off, only to happen upon a small drowning child—and Helmuth.

He gnashed his teeth in frustration at the thought of the man once more. Every fiber of his being said he should be out there, hunting Helmuth, not hanging out, not hunting for mermaids.

Wheeler reached out and touched his shoulder lightly. "Didn't mean to dredge it up."

Cody let out a shaky breath. "It's fine. And oddly enough, I was thinking about it all earlier today. I need to face my past demons."

"So people keep saying," added Wheeler. "Not sure I buy into the bullshit. Want to try to get hammered tonight? We can drink until we forget everything—including Costa Rica. It will take a shit-metric-ton of alcohol, but I'm always up for a good challenge. I'll admit when you called and said Helmuth surfaced and that he was linked to this area, I thought you'd want me to meet you to track him down." Wheeler glanced around the park. "Wasn't expecting you to suggest we keep with the norm. Know what I mean?"

"Wasn't my idea," said Cody. "I'd have gone with hunting the prick."

"I know," added Wheeler. "I was worried about you so I called Armand."

"Of course you did," exclaimed Cody. "I don't need a babysitter."

"That is debatable." Wheeler shrugged. "He

tells me you're not sleeping right. Something about dreams. They like before? Like Costa Rica?"

Cody touched his chest lightly. "No. I mean, I don't think so. They aren't exactly clear to me and they, um, feel like they might be sexual. Costa Rica wasn't sexual."

Wheeler kept people watching as he spoke. "But like before, you're not sleeping right. Easily agitated?"

Frustrated, Cody cast a disgruntled look in his friend's direction. "Why are you asking me all of this when it's pretty fucking clear you and Armand already discussed it in detail?"

"Because you need to learn to open up," said Wheeler, not the least bit riled by Cody's behavior. "You're the guy everyone goes to when they need something. The guy who is always there for everyone. Who is always levelheaded and keeps everyone calm. The guy who doesn't seem to let anything get to him. Until it comes to you. Then you're a shit-for-brains idiot who suffers in silence when he could have just opened his mouth and asked for a hand."

"You're kind of an asshole," said Cody with a sideways smirk.

"Yeah, I know." Wheeler grinned. "Doesn't change the fact I'm right and you know it. So, what's been eating you lately? And I'm not talking about Helmuth. Armand says you've been agitated for days."

Cody thought more on it before sighing. "Lack of sleep. And I feel like something is off. But I don't know what."

"That why you're seeing a wheel about a mermaid?" asked Wheeler with a soft laugh and a wink.

Cody grunted. "Armand told you about that too."

"Yes, but he wouldn't tell me where it came from, only that it was important you and I meet and it had something to do with a mermaid. When I was done laughing at him, he told me to be sure I was here on time. That you'd need a friend tonight. I was hoping you could enlighten me on the whole chick with a fish tail bit."

"Wish I could," confessed Cody. "But I'm as lost as you are."

"Ever get the sense you were sent on a fool's errand so you'd go out, get drunk, and unwind? You know, and not run headfirst into danger to go after Helmuth?" asked Wheeler.

"I think that is exactly what is going on," replied Cody. He stared down at his hands, remembering the loss of control he'd had and the partial shift in the SUV earlier.

"Armand mentioned there was an incident today," said Wheeler.

"Thanks for sugarcoating that for me."

Wheeler nodded. "We've all been there."

"True."

"Still having issues tonight?" asked Wheeler, no judgment in his voice.

Cody cracked his knuckles as his shark stirred deep within him, making itself known. "Yes."

Wheeler gave Cody the slightest of shoves. "Don't go losing it and turning into something I can't explain and will have to pee on or something to keep moist."

The visual the man painted was so vivid, Cody was jarred out of his oncoming rage. "Pee? You'd really pee on me?"

"If you were stuck in shark form on land, I'd do what needed to be done to keep you from drying out and dying or something," added Wheeler.

"Gee, um, thanks. But peeing on me won't

help, so how's about we *totally* take that option off the table?" Cody groaned.

Wheeler tilted his head. "Okay, but if you change your mind…"

"Yeah, positive that is *never* going to happen. I'd rather have the whiskey."

"What?" asked Wheeler.

Cody found it in himself to grin somewhat as he thought about Mac's offer to waste perfectly good liquor on him should he lose control and shift into a shark. "Long story."

Wheeler snorted, but his laughter faded rapidly, and a somber expression moved over his face. "Cody, I've never apologized to you for Costa Rica."

"There is nothing to apologize for," said Cody, meaning every word of it. "You didn't take me. An asshole did."

"But I could have looked for you," stressed Wheeler. "Hell, I could have realized you were missing. I thought you were off on a swimming bender like you did often. I didn't know you'd been taken. Had I known, I'd have done whatever it took to get you back. I wouldn't have caught a flight out, leaving you to be held and tortured for how many years? I'm a shitty best friend. I'm sorry."

Cody nodded. "You didn't know I was taken. How could you? How many times before that did I take off for weeks at a time to stay in shark form? Huh? How could you have possibly figured out that wasn't like every other time I did it?"

Wheeler bent his head. "I should have sensed it."

"Bullshit." Cody didn't like seeing his friend suffer for something that wasn't his doing. "Odds are, had you come after me, they'd have gotten their hands on you too."

Wheeler swallowed hard. "Do you think they got Kaiko?"

Cody licked his lower lip and clasped his hands before him. "Yes. When I got free and learned Kaiko was missing, my first and only thought had been that they managed to get their hands on him too. He wouldn't just vanish without a word to the Outcast Network. He'd have told us if he was planning to go off the grid fully. Doesn't matter how seat-of-the-pants he could be."

"Think he's still alive?" asked Wheeler.

Cody reflected on his time being held and all

that he'd been put through. He'd seen so many alpha males come through the various facilities he'd been kept at all around the world during his time being a captive that he'd lost count. Nearly all of them had died horrible deaths. "No. You?"

"No," whispered Wheeler. "When we do find these fucks, I want to help kill them all."

"The more, the merrier," said Cody with a half-smile, when he really wanted to jump up and head into PSI to see what, if anything, the twins and Armand had uncovered about Helmuth's whereabouts. Screw trying to be stealthy and going to the Para-Regs for help. Cody was about to storm the PSI castle.

"You've gone quiet," said Wheeler.

Cody looked down at the ground and got lost in thought a moment, his mind going back to Costa Rica once more. Not to Helmuth or the torture, but the little girl who had been drowning. "I wish I knew what happened to the kid."

"The kid?" asked Wheeler.

"That little girl who was injured and drowning," said Cody. "The one I tried to save before I was taken."

Wheeler shook his head. "No clue what happened to her. So much went on back then, that bit seemed the least important to me. Didn't you tell me later that you were sure you heard another boat approaching for her?"

"I did, but I'm not sure if she survived," said Cody, his stomach knotting more at the thought the little girl might not have made it. "She was so tiny, so vulnerable."

Wheeler nodded. "Put you in a pretty vulnerable position herself, didn't she?"

Cody's entire body tensed at the suggestion the child was at fault in any way—even small—with what had happened to him. "She didn't have anything to do with me being taken and tested on."

"I'm not saying a little kid orchestrated your capture, Cody." Wheeler leaned forward, his elbows going to his knees as he hunched partway over on the bench. "What I *am* saying is the timing of it all has bothered me since your escape —since you and I reconnected. Think about how statistically rare it is that at the same spot and second some random little girl is in the middle of the ocean, alone, and in need of help, you're there and so is The Corporation."

Cody hadn't really thought of that before, and it wasn't as if he hadn't had plenty of time to reflect on the events of that day. For most of his time in captivity, he'd dwelled on what had gone down that fateful day. On how restless his shark had been in the days leading up to his capture. About the dreams he'd had about someone he loved needing his help, and then how he'd happened upon the child in her hour of need. And how much of a total ass-face his shark side had been about allowing him to shift into human form.

He'd played the scene out, again and again, trying to imagine what, if anything, might have gone down differently had he been able to take human form. Would he still have been captured by Helmuth and the rest of the men aboard the vessel bearing Donavon Dynamics' logo, which they all learned later was a company owned and operated by The Corporation? Would Cody have been able to evade capture and make sure the child reached the shore? Or would he have still been taken and never truly know the fate of the little girl?

"Your face says you're still pissed I suggested it's too big of a coincidence that the girl was there with you right as you were taken," said Wheeler. "You're like a brother to me, Cody. I'm allowed to state my thoughts on something and worry about you."

"I know," said Cody. "But I'm telling you. She wasn't part of that. She was just a kid."

"Was she a kid they held and were testing on too?" asked Wheeler, posing another question that Cody hadn't ever asked himself before.

At the thought of it, his shark stirred awake, threatening to be an issue very soon. It didn't like thinking the child was a pawn in the sick fuck's games any more than he did. Was Wheeler, right? Had the little girl been a victim of The Corporation and Helmuth too?

An entirely new fear struck him. One he'd not considered before.

Suddenly, it felt as if Cody had been kicked right in the gut. Worry and fear for the little girl slammed into him, nearly knocking him from the park bench.

If she had been one of Helmuth's victims—or precious test subjects, depending on who you were asking—was she dead?

No.

He refused to believe she was dead and gone.

He'd clung to the hope the child had made it for seventeen years now. Giving in to any other line of thinking would do what the bad guys tried so hard to do for so long—break his spirit and his mind.

Nausea rose quickly and the next thing Cody knew, Wheeler was forcing him to bend forward, with his head between his knees as his breathing came in shallow, fast breaths.

"Calm down," said Wheeler in a hushed yet authoritative tone. "Hyperventilating and panicking isn't going to do jack to help the matter."

Cody tried to protest that he wasn't doing anything of the sort, but the fact he couldn't form any words because of his inability to take in enough air spoke to the contrary. He was panicking, and all because he was worried about some little girl he didn't even really know. A child he'd met briefly in passing seventeen years ago.

As he thought on it more, he realized that was precisely what he was doing.

In spades.

He took long, measured breaths, and after a few of those, his pulse rate slowed to something close to normal. It was then he realized sweat was beading on his brow. He swiped his hand over his forehead, moving away the moisture before sitting up fully and staring out at the people walking by. He shook his head, his thoughts still on the little girl.

"What if you're right? What if she was wrapped up in that entire thing? What if The Corporation ended up with their hands on her? Oh God, Wheeler, we've read the reports about what they've done to children. All the testing. The deaths. Who knows what else?"

Wheeler sighed. "Shit, Cody, I shouldn't have said anything. I don't know why I did. It's just, well, it's been seventeen years this week since it all happened, and I've had Kaiko on my mind lately. I'm sure the kid is fine. Bet she wasn't swept up in it all. She was just in the wrong spot at the wrong time."

Cody shot his friend a sideways look. "You don't really believe that, do you?"

Wheeler was quiet for a moment before shaking his head. "I don't think she was a secret operative for them or anything. Not with as little as she was. She wouldn't have been a willing pawn. That makes it even worse."

"You think she was taken by them too? The same day I was? The drugs they pumped through me once they caught me made it nearly impossible to focus or know what was real and what was imagined for weeks or months after. Was she there, close to me all along, and I did nothing to stop them from hurting her?"

"You can't blame yourself," said Wheeler. "You were hardly in a position to help yourself, let alone anyone else."

Cody's heart began to race once more. "Maybe she wasn't taken."

Wheeler sighed. "My gut says she was tied to The Corporation in some way. Man, it almost feels like she was bait for you. Their version of chumming the water. Crazy, isn't it?"

Cody went to protest but stopped. His friend's words felt oddly right. He paled, feeling as if he might be sick. "If they hurt her…if they touched her…I will hunt every last one of them down and kill them slowly. They'll beg me for death, but I'll make them wait for it. I'll rip their fucking throats out."

He tried to say more, but his mouth picked then to start to do a partial shift, a sign of just how far gone his control was. He bent his head fast to keep any humans from seeing the start of shark teeth. Explaining away five rows of jagged teeth wasn't something that could be done with any sort of ease. More of a worry was the fact that if Cody lost any more of his limited control, he'd end up fully shifted into a shark, right there in the middle of Johnson Square.

That would go over great in a day and age when everyone was walking around with a smartphone ready to record in real-time what was happening.

The I-Ops and PSI were already fighting an uphill battle to keep leaked information off the net. Having to try to sweep the net clean of video footage and talk of a man turning into a fucking shark would not end well.

Wheeler jerked up and stood fast. "You need to calm down, or I'm going to knock you out for everyone's safety. I may think of you like a brother, but I'll kick the ever-loving shit out of you until you're unconscious. Or I'll offer to pee on you again."

That made Cody laugh enough to return the shape of his mouth to human form. He looked up at Wheeler. "Thanks. Always willing to pee on me. Not sure what to say to that fetish you seem to have."

Wheeler shrugged and then winked. "You all right?"

Cody rubbed his upper chest. "Yeah. I think so. We should maybe change the topic. I'm not sure I can handle thinking that anything happened to that kid."

Wheeler snorted. "No shit. And, Cody, if she survived and all was fine, she wouldn't be a kid anymore. She'd be a grown woman."

That made Cody's breath catch.

Wheeler was right. She would be an adult now.

Chapter Nine

"WHERE IS RENE MEETING US? Did we decide on a bar yet?" questioned Gena as she and Bonnie walked down the sidewalk, in the direction of Johnson Square.

"You're still in a mood, aren't you?" asked Bonnie with a shake of her head. "I swear, you spent the entire drive back to Savannah pouting."

"Did not," said Gena with something close to a pout, serving to prove her friend's point.

Bonnie rolled her eyes. "For the billionth time, I'm sorry. I'd go in your place, but he didn't ask me."

Gena stared at her friend. "Because you disappeared again with that hot guy."

"Kahale," said Bonnie. "He is exceptionally good-looking, isn't he? And I didn't disappear, I finished the conversation I'd started with him before he'd gotten pulled away with the phone call. I can't help that meant you had more one-on-one time with the man single-handedly footing our research center bill."

"You keep reminding me he's our main funder," said Gena with a huff. "It's not like I forgot. I know how important his money is to the center."

"Yet when I met you out front by the van before we left, you were acting as if he was a leper. And when he asked you to meet him for lunch tomorrow, I really thought you were going to say no."

"Me too," said Gena.

When Bonnie had wandered off again with Kahale, shortly after lunch had been served, Gena had been left to dine alone with Helmuth. That had meant more awkward silence and a lot of staring at her on his part. Then, he'd asked her to meet him tomorrow for lunch on his yacht so they could talk about her thesis paper. She'd been about to tell him no when Bonnie had reappeared.

"There is just something about him," added Gena. "I don't know. I might be overthinking this."

Bonnie was quiet for a bit as they walked more. She then stopped and touched Gena's arm lightly. "Listen, if you're uncomfortable meeting him alone, don't do it. No amount of money is worth you being put in a situation you're not at ease in."

While Gena appreciated Bonnie saying what she did, they both knew deep down that the center needed the additional funding. Their passion for what they did was unrivaled, and Helmuth's offer to give them the money they needed couldn't have come at a better time.

Gena thought about her reactions to Helmuth and the things that had set her off about him. The more she focused on it all, the sillier it seemed. "No. It's totally fine. I'll meet him to talk about my thesis."

Bonnie snorted.

"What?"

"Nothing," said Bonnie with a shake of her head.

When they'd gotten back to the center, Bonnie had vanished into her office to change yet again and Gena had gone to her boat to do the same. Gena had used that moment to text Clara and Nicolette to see if they wanted to meet for drinks as well.

After a quick shower Gena had come out to find Bonnie there, on the boat, picking out something for Gena to wear for their celebratory evening out.

Gena's wardrobe wasn't exactly extensive. Since all she did was work, she had very few items to wear out and about that weren't shorts, t-shirts, dive suits, or swimsuits. Bonnie had managed to find a dress that Gena's sister had sent her for her birthday the year prior. It had still been in the same box it had arrived in. The sleeveless paisley dress was made of lightweight material and came to Gena's midthigh. It was done in blues with orange accents. It wasn't anything she'd have ever bought for herself because she wasn't the type to indulge, but even she had to admit it was comfortable and looked good on her.

Bonnie had gone with an all-white off-the-shoulder dress that fell above her knees. She had on a pair of sandals that were thankfully devoid of logos from her haul. Her hair was down, skimming her shoulders. It was strange seeing Bonnie in makeup since it wasn't something the women wore to work on a day-to-day basis. The woman was a total knockout and had been turning heads on their short walk to the bars.

Gena had gone with clear lip gloss and tied her hair into a new bun. Sadly, the bun was already coming loose. As the night wore on, she'd let it down, but it was too hot at the moment.

They reached Johnson Square and Bonnie drew to a stop, looking around.

"I can't remember if I asked but did, we pick a bar to meet Rene at?" asked Gena, moving her foot slightly because the smallest of pebbles had gotten between her heel and her flip-flop.

"We didn't. She said she'll meet us here on the square," replied Bonnie.

Gena glanced around, hoping to spot Rene.

"I cannot believe he gave us all the money we needed," said Bonnie for the tenth time since Helmuth had agreed to foot the extra bills. The woman had spent the car ride alternating from excited about the money to apologizing for leaving Gena alone with Helmuth more than once.

Gena stiffened as she thought about Helmuth. While he may have come through big time for them financially, there was no denying that he gave her the creeps. Yes, he'd done a very good deed, but still.

Bonnie nudged her as a cocky smile spread over her face. "Thinking about your romantic lunch date with him tomorrow?"

Gena nearly tripped over her own feet as she slid her foot back into her flip-flop. "Romantic? It's not romantic. You heard him. He's interested in my thesis."

Bonnie snorted. "Oh, he's interested in something all right, and hon, it's not your thesis."

"You think?" Gena asked as a sudden pang of anxiety swept over her. Was Helmuth interested in her sexually? She'd only just managed to talk herself into meeting him when she assumed it was strictly professional. Thinking he wanted something more from it all made panic well in her.

"He's hot," proclaimed Bonnie. "Really hot. Would it be overstepping as your friend to say that I hope you do him, and that he's so enchanted by your bedroom skills that he doubles his funding offer?"

Gena's head whipped around as she stared fully at her friend, her eyes wide.

"From the look on your face, I'd say that was a yes to overstepping," said Bonnie.

"It's not that, it's just…umm…"

"Um, what?" asked Bonnie before she grabbed Gena's arm. "Rene and I have talked about our past relationships, and our sex lives come up all the time."

"I know," said Gena, having gotten an earful on more than one occasion.

"But now that I'm thinking about it, the only time you've ever mentioned sex is when you told us about the dreams you've been having. With the hunky shark-shifter guy," stressed Bonnie, a knowing look in her eyes. "Gena, tell me you're not a virgin."

Biting her lower lip, Gena blushed. "My parents homeschooled us, and we all finished our schooling very early and were in college surrounded by people older than us. I know for me, it was hard enough adjusting to life in the real world after having been raised by the type of parents I have. Sex was the last thing I had time to think about. At some point, I got so focused on my education and my career that I didn't even stop to think about it one way or another. Then the dreams started."

Bonnie looked up as if a sign from the heavens would make the conversation better. "Good Lord, woman. Do not tell Rene about this. You know how she is. She'll make it her one mission in life to get you—"

"Not tell me what?" questioned an attractive blonde woman who came around the corner, seemingly out of nowhere. Rene had on a pair of shorts that barely covered her girlie bits or anything else. Her tank top was snug as well, and she looked to have opted out of wearing a bra.

That was a very Rene thing to do.

She also looked like a total knockout, as usual.

Gena just stood there, praying silently that Bonnie did not share the fact she was a virgin.

Bonnie squealed and hugged Rene. "We did it! We got the extra funding!"

Rene hopped up and down with Bonnie as the pair made loud, excited noises that drew the gazes of onlookers. Rene put her hands on Bonnie's forearms but kept jumping. "We got the grant?"

Bonnie's enthusiasm waned slightly. "Uh, no. We were passed over."

"No? I thought we were a shoo-in for it," said Rene.

Sadness touched Bonnie's eyes. "I don't know about that, but I thought we had a really good chance at it."

"Tell me Roberts didn't get it," said Rene.

"I'm guessing he did," said Bonnie.

"He's such a dirtbag." Rene's lip curled. "There is no way we were passed over without a little help from that dickhead. He runs with a lot of palm greasers. He probably knew we didn't get it before we did. You know he's somewhere gloating and talking about how women have no place in science and that our facility should have just been closed when he moved on to greener pastures. Weird thing is, I've been doing some checking on him and where he landed after us, and no one has ever heard of the place he's working for. They came out of nowhere."

Gena kept her thoughts on it all to herself because she didn't know Dr. Roberts as well as Bonnie and Rene, but even she had to admit that Roberts didn't seem like the type to go work for an unknown. He liked to toot his own horn and that was hard to do with a company no one in the scientific community had heard of before.

Rene's brows met. "I'm confused. If we didn't get the grant, how is it we got the funding?"

Bonnie thumbed in the direction of Gena. "We had the meeting today and as it turns out, Mr. Bigwig has a thing for girls with fish tails and Gena."

Rene's jaw dropped. "For real? Hold up, fish tails?"

Gena wasn't sure if she should take offense at just how shocked Rene appeared to be over the news Helmuth found her attractive. Since she wasn't convinced Bonnie was even correct—that Helmuth did have an interest in her that way—she refrained from comment.

Bonnie laughed. "Oh yeah. He asked her out for a lunch date tomorrow on his yacht. He couldn't take his eyes off her. Looked like a kid in a candy store."

Rene managed to appear even more stunned than she had been. "Did you explain to her that he was asking her out on a date? You know how she is with guys coming on to her. I'm not sure how it is she manages to date."

"She doesn't," Bonnie said under her breath.

Rene smiled. "I know."

Bonnie snorted. "Pretty sure she really thinks

he's interested in her thesis. He asked her on a lunch date tomorrow to discuss it in depth. I'm a huge nerd, and even I was bored by her paper."

Gena found it impossible not to laugh as well, knowing Bonnie was joking. At least she hoped she was. She'd put a lot of time, research, and energy into her thesis. Boring people to death had not been the end goal.

As she thought harder on it, she realized it more than likely did drag on in various spots. Moreover, Gena understood that not many people outside of the scientific community would find her thesis remotely interesting.

Rene cupped her mouth and teared up. "We really got the extra funding?"

Gena nodded. "We did."

Squealing, Rene grabbed for Gena and hugged her.

It took some doing to pry herself from the woman's grip, but she managed. Just in time, apparently, as Bonnie and Rene went right back to jumping up and down with excitement.

Rene tossed her arms out. "We have got to super celebrate tonight!"

"That is the plan," said Bonnie.

Gena was about to speak when the overwhelming urge to look past her friends in the direction of Johnson Square came over her. She did, and at first, she wasn't sure why it was she'd felt so compelled to focus on the area.

When she spotted two men sitting on a bench, somehow managing to fit notwithstanding their sizes, she froze.

It was him.

The man from her dreams.

The guy who started off as the shark who saved her life all those years ago before morphing into a man in the water. The same guy who then spent the rest of her dream, making her toes curl, and her body feel things she didn't even know was possible.

Reaching up quickly, Gena rubbed her eyes and blinked, sure she was seeing things.

Nope.

The guy on the bench still looked identical to the one she'd been dreaming of. If she was hallucinating, it was extremely believable.

He'd been drop-dead sexy in her dreams. In the flesh, he was indescribably alluring. That was if he was truly there on the bench, and she'd not had some sort of brain malfunction.

A number of ailments and issues that could

cause visual hallucinations came to mind. None of them were anything she was hoping for.

As she stood there, blinking in disbelief in the direction of the man on the bench, she couldn't help but notice the dramatic flip-flops her stomach was suddenly doing.

"Uh, is she okay?" asked Rene.

"Not sure. Does it look like she might faint to you too?" questioned Bonnie.

"Yes," answered Rene. "Should we make her sit down and put her head between her knees?"

"Pretty sure we should find a hottie who is willing to put his head between her knees," said Bonnie.

Rene laughed so hard she hiccupped.

Gena couldn't comment. All she could do was stare at the men on the bench.

They were both incredibly attractive, but the one with blond hair was downright godly. And there was no doubt in her mind he was the same man from her dreams.

That wasn't possible.

Of course, the odds of her walking along and running into the very stranger she'd been having naughty dreams about had seemed impossible to her five minutes ago.

Things changed.

On a dime apparently.

Then again, maybe the man just really, really, really looked like the man she'd been seeing in her dreams. Or perhaps her mind was filling in blanks with what it saw before it, rather than the truth of what it was.

A man who looked similar to the one she'd invented in her mind.

Very frigging similar.

Regardless, the man called to her in a way no other ever had. It was if he'd cast a fishing line and snagged her in the process.

Her heart felt as if it skipped a beat as she found it impossible to tear her gaze from him. Every ounce of her demanded she run to him. That she make contact with him. That freaked her out even more than the idea she'd been dreaming of him. Tossing herself at a man she didn't know, or any man for that matter, was not something she was known for.

Get it together. It's not the guy from your dreams. It's just a guy who really looks like him. Stop freaking out.

She tore her gaze from his.

"Gena?" asked Rene. "You all right there?"

"No," said Gena fast. "I mean yes. I'm fine. What were we talking about again?"

Bonnie looked concerned. "Getting the money."

"Right," said Gena, nodding. "Yay!"

"Has she eaten lately?" asked Rene. "Is this a low blood sugar thing or has she just lost her mind?"

"Might be both," said Bonnie, all smiles still.

"Could be the heat," supplied Rene. "It's hotter than hell tonight."

"Yes, he is," said Gena, her gaze flickering to the man on the bench. He was certainly hotter than hell.

"He?" questioned Rene. "Yeah, she's lost it."

"With as much time as she spends with us, it was bound to happen," offered Bonnie with a snort. "Surprised it took this long."

The women high-fived and then looked at Gena.

"She's still acting like a weirdo," said Rene.

"Weird is such a relative term." Bonnie waggled her brows. "Don't you think?"

Gena stared hungrily at the man on the bench who was in deep conversation with his friend.

Details from her dreams came flooding over her, making her body heat more. The things he'd done to her nearly made her moan just reflecting on them.

"Seriously, is the heat getting to her?" asked Rene. "Maybe we should head to a place with air."

"I'm fine," said Gena, still staring at the blond man.

He moved slightly on the bench and she darted behind Rene, allowing the woman to eclipse her view of the hot guy. If she couldn't see him, he couldn't see her.

Perfect.

Her upper neck flushed with embarrassment though she wasn't sure why. She had no reason to be. That being said, she found herself stepping to the left quickly as Rene moved, keeping herself hidden from view of the men on the bench.

Rene lifted a brow. "Uh, whatcha doing?"

"Being weirder than normal," said Bonnie with a big smile.

Gena gulped, her heart still racing, her body still hot. "Is he still there?"

"Is who still there?" demanded Bonnie, suddenly looking ready to rumble on Gena's behalf.

Absently, Gena pushed stray strands of her hair behind her ears as she continued to hide behind Rene. "The guy on the bench over there."

Rene laughed. "The two hot guys back over that way?"

Gena nodded. "The blond one."

"Pretty sure they're a couple," said Rene.

Chapter Ten
―――――――

SEVERAL MINUTES TICKED by as Cody sat on the bench in the park, trying to wrap his mind around what Wheeler had pointed out. With the time that had passed, the little girl wouldn't be little anymore at all. She would be fully grown. As he ran the date of events through his head once more, he realized she'd be around the age of twenty-seven now. Within seconds he was trying to imagine what she'd look like now.

Quickly flashes of a woman with long dark hair and pair, creamy skin ran through his head. They were fleeting and elicited responses in him physically that he wasn't sure how to properly process. The way he imagined her to be as an adult was sinfully sexy

His frantic thoughts skipped quickly to if she was safe and happy now.

If so, what was she doing now?

Where was she living?

Did she have someone special in her life?

Was she married?

Cody's entire body tensed at the idea she might very well be married with a family of her own. His shark thrashed around within him, unhappy with the idea any man would have gotten close enough to her to touch her let alone bed her. For some strange reason, the idea of her possibly being married set him on edge. He wasn't sure why.

He wanted to know she was alive, safe, and happy. He just wanted that happiness to have been found in a convent or something of the like. Anywhere with vows of celibacy. Not with a man.

When Cody recognized his feelings on the matter as jealousy, he lurched and ran his hands through his hair, shaking his head as he did. Why in the world would he be jealous of what some random girl he saved years ago was doing now?

He could find no explanation for his feelings on the matter.

He let out a frustrated growl at the idea a man could have dared to touch her.

It was official.

He'd lost his damn mind.

No matter how illogical the feeling was, it was real to him and that freaked him out.

Wheeler snickered. "Mind blown?"

Cody nodded. "Honestly, my mind was less blown when I was being held and mind-fucked by assholes."

"Took that better, did ya?" asked Wheeler, his lips setting in a thin line. It was easy to see the man was amused that Cody was losing his shit over the fact the girl wasn't little anymore.

Cody swallowed hard. "Yes."

"Want me to change the subject?"

"God yes," said Cody, desperate to talk about anything other than the girl or Wheeler's urination.

"Remember that time we were all in that pub in Australia, near the port?" Wheeler asked, reminiscing about the days of old.

Simpler times.

"I've spent a lot of time in pubs in Australia," replied Cody. "You'll need to be more specific."

"The redhead," added Wheeler.

"Redhead for me or for you?" asked Cody, as Wheeler tended to have a thing for women with red hair.

"You," returned Wheeler.

Instantly Cody thought back to the hottie he'd spent the night with all those years ago. She'd been in the market to land a serviceman, and she'd managed to snarl Cody. Not that he'd needed much bait. Back then, a cool breeze could turn him on.

Those days were long gone.

"The good old days," said Cody.

His friend nodded. "I went home with twins that night. Those were *great* fucking days."

"I bet." Laughing, Cody adjusted slightly on the bench. It wasn't made for comfort. That was for sure.

"Good to be back?" asked Wheeler.

Cody had gotten back to Georgia at dawn's first light. "Yeah. Colorado is landlocked. After a few hours, I get twitchy, and if I stay too long, I get hives. Wish that wasn't true."

A fly landed on Wheeler's cheek, but the man made no sign of noticing or caring. It crawled around on his face, and Cody nearly smacked it away himself. He resisted as Wheeler stared out at the humans as they went on about their business, none the wiser that they were so close to apex predators.

So close to danger.

"I can hear their hearts beating," said Wheeler in a hushed whisper, while rubbing the palms of his hands on the tops of his jean-clad thighs. The insect picked then to fly away as if it sensed just how on edge the man was and wanted no part of it.

Cody stiffened as he realized his friend was struggling with his vampire side again. It wasn't the first time he'd seen Wheeler struggle with the darkness he carried. But the times were getting closer and closer together, and that was worrisome. The last thing he wanted was for Wheeler to end up like a number of the Outcasts had over the years—insane and a danger to themselves and others.

A few had even been turned into something far worse at the hands of a madman, but Cody didn't want to think upon that more at the moment. Right now, he simply wanted to assist his friend.

"Sure. You're feeling peckish and I'm sitting here, all full of blood and stuff. That isn't the least bit concerning. Nope. Not at all. Where is a mobile blood bank when you need one? If I donate to the cause, do I get a cookie when I'm done?" asked Cody, wanting to insert humor into a non-funny situation in an attempt to lighten the mood. "Hey, would a bloodmobile be considered a food truck for your kind?"

Wheeler stopped rubbing his palms on his thighs obsessively. He did take a few deep breaths before running a hand through his ear-length brown hair. The pair were matched in height and build, but that was where the similarities ended. Wheeler's dark hair was a sharp contrast to Cody's naturally blond locks. Though Cody did have some brown hair around the nape of his neck. It was more of a medium brown, but it counted.

At least he assumed it did.

Wheeler grinned, his gaze darting to the street. "Yeah. If mobile blood banks had a bell and rang it while driving through town, I'd come running."

"A nice catchy tune would be good. How about something appropriate to a funeral, since most vamps are dead and all—present company excluded," said Cody.

Wheeler laughed. "'Taps'?"

"Totally." Cody hid his grin, pleased his joke had helped Wheeler gather additional control. That had been the intent. He took a deep breath in and caught the scent of the water, not far from where they sat. "I like knowing there is a big body of water close by, should I need it. And that if push came to shove, I could get from it to the ocean quickly. Colorado seriously was starting to make me twitchy."

"I bet," said Wheeler. "I'm shocked the twins didn't offer to find you a saltwater pool to take a relaxing shift in. Nothing like a great white in the pool while they throw some shrimp on the barbie."

"Funny," Cody said sarcastically at Wheeler's jab about Cody being from Australia. "They offered it up as a suggestion for how they were going to deal with me if I sharked out on them."

"Ah. This sharking-out. Did it have something to do with the crazed hippie guy and his cult or did this run more on the lines of Helmuth?" asked Wheeler.

Cody exhaled long and loud. "I take it when Armand called you, he got into being worried about me?"

"He did," said Wheeler. "He's right to be worried about you. Helmuth already found a way to capture you and hold you against your will once in your life. Want to give him another shot?"

"No," said Cody softly, staring out at the park. "I want to kill him. I want to feel my hands around his throat a second before I snap his neck."

Wheeler nodded, saying very little on the matter for what felt like forever. When he did speak, it wasn't what Cody wanted to hear. "From what I'm told, snapping his neck won't kill him. Didn't two pretty fucking powerful ops already try to stand against him, and he came back from that with what looks like relative ease?"

"Yes. But this will be different." Cody leaned back on the bench, extending his long legs, putting one ankle over the other. He and Wheeler both stood well over six foot, and the bench they were on wasn't exactly made for men their size.

Still, they made it work.

"Because you're going to let blind rage lead the charge?" asked Wheeler.

"You're something of a buzzkill, dude," said Cody with a grunt. "Want to start in on the kid from all those years ago once more, since you're on a roll and all?"

Wheeler snorted. "Just keeping it real. And trying to keep you alive and not locked away in a containment tank or cage again. I'd think you'd want that too."

Cody did want that. "You okay?"

"I'm not planning to drain anyone dry right this second," said Wheeler, grinning, though it wasn't full, and Cody suspected that meant the man was still struggling with his vampire side. If he was, fangs would show when he smiled all the way. And fangs weren't something Wheeler was a fan of flashing.

Cody didn't much care if the man vamped out or not so long as no one was hurt in the process, but he knew it bothered his friend. It had taken Cody some time to become comfortable in his own skin after his supernatural awakening. It was taking Wheeler far longer.

But his change came with a bloodlust Cody knew he couldn't relate to. Not at the level Wheeler suffered.

His cell buzzed, and he withdrew it from his pocket to find he had a text from Armand. Since Armand wasn't exactly a huge fan of texting,

Cody had to wonder what had prompted the action. When he saw it was regarding Bill and Gus, he got a better understanding.

He shook his head when he read it and realized Wheeler was reading over his shoulder.

"Uh, who are Bill and Gus, and why did Armand just refer to himself as Count Dick-u-la?" asked Wheeler.

Cody had forgotten that Wheeler hadn't had the pleasure of meeting Bill or Gus just yet. "The two humans who started out with Casey Black."

Wheeler scratched his scruffy chin. "Didn't I hear about them stealing Duke Marlow's sports car and wrapping it around a tree or something? I think it was Westin who was complaining about them in a group text. They were staying with him and his mate in Tennessee, last I heard. Or do I have the wrong human pets in mind?"

Cody grinned. "Those would be the ones. They're steadily making the rounds. Pray they don't show up for you. When they do, insanity follows, chaos occurs, and someone walks out of there pregnant."

Wheeler laughed long and hard. "I can't wait to meet them."

"Might get your chance," said Cody. "They

insisted on flying back with me. The twins and Armand are currently human-sitting. Not sure but Armand may drain Bill dry sooner rather than later."

"Takes a lot to get under Armand's skin," said Wheeler. "He tends to ignore most people."

"There is *no* ignoring the force known as Bill."

"Now I really can't wait to meet him," added Wheeler.

Cody glanced at his friend. "Um, Gus, he, erm, seems to think I needed to be here tonight, with you, because some woman he thinks is a mermaid is in danger."

Wheeler stiffened and then patted himself all over in a dramatic fashion.

"What are you doing?" asked Cody.

"Making sure I didn't bring your mermaid in my pocket or anything."

Cody groaned. "You know, you have a really shit sense of humor."

"I try," added Wheeler before wiping the smile from his face. "So he thinks a woman who's a mermaid is in danger, meaning, he thinks mermaids are real?"

"Yes."

"So, he's crazy?"

Cody wasn't so sure anymore. "Maybe. Maybe not."

"What do you think?" asked Wheeler. "Is he right about some mermaid chick being in danger?"

"Honestly, I don't know what to think. He's been right about a lot of things."

"And Gus said you needed to be here? With me, tonight?" asked Wheeler.

"Yes."

Wheeler glanced around in a wild manner.

"What in the hell are you doing?" asked Cody.

"Looking for mermaids, dipshit," answered Wheeler. "Drinks are on you if I find one first. Oh, do you think she'll be wearing a shell bra or starfish over her nipples? I'm totally fine with either."

"Asshole."

Wheeler nudged Cody's shoulder as a hot blonde woman sashayed toward them, wearing a pair of shorts that left little to the imagination. Her tank top was dressy with sequins on it that caught the glow of the streetlamps just right. "How about that one? She it? She your mermaid? Maybe she made a deal with a sea witch to get some legs for the night. I hope there is a singing crab."

"What are you talking about?" asked Cody, his gaze following the blonde as she approached. "You hope you get crabs that sing?"

"Uh, no. I might have a soft spot for children's movies," confessed Wheeler. "We're not going to talk any more about that though. Hey, even if she's not the mermaid we're supposed to find, she might be the one to pull you out of your funk. What do you think?"

The blonde's tank top tugged at her ample breasts, and Cody glanced down at his jean-covered lap, willing his cock to respond. She was precisely the type of woman he used to go for—back before he broke.

Nothing happened.

His body seemed no different than before, and he didn't feel any pull to the woman.

"Anything?" asked Wheeler, clearly knowing Cody far better than he should.

With a sigh, Cody shook his head. He'd pretty much given up the idea of having a sex life again.

"You know, there was a point in my life that this conversation would have been weird," added Wheeler.

"You're saying talking about my inability to get a rise for anything is weird?" asked Cody with a smirk.

"Nah. The mermaid part is the weirdest part of the night," replied Wheeler, his attention back on the blonde.

"More than you offering to pee on me every chance you get or you confessing to liking children's movies?" asked Cody. He got a mental image of Wheeler sitting home alone watching children's animated cartoons and movies. It was hard to keep from laughing.

"Mermaid still wins."

The blonde woman paused in her step, looking them over slowly. Cody quickly felt as if he were cattle, being sized up at market. Oddly, it didn't bother him in the least.

Wheeler leaned in toward Cody. "Is it me or is she undressing us with her mind?"

"I'm not the one who can read minds," said Cody in a hushed tone. One humans couldn't hear. "You tell me. Is she?"

Wheeler's gaze narrowed on the woman, and he burst into a loud fit of laughter, startling the woman out of her state of fixation.

Her cheeks pinked and she hurried off, her breasts bouncing more as she did.

Still, Cody's cock didn't take note.

Wheeler faced him. "She was vividly picturing us undressed and in bed."

"Cool," said Cody, totally fine with being objectified. "At least someone is getting a rise out of the evening."

Wheeler laughed more.

"What's so funny?" asked Cody.

"She was picturing *us* in bed naked, together. *You* and *me*. Not with her. She assumed we were a couple," said Wheeler.

Cody snorted. "Of course. Offer to pee on me in front of her. That would totally sell it."

Wheeler's tastes didn't run toward the same sex. Neither did Cody's. Then again, it seemed as if Cody's interest hadn't run, walked, or crawled in any direction for years. For a short period, he thought he might be able to kick-start his sex drive once more. He'd met a woman who appealed to him on a certain level, holding his interest. But that hadn't worked out for him or them. Mainly because they'd realized quickly that a romantic thread simply wasn't there. But a strong friendship one was.

It had been for the best that his cock and his heart hadn't gotten on board with dating her. Especially since Nicolette, the woman in question, was newly mated to a man Cody knew well. The ancient Viking she'd ended up with was a good guy until the thought of anyone else boning his mate came into the picture. Then he was downright deadly.

"How long did Gus say we had to sit here until the mermaid showed?" asked Wheeler. "Did he say if she'd come by way of a shark tornado or a hurricane full of alligators?"

"He didn't," said Cody, staring at his friend as if seeing him for the first time. Wheeler was a very strange man. "He just said I had to go about my normal routine with you tonight for events to line up."

Wheeler checked his watch. "So, you're saying we're going to be drinking very soon then."

"Oh yeah. For sure. Good news, if we do manage to get drunk enough, we might very well see a mermaid. Of course, we'll be hallucinating it but whatever. Win."

"That her?" Wheeler motioned to another woman. This one had short red hair.

Cody shook his head. "I don't think so. Then

again, I wouldn't know, since they aren't real and all."

Wheeler grunted. "It would be nice if she showed up with a sign or something, announcing herself. Daryl Hannah kind of hot with a fish tail would work."

"There are times I have no idea what you're talking about," said Cody with a nervous laugh. He then wiped his palms on his jeans. "This is totally a ploy to get me away from PSI for the night so the guys can hunt Helmuth, isn't it? They think I'm a liability because of my control issues when it comes to him, don't they?"

"Maybe, but Armand would have mentioned that to me," said Wheeler, his candor appreciated. "In case you're wondering, he didn't. How about we go park our asses on some barstools and drink until we trip over our own two feet?"

Cody thought of the inebriated college boys from before and snorted. "We might be too old for that."

Wheeler laughed. "We're too old for *everything*."

True.

They were.

"Hey, was the lady at the crosswalk the

mermaid?" asked Wheeler, a shit-assed grin on his face. "The one with the little dog? Did Gus give you an age range on her? Did he mention if she was a dog lover?"

Groaning, Cody put his head down and covered his face with his hands. "You're a huge help."

"I am," said Wheeler before bumping Cody's leg with his. "What about one of those women over there?"

"I'm not looking because I'm almost afraid of who you'll suggest could have a fish tail next," returned Cody.

"Fine. They're probably being told we're a couple anyways, since the blonde apparently knows them."

Curious, Cody followed the direction Wheeler was looking in. He spotted the blonde from before standing near two women. They were all beautiful. There was no denying that much—but only one called to him, making him take note.

Cody sat up fast, his gaze locked firmly on a woman who seemed to be in her mid-twenties. Her long dark hair was pulled up in a haphazard bun with tendrils falling over her shoulders. Her large brown gaze was centered on the blonde as she laughed at something that had been said.

For a split second, Cody was reminded of the little girl from long ago. The one from Costa Rica. She'd had hair as dark as the woman's, and her eyes had been wide and brown as well. Knowing he had the child on his brain from having only just talked about her, Cody dismissed the similarities.

In the next breath, random flashes of the woman he was sure he'd been dreaming of came to him. As they did, he couldn't help but notice that the woman near the park bore a striking resemblance to the one he saw in his dreams.

His shark struck at him from within, seeming to want to communicate something important, but it was as stunned by the woman near the park entrance as he was.

As her full lips curved upward, Cody's cock came to life as if someone had shocked it with electricity. He jerked and grabbed himself through his jeans, his attention never leaving the woman who was just outside the park entrance, near the street. She was around five foot six or so. Her friends were a touch taller, making her appear short. As his gaze moved over her, his cock throbbed with need and his body heated to the point he was sure he'd burst into flames.

His shark was basically stunned into submission, also captivated by the female.

The second he caught the scent of the open ocean in its purest form, he knew it was her. That she was the source.

And she was divine.

Wheeler leaned in close to Cody's ear. "I'd like it noted that I'm not as shit at helping as you think. Pretty sure I just pointed out a woman who can help you out of your no-sex funk. That or the idea of me pissing on you is really a turn-on for you because, um, you've pitched a tent there, buddy."

Cody glanced down at his lap and noticed his jeans were bulged as his hard-on did its best to gain the room it needed and wanted. In a state of shock, Cody turned his head slowly, searching Wheeler's face for any sign of what to do next. "Is it her?"

Wheeler's expression softened. "If we're going by *little* shark's vote down there, I'm going to say yes. She'll more than work to help bring you out of your super-long dry spell. Now, if you're asking if she's the mermaid, I can't answer that. But I can offer to spritz her with water to see if her legs turn into a fish tail. I like to think of myself as a helper. A true friend. But if she calls the authorities, I don't know you."

"You think I should talk to her?" Cody asked, his voice squeaking as he did. It was embarrassing but Cody didn't care.

Wheeler was motionless for a few tense seconds before the man burst into laughter. He whipped out his phone and snapped a picture of Cody.

"What in the hell are you doing?" demanded Cody.

Wheeler offered an amused smile. "So I can show everyone later how pale you got when you were finally about to get laid again."

Cody lowered his head. "You're a dick."

"Yep. A dick who thinks this is kind of hilarious," said Wheeler, taking yet another photo.

"I'm gonna shove that phone up your ass," warned Cody.

"Nah, you'd have to stop clutching the bench seat for dear life first. You're pussing out on talking to a hot chick and possibly getting some action. Who are you? The Cody I know used to be able to blink twice and girls would toss their panties at him. Where did he go?"

Cody was about to argue that he wasn't clutching the bench when he realized that's exactly what he was doing. He didn't remember grabbing it. All he remembered was seeing the woman from across the way and feeling as if he'd been sucker-punched in the gut.

And then horny.

Really fucking horny.

The tent in his jeans showed no signs of going down anytime soon.

Cody exhaled a shaky breath. "Wheeler, I need you to be a friend here. Tell me what to do. Please. I'm kind of freaking out."

"Kind of?" echoed Wheeler.

Cody glanced at him, desperation showing in his gaze. "Something isn't right."

"I call your *little shark* now working again right in my book," said Wheeler. "But I'm kind of all about getting laid, so take my thoughts on the matter with a grain of salt."

Cody sighed. "That isn't what I mean. Well, it is, but it's not."

"That totally cleared it up."

Cody's shark felt as if it was swimming in

circles deep in the pit of his gut, with the threat of breaching any second. It was as wound up as he was over the woman.

Wheeler wiped the amused grin from his face. "Seriously, go say hello. I'll go with you. I'll be your wingman."

A pained look came over Cody. "I really have to talk to her?"

Wheeler rubbed his temple, shaking his head as he did. "When this evening started, I had a best friend who was not a total pussy. What happened to him?"

"He got an erection and all the blood went from his head to his dick," said Cody quickly. It was the truth.

Wheeler snorted. "Okay, get up."

"I don't think I can stand," said Cody, nodding to his groin.

Wheeler blinked several times. "I'm not offering to fix that problem for you, so figure it out. Want me to talk about pissing on you again? Will that kill your hard-on?"

"I don't think so," said Cody. "Pretty sure only one thing will fix it. Her."

Wheeler looked to be trying not to laugh.
He failed.

"Then go say hello to that *one thing* before she leaves, and you miss your chance," said Wheeler with a nod of his head at the woman and her friends.

"She's leaving?" asked Cody, his gaze whipping around in the direction of the woman. She was still there, talking with two other females. Cody growled. "Don't scare me like that."

"Tell little shark there to settle down long enough for your balls to descend since you're acting like you're twelve or something," said Wheeler, crossing his arms over his chest. "Pussy."

Cody's mind raced with too many thoughts to track or make sense of. He did his best to focus, and the first thing he was able to concentrate on was Wheeler's remark. "Hey, did you call my dick little?"

"Wondered if you'd catch that," said Wheeler with a snort. "Shall we go say hello to the woman who managed to resuscitate little shark *now*?"

Cody froze. "No."

Wheeler leaned back on the bench. "Okay then, we'll just sit here waiting for divine intervention or for you to grow some balls. Whichever comes first. A little tip, you won't be *coming* anytime soon if you don't actually meet her. Hey, let's go ask if she's hiding a fish tail. Wouldn't that be something if she was a mermaid? It would explain your sudden attraction to her. Your shark would view her as lunch."

As Cody's heart raced, he had a sneaking suspicion his shark side saw her as something else. Something he wasn't sure he could wrap his mind around at the moment.

Chapter Eleven

BONNIE'S ATTENTION went in the direction of the men on the bench as Gena tried once more to hide behind Rene, though it didn't work as planned.

Bonnie pursed her lips. "Um, I'm not sure they're a couple."

Rene sighed. "I don't know. I think they might be."

Gena began to relax. If that was the case, the blond on the bench couldn't be the man from her dreams.

Bonnie snorted. "Uh, then why is the blond staring over here like he's about to leap up, run over, and hump Gena's leg?"

"What?!" exclaimed Gena, leaping to the side again to use Rene as a human shield.

"Really?" asked Rene, spinning around to see for herself. "Huh. I'll be damned. He *does* look like he's about to do that."

Gena stepped closer to Rene's back and leaned to the side, looking around her friend in a discreet manner. When she found the hot guy was indeed wearing the very expression Bonnie had described, she yelped and jerked back behind Rene once more.

In that moment, she felt every bit as naïve when it came to the opposite sex as Bonnie and the others liked to tell her she was.

Rene glanced over her shoulder at her. "Are you hiding?"

"Um, no?"

Rene glanced at Bonnie. "She might very well be hopeless."

"I know, right? The girl has a date tomorrow with a hot loaded guy and has caught the eye of that delicious specimen of manliness over there," said Bonnie, pointing rather obviously at the blond man. "But look at her. She's about to skulk away in the bushes, hiding under the cover of darkness."

Gena glanced around, wondering if the whole skulking away thing was viable or not. Sadly, it didn't seem to be the case. Had it been on the table, she'd have taken it in a heartbeat.

Rene flashed a wider smile at Bonnie. "Did you talk about hot guys like this when you were with Ruby?"

"Yep," said Bonnie. "Ruby was secure enough in her womanhood not to care about that. She left because all I do is work, and she hates the place we work for and because I never made time for her. Not because I announce when I see a beautiful, sexy person, man or woman. Besides, she'd have ranked him. One to ten thing. Betting the two on the bench would have gotten tens from her."

"Oh, they're twenties, for sure," said Rene. "Is Mr. Bigwig a twenty?"

"Oh yeah," said Bonnie.

"No," offered Gena, from behind Rene still.

Bonnie glanced at her. "You didn't find him attractive? You were looking at the same man I was, right?"

"Yes, he's attractive, but there is just something off about him," said Gena. "I don't know. I can't explain it. Can we go to the bar now and stop standing out here in the open?"

"Why? Worried about the sexpot who is eyeing you up?" asked Rene with a laugh.

Gena stiffened. "He's still staring over here?"

The women both nodded and replied in unison. "Yes."

Gena took a deep breath. "Bonnie."

"Yes?"

"It's him," whispered Gena.

"Him?" questioned Bonnie.

She eyed the woman. "From the dreams."

Gena expected her friend to laugh. When Bonnie's expression turned from amused to shocked, Gena's gut tightened more.

"For real?" asked Bonnie.

Rene lifted a hand. "Am I following this discussion right? One of them is the guy Gena's been dreaming about?"

"You told her about the dreams?" asked Gena, stunned.

"Erm, yes," confessed Bonnie. She then looked at Rene. "Go ask if he's hung like a horse but can change into a shark. Hurry, I need to know if I'm right."

"Right about what?" asked Gena.

Rene made a move to go toward the park.

Gena grabbed the woman around the waist, still planted behind her, holding firm. "No! You're not to talk to them. Ever. None of us are talking to them. We're going to walk really fast in the other direction and pretend this never happened. Maybe he didn't actually notice me. Bet he was staring at you two. You guys are babes. I'm a bookworm nerd."

"You think?" asked Bonnie as she looked to be fighting a laugh.

Rene snorted. "Yeah, I don't think he was staring at us."

"You can't know that," said Gena from her hiding spot. She tugged lightly on Rene's waist, trying to get the woman to walk sideways away. She didn't care how ridiculous it would look to others. She wanted distance between herself and the man from her dreams.

It was all too much.

Too surreal.

She needed time to think clearly.

Bonnie looked at Gena, grinning more. "You don't want to meet him? What if it's fate?"

"It's not," said Gena, fast. If by some crazy chance the guy was really the man she'd been dreaming of, facing him while thinking about all the naughty things they'd done to one another in her dreams would leave her passing out. "I don't want to meet him. He doesn't want to meet me. We should go now. Like right now."

"Why? Worried he's going to want in your panties?" asked Rene.

Gena moaned slightly at the thought of the man being in her panties. If her dreams were in any way an indication to his bedroom skills, he would have her melting in the palms of his hands in mere seconds. "More like hopeful. Wait, I mean, no!"

Her friends laughed before they parted as if they were the Red Sea, leaving Gena fully exposed to the man's view. She froze like a deer in headlights, the sound of her blood pumping filled her head.

Rene nudged her.

Gena didn't move an inch.

Bonnie let out a long, dramatic sigh. "Want me to go talk to him for you?"

"No!" shouted Gena before wincing at her own outburst.

Just then, the blond stood, but the act looked stiff.

His friend rose to his feet as well, staying close to the man. He put his hand on the blond's shoulder and said something to him.

The blond nodded, his gaze never leaving Gena.

Gena looked to her friends for help on what to do or how to react.

She found them grinning from ear to ear.

"This isn't funny," she said sternly before she started to laugh herself.

The absurdity of it all got to her, and she giggled more. Before she knew it, all three of them were practically cackling, feeding off one another's snorts and laughs.

Gena bent her head, clutching her side as she laughed more. "You're right. I'm hopeless. We should go now before I make a bigger fool of myself in front of the man."

"Too late," said Bonnie.

Looking up, Gena found the hot blond standing directly in front of her. His friend was by his side, appearing cautiously entertained.

Gena had thought the man was sexy from a distance. Seeing him up close really drove home just how genuinely magnificent he was. And it left no room for error. He was the mystery man she'd been dreaming of.

The scientist in her screamed at the improbability of it all. Yet there he was in the flesh. The proof was in a pair of jeans that fit him just right.

She just stood there, her mouth agape, no sound coming from her as her brain spiraled.

Say something.

Anything.

Make a noise.

Breathe.

She moaned as her gaze slid over the bulge in the front of his jeans. It was huge.

Make any noise but that!

Bonnie and Rene got a kick out of her inability to speak.

Gena didn't find it quite as comical. Then again, she wouldn't.

The man with the blond pulled out his cell phone and took a picture of his friend, who appeared to be equally as lost for words as Gena. That was at least somewhat comforting…until she wondered why.

Had he actually had dreams with her in them too?

If so, had they been sex dreams?

As Gena reflected on all the things the man had done to her in the dreams, she began to breathe faster as her anxiety kicked into high gear. They'd done things in the dreams that she'd been too embarrassed to even tell Bonnie about. Things so racy they made her want to toss a glass of cold water over her upper chest to relieve the heat that seemed to be emanating from there at the moment.

"Is anyone going to say anything?" asked Rene.

No one other than her spoke.

Bonnie and the blond guy's friend snickered.

Gena cast a pleading look at Bonnie, who shrugged.

"You've got this," said Bonnie.

No.

She really did not have it.

Having it was the furthest thing from the truth.

Her attention returned to the man from her dreams. She stared at the astonishingly handsome specimen of a man and tried to will her hormones to behave themselves. It didn't work. Her insides shouted at her that he was baby-making material. And while she'd never given much thought to having a family of her own, all she wanted to do at that very second in time was procreate with the man.

She understood the root of the response. Still, understanding fundamental biology and living it were two very different things. The textbooks and college lectures neglected to mention the mindlessness that accompanied the urge to reproduce or the fact she was fairly sure she was a lovely shade of plum from blushing and excitement.

No. That had never been brought up in her studies.

Nowhere in her education had sex dreams with mystery men who turned out to be real come up either.

It would have been handy to have that in her arsenal for adulting. A nice defense at the ready in the event the most spectacular male she'd ever seen in her life appeared out of nowhere.

Which was precisely what happened.

From the look of him, he had to be easily six and a half feet tall. Maybe slightly more. He would undoubtedly breed some hardy stock.

It took her a second to realize someone was giggling.

Bonnie eased close to her and lowered her voice. "Breathe, hon."

Gena did, and it helped.

A little.

Her gaze eased over his strong jawline, down his corded neck to his shoulders, and she nearly shivered in delight at the idea of what his robust frame looked like over her in bed. In her dreams, he'd taken her every way and everywhere.

Moisture pooled at the apex of her thighs, and his nostrils flared as he took a deep breath. He stepped toward her fast, crowding her space, and she welcomed the intrusion. In fact, she hoped he got a heck of a lot closer even. Horizontally would be best.

A mix of colors, from white-blond to light brown, danced through his shoulder-length hair. It was all she could do to keep from reaching up and running her hands through his glorious locks. Truth be told, the idea of running her hands all over him seemed like an excellent idea.

Best she'd had all day.

Possibly all week even.

His entire body seemed to be toned to perfection. It wasn't as if she hadn't been around physically fit men in her life, but the hunk she was staring at put them all to shame.

The strongest urge to get the man naked to simply see if he was as perfect as he'd been in her dreams came over her. At the thought of him minus clothing, a trickle of sweat moved down her spine.

"Are they going to do it right here in the open?" asked Bonnie.

"I sure the hell hope so," said a man with a slight Southern drawl. He snapped another photo with his phone. "Don't mind me. Keepsakes."

Rene laughed. "I hope they say hi to each other first. Neither one has said a word."

Gena came to her senses and took a massive step back from the hot blond guy. "Um, hi?"

When he smiled, she thought her knees might actually give out on her. "Hi."

"Awkward," whispered Bonnie in a not-so-quiet way.

The blond licked his lower lip and just stared at her.

The man next to him shot forward and extended a hand. "Hi there. I'm Wheeler. The suddenly silent guy next to me is my buddy, Cody. We were just about to head over to Stanley's for drinks. Would you three be up to joining us?"

"We would love to," replied Bonnie with a laugh.

Gena took Wheeler's hand and shook it.

Cody growled lightly, his gaze narrowing on his friend.

Wheeler lifted a brow and took his hand from Gena's. "One of us had to break the ice. It was downright unnerving the way you two were staring at each other. I only made introductions. I didn't ask if she wanted to skip the nonexistent small talk and do it with you."

Bonnie laughed so hard she sounded like a seal barking.

Rene joined in.

Gena stood there, turning yet another shade of red. She had to wonder if she could blush any more than she already was.

Cody exhaled slowly, his hands shaking a bit. "Is that an option? The skipping the small talk and just doing it with me?"

Wheeler sighed and put his hand to Cody's cheek. "Aussie, focus. You're kind of making a fool of yourself here. That what you want?"

"No," said Cody.

Wheeler patted his cheek. "Good. Now, how about I go over to Stanley's and grab us a table while you actually talk to this lovely young woman and her friends."

Bonnie glanced at Gena, smiling wide. "You okay if Rene and I go with Wheeler to grab a table? The bar is across the street, down a bit that way. Maybe a two-minute walk. It would give you a chance to talk to Cody…unless you don't want to. We'll stay if you're uncomfortable at all. I know Mr. Bigwig was off-putting to you."

"Mr. Bigwig?" asked Wheeler.

Bonnie tipped her head. "Loaded hot dude who asked Gena out on a date when we met him earlier today."

Cody stiffened. "What? Someone asked her out on a date?"

"It's not a date," Gena said quickly, though she wasn't sure why she felt the need to clarify. With a clearing of her throat, she composed herself and met Bonnie's gaze. "I'm fine if you go ahead with Wheeler. We were planning to go for drinks anyway so Stanley's will be perfect for celebrating."

"Celebrating?" asked Wheeler.

Rene and Bonnie began to jump up and down

again as if they'd never actually stopped from before.

"We got the funding!" they chanted.

Wheeler nodded but didn't seem to be paying attention to anything except their bouncing cleavage.

Bonnie and Rene hurried past Wheeler in the direction of Stanley's, leaving Gena standing with Cody.

She was about to attempt small talk once more when Bonnie turned back, about twenty feet away, cupped her hands around her mouth and proceeded to shout, "Ask if he's dreamed of you too!"

Heat rushed over Gena so fast that she swayed.

Cody grabbed for her, and the second his hands made contact with her bare skin, additional heat assailed her. Breathless, she stared up at him, unable to look away. One second he was helping her stay upright, and the next he was fixated on her lips.

She parted them as a small gasp came from her.

Dipping his head, he captured her lips with his—and Gena shut off, gripping his T-shirt as his tongue pushed into her mouth. It explored her tongue, easing around it in an expert manner. She held tighter to his shirt, savoring his taste and his kiss. It was exactly as it had been in her dreams.

His hands found her waist and he lifted her off her feet, kissing her deeper and faster. Within seconds, she was gasping and eating at his mouth.

Growling, he bit at her lower lip, making her hormones shout in triumph.

As they were busy making plans for procreation, her common sense decided to show up to the party.

Better late than never.

When Gena realized what she was doing—making out with a man she'd known all of thirty seconds (not counting dreams) on a sidewalk, out in the open, where anyone and everyone could see—she froze, her tongue still laced around his.

Cody stiffened and broke the kiss slowly, still holding her off the ground with ease by way of her hips. "Shit. I didn't mean that. I'm sorry."

Unable to look away from his full lips, Gena gave the slightest of head nods before reaching up and touching his lower lip. Her fingers buzzed with warmth as she did. Her jaw went slack at the same second he inhaled deeply, growling once more.

If the man kept that up, she'd be naked and having her way with him, public space be damned. Evidently, her hormones had been put on the back burner long enough and were dangerously close to throwing a coup. One she'd end up spread-eagle for—if she was lucky.

Clapping drew their attention to the side, where they found Bonnie, Rene, and Wheeler all standing down from them just a ways, smiling. They continued to clap before Wheeler lifted his hands and put his fingers in his mouth, whistling loudly.

Rene laughed. "That so beats saying hi! Wonder what they'll do for the next step in the getting-to-know-you stage of the game."

"Bet whatever it is, they do it minus clothing," said Bonnie, appearing amused as well.

Wheeler grinned but his smile wasn't quite as big as the others, as if he wasn't one for showing his teeth. "That would be my guess too."

Cody lifted his brows slightly as he wrapped his arms around Gena protectively, drawing her against his steely frame. He sheltered her from the view of the others and it took her a second to realize he was laughing silently.

Her face burned with embarrassment. If he'd have been data, she could have easily figured him and the situation out, but outside of a research setting, she was as hopeless as Rene and Bonnie liked to accuse her of being.

He winked. "Wrong that I hope they're right? That the next step happens minus clothing?"

"Yes, minus clothes," she said, her head still in a fog of sorts as she tried to rationalize how it was the man from her dreams was not only real but had already crammed his tongue down her throat.

Cody laughed harder.

"What?" asked Gena before thinking more on it all. It hit her then. She'd agreed to getting naked with him. Jerking away, she took a deep breath and then began to straighten her dress as if it had been jumbled.

She then practically ran at her friends. When she got to them, they were cackling.

They looped their arms through hers and proceeded to drag her in the direction of Stanley's as Wheeler and Cody followed close behind.

Chapter Twelve

CODY WRAPPED his hand around his beer as he leaned against the bar, his gaze never leaving Gena. She and her friends were throwing darts as they shared a pitcher of beer. Gena had barely touched any of the alcohol. Instead, she'd spent the forty minutes they'd been at the bar doing her best to stay hidden from his line of sight.

He'd have been offended if he didn't find the act somewhat adorable.

At the moment, she was trying to use the tall blonde as a shield once more. It was kind of cute, watching as Gena snuck peeks at him when she thought he wasn't looking. She was curious about him. That was good. Because he wanted to know everything about her.

Like had she really dreamed of him too, as her friend had suggested? If so, had her dreams been racy?

Wheeler poured himself a shot of tequila and faced the women as well, putting his elbows on the bar behind him. "Is it me or is Stanley's busier than normal?"

He was right.

The bar was fuller than normal for the night of the week and time. The place normally played classic rock or even soft rock from the past through its sound system. Tonight it was playing music with more of a dance beat to it.

Cody hated it.

Wheeler had been doing whatever it was he did that kept humans from getting too close to them and Cody was thankful. He just wanted to observe Gena, even if she was doing her very best to look as if she wasn't interested in him as well. He didn't want to deal with anyone else.

"You should blink or something," said Wheeler, pressing shoulder to shoulder with him.

"What?"

Wheeler nodded in the direction of Gena, who was watching Bonnie as Bonnie took a turn throwing darts. "You've been watching her for a long time. Blink. It will make you slightly less creepy."

Cody brought his beer to his lips and before he took a drink, he spoke. "I'm not creepy."

"Okay, sure. *And* I don't have issues with bloodlust," said Wheeler, sarcasm dripping freely from his every word. "Any other lies we're telling ourselves tonight? Like, say, oh, I don't know, why it is that your *little shark* picked that little human to swim to shore for?"

The man's analogies were something indeed.

"Stop calling my dick little," snapped Cody, only to find Rene walking toward them. She held an empty pitcher. From the look on her face, she'd overheard at least part of their conversation.

Wheeler chuckled and raised his shot glass in Rene's direction. "To him not being little."

Rene smiled and gave Wheeler a good once-over. "What about you?"

"One way to find out," said Wheeler, never missing a beat or an opportunity to get laid.

Rene pressed in close to him, pitcher in hand, as she motioned for the bartender. "I don't know. I'm told there is more than one way to skin a cat.

I'm sure there is more than one way to find out about you. All of you, that is."

Wheeler poured himself another shot and glanced at Cody. "If I go home with her tonight, you're sleeping in your van, got it? Not the house."

"The two of you live together?" asked Rene. "Are you sure you're not a couple?"

Cody snorted.

The bartender took the pitcher from Rene and began to fill it. She used the time to focus on Cody. "Are you going to keep watching her without saying anything? It's creepy."

Wheeler chortled. "Already said as much to him."

"Talk to her," said Rene.

"Pretty sure talking isn't what he has his heart set on," added Wheeler, earning him an elbow to the gut from Cody.

Wheeler didn't seem to mind as he downed another shot.

Rene smiled and took the full pitcher of beer back in the direction of the table she was sharing with Bonnie and Gena.

Wheeler watched her walking away as if the act was soft-core porn.

"Really?"

Wheeler shrugged. "What? She's hot."

Cody's gaze locked on Gena. Little shark picked then to harden again, making itself known in a not-so-little way. So far in one evening his dick had gone from not working to not wanting to shut off. All he wanted to do was go to Gena, inch up her dress, and find paradise in her silken depths. "No. She's the most beautiful woman I've ever seen."

"Uh, we still talking about the same person?" asked Wheeler. "Because I'm thinking we're not."

"Hmm?" asked Cody, his concentration off as Gena's scent wafted over him, doing nothing to help his cock calm down. It anything, her scent made his erection all the more difficult to manage.

Wheeler propped himself against the bar and crossed one ankle over the other as he leaned. Everything about his posture screamed self-assured. That summed the man up perfectly. "Planning to keep at least fifteen feet from her at all times the rest of the night?"

Cody sipped his beer. "I make her nervous. Can't you sense it on her?"

"Yes, but I don't sense she's scared *of* you," admitted Wheeler. "What I'm getting is that you excite her. Since I already saw the tent you pitched when you first saw her, and the one I'm doing my best to avoid drawing attention to now, I'm going to go out on another limb here and say she excites you too."

"God yes," breathed Cody, watching as Gena went to take her turn at darts.

Rene bent slightly near Gena and whispered to her, but the supernatural males could hear it with ease. "He's still looking at you."

"Stop," returned Gena, also in a hushed tone, throwing a dart that went wild and hit the wall near a light-up beer sign instead of the board. "He is *not* looking at me."

"He's hot," said Rene in a sultry manner. "They both are. Admit it."

Gena lowered her gaze and nodded. "Yes. They are."

Cody found himself giving his friend a dirty look. "Asshole."

"I'm an asshole because she thinks I'm hot too?" asked Wheeler, seeming somehow even smug than he had been only seconds prior.

Cody had half a mind to kick his foot out from under him and watch him fall on his ass. It would serve him right.

How dare he be a guy Gena thought was good-looking.

Asshole.

"Which do you think is hotter?" asked Rene, her gaze flickering to Cody and Wheeler as a grin spread over her face.

"I don't know," said Gena, lining up to throw another dart. "I don't want to talk about it anymore."

"Okay. If you're not interested, I'll see if they want to take off with me and have some between-the-sheets fun," said Rene with a shimmy of her shoulders.

Wheeler groaned lightly as if in pain. "Please, please, please let that be true."

"You're an asshole," said Cody.

His friend snorted. "You already said that."

Gena's hand tightened around the dart and she lowered her arm, no longer lining up a shot.

Rene touched her shoulder. "What's wrong? Was it something I said?"

Gena remained quiet.

"You know, if someone was throwing their trash in the ocean, you'd yell to the point you were blue in the face and probably deck them a good one," said Rene. "So how is it you can be outgoing and vocal when it comes to that but clam up when it comes to staking your claim on a guy you find attractive?"

Bonnie poured herself another beer and took a sip. "Probably because Gena isn't exactly sure how to deal with it all. Hitting something is easy. Telling it you think it's hot is very different."

"Yes, that," said Gena with wide eyes and an enthusiastic nodding of her head.

Rene licked her lips. "So, do you find one of them more attractive than the other? And you haven't said anything about the kiss you and the one I'm guessing you do find hotter shared. Any reason why? Is he a shit kisser?"

Wheeler choked on the shot he was doing as he laughed.

Cody grunted.

Gena glanced nervously over in Cody's direction and he stared up at the ceiling quickly, trying to appear as if he hadn't been looking at her.

"Smooth," said Wheeler from the side of his mouth, barely moving his lips.

"Asshole."

"He's a really great kisser," said Gena with a breathy sigh.

Cody had to fight to keep from jumping up and down with the knowledge she thought he kissed well.

"Contain yourself there, Sparky," said Wheeler.

"He's a great kisser and we know you think he's hot," said Rene with a small laugh. "And I feel safe saying he's way into you, too. Why hide over here? Talk to him. Unless I have it all wrong and it's you that aren't into him like that. Maybe the kiss was a fluke or something."

"Oh, I'm into him," said Gena. "I keep thinking about the kiss and then I keep wanting to go over there, grab him, yank him out back and pin him to the ground while I have my way with him."

Cody kept glancing up. "Please, please, please."

Wheeler huffed. "Now who is the asshole?"

"Still you," said Cody as he looked back at Gena to find her staring at him as well.

This time, neither of them averted their gazes.

"Bet he's got a rocking body. And I have it on good authority he's working with some impressive equipment in the nether regions as well," said

Rene, still bending slightly to be closer to Gena's ear. "You should totally take him home for a test drive. He'd be one heck of a way to celebrate the funding you secured us."

"I didn't secure anything," countered Gena. "That was all Bonnie. She's put so much hard work into the team. Clearly it was noticed."

Rene touched Gena's arm lightly. "Listen, I'm normally all for being as wild and crazy as a woman wants to be with their sexuality, but I have a hinky feeling about this lunch date Bigwig asked you out on."

"It's not a date. He just wants to discuss…" Gena fell silent a second and then gasped. "Ohmygod, it is a date, isn't it?"

Bonnie eased up closer to the other women. "Oh yeah, hon. It's totally a date. He was on you like flies on honey the second he saw you. Granted, not as on you as the blond god over there, but still. You're having a very male-tastic day. Run with it."

Rene stiffened. "Maybe we should go with her on this lunch thing tomorrow."

"*We* weren't invited," said Bonnie, grinning. "He only has eyes for her. Really wondering how this is going to play out, since she's now met another hottie. My money is on her waking up in his bed come morning. Awkward to then go on a lunch date with some other guy, but you're a grown woman who is not in any relationship, let alone a committed one—you do you, hon."

Gena tossed her hands in the air, still holding the dart as she turned to face her friends fully. "I'm not waking up in any man's bed. And I'm not going on any romantic lunch with the guy funding our project. I'll reach out to him in the morning and let him know I can't make it. Unless you think it will hurt our funding. If you do, I could maybe still go but I don't know how I feel about going out on a boat alone with him."

Bonnie offered a sympathetic smile. "If you're not comfortable, then don't go. We'd never really push you to go on a date with a guy for us to stay funded. Not our style. We'll joke, yes, but that is where it ends. If you want, I'll reach out to him tonight and tell him something came up and you won't be able to meet with him. If he really wants to talk to you about your thesis, he can set something up through me and come to the center. A place you feel more comfortable. But he seemed like a nice guy to me. Eccentric for sure. I mean, come on, huge shark paintings…and let's not forget his fetish for mermaids."

Gena nodded. "I'd like it if you called him for me. Thank you."

"Not a problem," offered Bonnie.

Chapter Thirteen

AT THE MENTION OF MERMAIDS, Cody and Wheeler jerked upright, each taking notice. There were coincidences and then there was that.

Cody glanced at Wheeler. "You heard what I heard, right?"

Wheeler nodded. "I did."

Rene tipped her head. "Bigwig has a thing for mermaids? Really?"

"He has this massive fountain out in front of his place along with inlaid tiles forming one at the entrance," said Bonnie. "And don't even get me started on all the mermaid stuff he has in the house. He has this one ginormous oil painting in his den that has a mermaid on it. She looks a lot like the fountain one but with more details and in full color. Not to mention, she looks like Gena. Like, *just* like her. It was so weird."

"For real?" asked Rene.

Gena cringed but nodded. "Yes. I didn't like the way he stared at the painting either."

"Like he wanted it to come to life to do it?" asked Bonnie with a laugh.

Gena shook her head. "No. It was as if he wanted to own it, possess it, control it."

Rene stepped back. "That is all too weird for me. I say we don't let her go anywhere alone with him. Not until we know more about him. I have a bad feeling."

"You didn't even meet him or see his oddities," said Bonnie, chuckling. "You're overreacting. He's rich and eccentric. And let's not forget, nearly fully funding us now."

Gena set the darts on the table. "Bonnie, for a man who claims to be all about protecting sharks and conservation, why would he have that huge painting of the great white in a holding tank being tortured? I know he gave me an explanation, but it felt forced and wrong. Like it was a lie. Not the real reason. When he looked at that painting, I swear to you that he seemed almost gleeful about it—about seeing a shark being tortured like that."

For a split second, all Cody heard was his own heart beating. Everything else faded away as he focused on what Gena had just said. Flashes of his time in captivity came flooding back to him, and he remembered vividly what it had been like to be forced into shark form, held in a tank, and tortured.

He clutched his beer so tightly that one second he was holding it, and the next, beer was exploding all over his hand and arm as the bottle shattered. Glass sliced through his palm, ripping him from his remembered pain of the past. With a jolt, he stood there, realizing he'd lost control of his strength to the point he'd broken the beer he'd been holding and cut himself.

In the next second, Gena was there, snapping her fingers, demanding a clean towel from the bartender. She went from quiet and shy to totally in control as she then proceeded to check his palm and remove a chunk of glass.

Her wide brown eyes found his face. Worry showed.

"What happened? Are you okay?" she asked, holding his hand in hers as she then went to work wrapping the clean towel around his wounded hand. "We need to get you over for stitches. Now."

The edges of his lips drew up slightly as she continued barking orders at him.

He'd thought she was adorable when she was shy. Seeing she was quite capable of laying down the law when the need arose only served to turn him on more. He didn't even know that was possible. But the woman was finding new ways to heighten his need for her.

She pressed her small frame against him, holding the towel around his hand. "I can call for a ride for us since you've been drinking."

"I'm fine, thank you though," he said, liking having her so close. "I don't need any stitches."

"Fine?" she asked, her eyes managing to widen more. "Uh, no. You cut the heck out of your hand. It needs to be looked at."

Cody used his uninjured hand to push stray strands of her dark hair back from her cheek. "It's okay. I promise. It's not as deep as you think. I'm guessing it's already stopped bleeding."

Explaining he was more than human and could heal something as small as what had happened with ease wasn't something he relished having to do. Lying was the next best option.

For now.

Wheeler made quick work of the broken pieces of the bottle on the floor, gathering them with care and then boldly walking back and behind the bar to the trashcan. The bartender glanced at him, and Wheeler locked gazes with the man. "Nothing out of the ordinary here. All is good. Go on about your business."

Nodding, the bartender went back to mixing drinks. "All is good."

Cody wished he had the gift of mesmerizing like Wheeler did. It would come in handy. Especially with convincing Gena he was totally and completely fine, and that the night didn't need to be cut short for him to get medical attention.

Gena kept her hands around the towel, meaning she was left standing toe-to-toe with Cody.

That was nice.

Better than nice.

The smell of the ocean filled him once again, and he lowered his head, inhaling deep near her hair.

She stilled. "Um, what are you doing?"

He tensed. "Sorry. I should probably lie and tell you nothing, but the truth is, I was smelling you."

"Oh, that isn't off-putting in the least," said Wheeler, returning to his post near the bottle of tequila. "Tell her you live in your mother's basement or something. You know, really drive home the ick factor."

Do something, pushed Cody with his mind at Wheeler. *Make her forget I cut myself and that I was smelling her.*

You want me to mind-meld your date? asked Wheeler via their mental pathway.

Cody was about to point out that Gena wasn't technically his date when he decided it didn't matter what she was. *Yes. Make her forget. I don't want to freak her out.*

Fine, but you owe me.

Wheeler smiled and touched Gena's shoulder lightly.

The act set Cody's shark on edge once more. It didn't like an unmated male making contact with his woman.

My woman?

Wheeler glanced at him. "What?"

"He didn't say anything," said Gena, appearing confused.

Dude, did you just call her your woman? asked Wheeler.

Cody's mind raced. Had he?

He thought on it more and the panic set in.

He had.

"Guys?" asked Gena.

"Right," offered Wheeler, keeping his hand on her shoulder. "Cody didn't cut himself. It just looked like he did. Everything is fine here."

Gena stared at Wheeler for what felt like forever before she slid her gaze over to Cody, very slowly. "Does he actually believe what he just said? Of course you cut yourself. I dug glass out of your bloody palm."

I told you to do your mind thing on her, snapped Cody.

Wheeler paled considerably. *I did.*

Well, do it again, but this time do it right. Tell me you haven't suddenly lost your touch.

Wheeler spun around and motioned for the bartender. When the man arrived, Wheeler stared into his eyes. "Take this lovely young lady into the back and get her your first-aid kit. You have one of those here, right?"

"Yes," said the bartender before focusing on Gena. "Come with me, and I'll get you our first-aid kit."

Gena hurried around and behind the bar, disappearing into the back.

Wheeler faced Cody. "Dude, I still got it. It just didn't work on her. She's immune."

"Immune," snorted Cody. "Don't be ridiculous. You can do it to *any* human."

Wheeler did a long blink.

Cody's mouth went dry at the implication. Gena wasn't human?

"No," whispered Cody. "You think?"

Wheeler eyed him. "The last time the mind-meld didn't work was when I tried it on Nicolette. I'm not saying that means she's a supernatural. All I'm saying is the last time my gig didn't work on someone, they weren't human. Take that as you may."

Cody had known Nicolette wasn't human long before Nicolette knew. But he'd never thought to tell Wheeler as much when he'd asked the man to look in on the women whenever Cody couldn't be in town.

While Wheeler was right—the fact he couldn't mind-meld Nicolette was not definitive proof that

Gena was also a supernatural—it did lend credence to the theory.

Wheeler grunted. "It would have been great if you'd have given me a heads-up that Nicolette wasn't human. I tried to make her want to go home and away from danger, but she was immune. I thought it was weird too since no human I've ever met has been able to resist obeying me. Turns out, she wasn't human—again—thanks for the notice on that ahead of time. My gut is telling me this is like that. In related news, Garth was a hot mess when dealing with her too—like you are with Gena. He did a lot of stupid shit too. Like you."

"I'd smell it on her. So would you." Cody attempted to wrap his mind around his friend's words. "What are the odds I'd be in the park with you at the same second a woman who makes little shark stand at attention appears? And that woman just happens to be immune to your influence?"

Wheeler pursed his lips. "Oh, so you can call it little shark, but I can't?"

"It's *my* dick," Cody grunted. "Back to the actual subject."

"You mean the subject of Gus telling you to

meet me about a mermaid, only for you to go ga-ga over Gena when you saw her? Then, while standing here, you break a bottle when you hear her mention mermaids and sharks in tanks? Or the part about her being immune to my mental push? Or the bit about you telling me she's your woman? Enlighten me. What subject are we getting back to?"

"When you put it that way, I'd rather talk about my dick," said Cody.

"I'm sure you would," said Wheeler, pouring himself another shot.

Gena came out from the back of the bar with the world's smallest first-aid kit and a disgruntled look on her face. She was back to Cody quickly and set the kit on the bar top. The angle that she was at as she leaned for supplies from the kit gifted Cody a glimpse straight down the top of her dress.

Little shark picked then to twitch, and Cody winced, worried he'd lose his shit even more than he had and come in his jeans. He was having that kind of day.

Gena looked up at him, frowning. "You're in pain. Please let me take you over to get it cleaned and stitched."

Wheeler fake coughed. "Pretty sure that's not what's bothering him."

"Asshole," spat Cody before thinking better of saying it in front of Gena.

She lifted her brows. "You two sound like my brothers. They go at it like this. But don't dare come between them or there will be heck to pay."

Wheeler gave him a stern look.

Cody was lost.

Livingston, talk to her. Ask about her brothers. It's an opening to having a real conversation with her, pushed Wheeler down their mental path.

Cody nodded. "Right. Brothers. You have them?"

Smooth.

He grunted as he looked at Wheeler.

Gena giggled and the sound made his chest flutter. "Brothers. Yes. I have two. You?"

"Hundreds if you're counting the men I served with. None if you mean biological," said Cody, surprised he'd volunteered that much about himself.

"You served?" asked Gena, giving him a smile that made him want to kiss her again.

"I did," he replied.

"With Wheeler?" she questioned.

"Yes," said Cody, fixated on her lips.

I can't watch this train wreck, said Wheeler. *Remember when you could just glance at a woman and she'd toss her panties at you and you actually knew what to do with said panties? Those days are long, long gone. You're like a born-again virgin, but with even less game.*

"Bite me," snapped Cody.

Gena stiffened. "Uh, okay?"

He cringed. "Not you. I mean, you can bite me if you want… No, I don't mean that. Wait. I do. Never mind. Ouch, uh, my hand. So much pain. I probably need to be looked at."

Wheeler turned around, faced the bar, lowered his head and proceeded to laugh to the point he stopped making any sound.

Gena exhaled slowly. "Am I the only one feeling tongue-tied and like I'm saying all the wrong things?"

"No!" shouted Cody before he gathered something that he thought might be control. He wasn't sure since he'd had very little of it since seeing Gena. He also seemed to be missing his dignity. That had abandoned him at first glance of her as well. He cleared his throat. "You're not the only one. I feel like I'm having an evening full of opening my mouth and having stupid fall out."

Wheeler pressed to his side. "Because you *are* having an evening of opening your mouth and having stupid fall out."

Cody groaned and found Gena smiling as she watched them both. "We still remind you of your brothers?"

She beamed. "You do. And like the two of you, they're not technically biological. None of my siblings are. We're all adopted, but we're family regardless."

"How many of you are there?" asked Cody, proud of himself for getting out at least one sentence that wasn't off-the-cuff or nonsensical. Maybe a conversation wasn't completely out of the realm of reason.

"Four in total. Two boys and two girls," she said.

"Bet that kept your parents busy." Cody wanted to keep her talking. If she was conversing with him, she was close, and he liked having her close.

She wrapped her hands around the towel on his hand and Cody found himself placing his free hand over hers. "They went from having no children to getting four in one day. They did okay with us all though. My childhood was spent outdoors for the most part, learning, exploring, burning off excess energy. For the best really. If you ever met my brothers, you'd realize just how important it was they burned off energy."

Cody smiled. "They have a lot of it?"

"And then some," she said. "My sister and I weren't quite as high-strung. But don't let that fool you. We were still a handful. But my parents never batted an eye at the challenge. They opened their hearts and their home to us."

"Sounds nice," he said.

"What about you? Are you close to your parents?" she asked.

Cody stiffened. He didn't want to get into his personal life. Lying to her felt wrong, but telling her his parents had passed away decades before she was even born wasn't exactly an option either. "Not anymore. They're both gone now."

Sadness touched her eyes as she eased closer to him. "I'm sorry."

Nodding, he stared down at her, wanting more contact with her than he was currently getting. Her lips called to him, tempting him in a way that left him teetering on the edge of kissing her again.

Gena ran her hand over his forearm, stopping just shy of his bandaged hand. "Does it hurt?"

"No," he said, before the edges of his lips began to pull up. "Unless it will get me sympathy from you then yes, ouch, horrible pain."

She snorted and eased against him, her forehead finding his chest as she proceeded to laugh. The act was one a couple who had been together a long time and felt comfortable with one another did. Not two people who had only just met. It meant she felt a connection to him as well. That made him even happier.

She was more at ease near him.

That was a good thing.

His free hand found her cheek. He ran his hand over her smooth skin before pushing his hand through her hair and cupping her head to his chest. It was gutsy and he knew it, but he had to have her closer to him.

She didn't pull away.

Instead, she pressed against him fully, her arms easing around his waist.

They stood there, neither saying a word as they held one another. It should have been odd. It wasn't. It felt right. Like the woman before him had been made to fit against him, made to be held by him. She fit perfectly to his size and shape, and no adjusting needed to be done.

Chapter Fourteen

CLOSING HIS EYES, Cody savored having Gena in his arms. He couldn't recall a time in his immortally long life that he'd ever really and truly held a woman, just for the sake of keeping her close to him. He'd never had the desire to do so before. But now, he wanted to keep his arms wrapped around her forever.

If he was holding her, she was with him.

And that's what he wanted.

Her, with him always.

It took him a second to realize he was starting to growl. The noise had been automatic and as possessive as he felt. Like his shifter side was completely on board with the idea of keeping Gena for all eternity.

He'd have explored it all more, but a woman who'd had a bit too much to drink bumped into Cody.

Gena reached out fast, steadying the woman with one hand while giving her a firm look.

The woman ignored her and set her sights on Cody. "Well, hello there, big boy."

Wheeler tried to play interference.

Gena, who was a few inches shorter than the woman, put her hands on her hips and proceeded to rake her gaze over the newcomer. "Do you mind?"

Bonnie and Rene approached and artfully positioned themselves between Gena and the drunk woman.

Rene took note of Gena's stance. "Everything okay?"

The tipsy woman laughed and bit at her lower lip, still staring at Cody. "Mmm, yes. He's yummy. Oh, so is he," she said, pointing to Wheeler.

Wheeler waggled his brows. "Thanks."

Bonnie launched into action. "Okay, let's find who it is you're with and let them know you need coffee, not more to drink."

The woman jerked away from Bonnie and

nearly tripped over her own two feet. "They're hot."

She then stumbled slightly and pointed somewhere in the vicinity of Wheeler and Cody as if she might be seeing double. "I'm going to touch them. See if they're as hard as they look."

Wheeler couldn't have looked happier if he tried. "I love Stanley's."

Gena planted herself in front of Cody. "Make a move to grope *my man* and you're going to have me to deal with. I'm scrappier than I look. Ask Bonnie."

Wheeler slapped Cody's arm so hard it actually hurt. "Did she just call you her…?"

Bonnie and Rene were staring at Gena with dual shocked expressions.

"Did she call him her man?" asked Rene.

Gena shook her head. "What? No. Why would I say that? I just met him. A bit early to be calling him mine. You two are so weird."

Rene glanced at Cody. "Yeah, weird."

Bonnie nodded before clearing her throat. "Okay, lady-who-needs-caffeine-not more-to-drink, let's go. You do not want to take on Gena."

It took Rene and Bonnie to steer the woman

away, but they finally managed, leaving Gena alone with Wheeler and Cody.

She turned to face Cody but didn't exactly talk to him so much as she talked *at* him while she opened the first-aid kit and began pulling out things to clean his nonexistent injury.

"Thinking he doesn't need looked at," mumbled Gena to herself as she fumbled with a sealed roll of gauze. "Fool."

She dropped it and then bent to retrieve it.

While she was getting the gauze, Cody stared desperately at his friend.

The cut is healed, said Cody mentally to Wheeler.

Wheeler grabbed for Cody's hand, yanked open the towel and, in the next second, let a nail lengthen, slicing him open again.

Asshole, snapped Cody.

Hey, I'm a helper, added Wheeler.

Cody winced but said nothing as Gena stood with the still-sealed roll in her hand. She looked at his bloody hand and shook her head. "Seriously, that needs checked and possibly stitched."

He held it up and offered a pouty face, hoping she'd simply take pity on him and stop scolding him.

Her expression softened, and she set about cleaning the fresh wound and then wrapping it in gauze. Before she had the bandage taped, Cody could feel his skin healing over. Thankfully, it happened under the cover of the gauze where Gena couldn't see.

Explaining that away would be difficult, especially since she was apparently immune to Wheeler's compulsion.

She put her hand over his injured one gently. "There. It's not perfect but it's better than nothing. If it keeps bleeding, you're getting it looked at. Understand me?"

"Domineering," said Wheeler, waggling his brows. "I like it. If you spank him, can I watch?"

A second before Cody was about to give Wheeler a piece of his mind, he caught the faint scent of shifter and Fae and stiffened. He grabbed for Gena, pulling her against the security of his body as he stared around, trying to find the source of the smell.

She winced.

He released her quickly. "Sorry."

Gena glanced up at him. "Don't be. Just try not to hug so firm next time. I might pop."

Wheeler snickered and nudged Cody once more. "So might he. Different way though."

Cody ignored the sexual innuendo and scanned the bar for signs of the supernatural he'd caught the faint scent of. Since the place was so crowded, it was difficult to pinpoint the exact location it was emanating from. It didn't help that the bar smelled heavily of sweat, perfume, body lotions, and cologne. More so than normal due to the sheer number of patrons as well as the heat that was blanketing Savannah.

Then there was the obvious distraction to his senses. The one scent that continued to supersede all others.

Gena's.

And it was the embodiment of perfection. A distracting embodiment, but one all the same.

Wheeler stiffened and stood up straight, shoving the half-empty bottle of tequila behind him more on the bar before facing forward, trying to look semi-respectable.

"Wheeler?" asked Cody. The man wasn't exactly known for his abundance of concern over what others thought of him. If he was taking a second to get his shit together, something was certainly going on.

Just like that, Cody's brain connected the dots between the scent of the supernatural that had found him, and who said supernatural was.

A young woman he'd come to know well over the past few years. One he considered a friend.

Clara.

She was best friends with Nicolette, the woman Cody had attempted to date, but had found *little shark* wasn't on board with the idea of having sex or anything that resembled as much—at least not with her. It was all for something more with Gena though.

Clara had been part of The Corporation's twisted scheme to create a master race of supernaturals, as had Nicolette. Both women had been tested on in horrific lab settings as small children.

From what Cody had managed to find out about it all, the labs, and those running them, were despicable. The children who were tested on had been subjected to the same gut-wrenching experiments as Cody and the other Outcasts.

Doing it all to an adult male was bad enough. Putting small, innocent children through the torture was unthinkable. Yet both women had endured just that. They were liberated from the lab they'd been held in by PSI some twenty years prior when they were very young. From there, they'd been placed into homes with loving, trustworthy supernatural parents.

In the cases of Clara and Nicolette, they'd been placed into the care of supernaturals who had remained in close proximity to one another throughout the girls' lives. Nicolette had been adopted by her uncle (who happened to be a member of the Fang-Gang), and Clara had been adopted by a couple the uncle knew and trusted.

The girls had been raised close to one another and had been best friends since day one.

Clara and Nicolette had met Cody at Stanley's on more than one occasion in the past for drinks, so it wasn't exactly shocking to see her there. But Cody hadn't called her to set up the meeting and he knew Wheeler wouldn't have either. Wheeler had watched over Clara and Nicolette from a distance more than once since Cody had come to Savannah, but the man had never been formally introduced to them.

Cody tensed, worried something had possibly happened to Nicolette since Clara had shown up at Stanley's apparently alone and without Cody calling first. "Clara?"

Gena turned in Cody's arms and let out a

loud squeal. She pulled away from Cody and rushed in the direction of Clara.

Clara's long brown hair was pulled up in a sleek ponytail, and she had on a pair of dress slacks and a silk blouse. She'd more than likely come from work. She indirectly worked for the Para-Regs, but she wasn't supposed to know that.

That wasn't much of a shock to Cody. He'd grown used to the secrecy a supernatural was forced to employ in his life. It was sort of par for the course. Clandestine organizations that operated under the public's nose, while staying hidden from humans were a dime a dozen.

Clara and Gena embraced and then Clara stepped back, holding Gena's hands, keeping her at arm's length. She looked Gena over slowly, smiling wide. "Ohmygod, babes. You look hot. Who got you to wear a dress finally?"

Gena laughed. "Bonnie."

"I really have got to meet this woman. You talk about her so much that I feel like I know her," said Clara, her gaze flickering toward Cody.

Gena tugged on Clara lightly. "She's here with Rene. I've talked about her to you as well. Come on, I'll introduce you to them. They've been wanting to meet you and Nicolette too. Is Nicolette here?"

Clara pressed a thin smile to her face. "No. She couldn't make it tonight. I got your message about meeting up for drinks and wanted to swing by to tell you the news in person."

Gena was the reason Clara was at Stanley's?

Cody simply stood there, dumbfounded at the knowledge that Gena knew Clara and Nicolette. Not to mention she'd just happened to be in the square at the same time as he and Wheeler. She just happened to remind him of the flashes he could remember of the woman from his sex dreams. And she just happened to make his cock spring back to life after being dormant for seventeen years.

There was such a thing as coincidence and then there was what was happening with him and Gena. None of it was random or happenstance. He was starting to see that clearly now. He just wasn't sure what to make of it and had to wonder if Gus's whole mermaid bit was somehow related to Gena too.

"News?" Gena paused, tipping her head. "What's going on? Is Nicolette okay?"

Clara smiled wide. "She is. Well, if you count

off the market and living in Virginia with a super-hot Viking guy okay."

"What?" demanded Gena, her voice loud enough to cut through the noise of the bar and draw the attention of other patrons. She didn't seem to notice or care. "She's living in Virginia? Since when? And with a Viking dude? I didn't even know she was dating again let alone serious enough with some guy to move to another state with him. Does Landros know? I can't see him being okay with that. He's very overprotective of you two."

Wheeler's sharp intake of breath mirrored Cody's as the name Landros fell from Gena's lips.

Landros was Nicolette's uncle, who just so happened to work for PSI. Not to mention the guy was a vampire.

Do you think she knows supernaturals are real? Wheeler asked via their mental pathway. *Fuck. Is my gut right? Is she the one?*

Cody merely stared at Gena, too shocked to do anything more.

Wheeler leaned against Cody more. *Holy fuck nuts, you don't think she's really got a fish tail, do you?*

With distinct slowness, Cody turned his head

toward Wheeler. "I don't know what to think at this point."

"It's super recent," said Clara, giving him a knowing look. "The guy she's living with is a great man. His name is Garth and he's in the military, kind of. I'm sure you'll meet him soon enough. It was all really sudden but she's totally happy and safe and I trust the guy implicitly. So does your beach bum buddy over there."

Gena glanced over her shoulder at Cody and her brows met. "Hold on, you know Cody?"

Wheeler laughed. "Notice Gena knew exactly who, of the two of us, the beach bum is."

"Asshole," said Cody, in a low tone.

"I do know him," said Clara, her smile widening. "He's a great guy. I've known him a couple of years now. I think Nicolette and I have talked about him a little to you before too."

Gena's gaze darted away a second and then widened more. "Tell me he's not the same Cody that Nicolette mentioned dating briefly. The one who crashes at your place at random."

In that moment, Cody wished he could go back in time and not make an attempt at dating Nicolette. That they'd just kept the relationship totally platonic, not that it had ever gotten hot and heavy.

Guilt that he couldn't explain filled him.

Wheeler tipped his head in Cody's direction and smirked. "Why do I feel like you're in trouble?"

As Cody stared at Gena and saw the hurt and uncertainty in her dark gaze, his stomach clenched and he darted forward, going straight to her. "Honey, I swear to you that Nicolette and I are only friends and saying we dated is kind of a stretch. It never took off romantically. I swear. We never had sex."

Gena lifted a brow. "Why are you telling me this?"

Clara lifted a hand as if in a classroom setting. "Uh, I want to know why you called her honey?"

"I got this one," said Wheeler, laughing from his position near the bar. "It *is* hot and heavy between him and Gena and it's certainly romantic between them."

Gena tensed and her cheeks turned a brilliant shade of red.

Clara's eyes widened. "Shut up! Really? Since when? How did y'all meet? When did you meet?

How long have you two been seeing one another? Why didn't either of you tell me?"

"They just met tonight," offered Wheeler.

Confusion coated Clara's face. "But I could have sworn I saw Gena and Cody embracing when I first came in. Did I see that?"

"You did," said Wheeler.

Clara grabbed Gena's hand. "Girl, you are not the type to hug any guy you just met. Hell, do you even hug guys that you've known for years? What is going on?"

"You should have seen them kissing earlier," added Wheeler, ever the helper. "It was darn near X-rated for a moment there. I thought articles of clothing were about to start flying in every direction. To hell with the fact they were in public and had known each other for about ten seconds. It was lust at first sight."

Gena's shoulders slumped and she eased back more, clearly uneasy with the direction the conversation was going.

Cody didn't like knowing she was uncomfortable. He filled the small space between them and ran his hand over her back lightly. She instantly eased over in his direction and he lifted his arm. She came to him and pressed against him. He wrapped his arm around her and stared over her head at Clara.

Clara blinked several times before her gaze snapped to Wheeler. "Holy crap. Are you thinking what I'm thinking?"

"Depends," said Wheeler with a shrug. "Are you picturing yourself minus clothing?"

Clara grunted. "No."

"Then we're not thinking the same thing at the moment," said Wheeler, making Gena laugh slightly.

"You have got to be Wheeler," said Clara.

"My reputation precedes me?" asked Wheeler.

With a snort, Clara rolled her eyes. "Something like that."

Cody kept Gena close to him. "I'm curious how it is you and Gena know each other. You never mentioned her to me before."

Clara grinned. "Yes, Nicolette and I did. We told you that we had a childhood friend move to the area not long back. That we were all adopted around the *same time*."

The way she stressed "same time" made Cody's gut clench. Was Clara telling him Gena had been part of the experiments as well?

Cody's entire body filled with dread and the burning need to grab Gena and get her the hell out of Savannah. He couldn't explain it.

Bonnie and Rene approached, laughing about something.

Gena eased back from Cody and squared her shoulders. "Guys, this is my friend Clara."

Bonnie smiled wide and extended a hand to Clara. "Nice to meet you finally."

"You too," said Clara before taking Rene's hand and shaking it as well. "I've heard a ton about the two of you."

"Oh Lord," said Rene. "We're going to need to explain ourselves, I'm sure. We know we're terrible influences on Gena."

Clara laughed. "No way. You two are great. She really likes you both."

Bonnie nodded to Gena. "We're going to step outside so I can call your lunch date for tomorrow and let him know that isn't happening. Want to come too?"

Gena nodded. "Yes. But I don't want to talk to him. He gives me the creeps."

The moment Gena was out of the bar, Clara lurched forward and grabbed Cody at the arm. "What in the hell is going on?

"I was hoping you could tell me," said Cody, his body still screaming at him to get Gena far from the area.

Wheeler stared at them both. "You said you were all adopted around the same time. The way you said it left us wondering…"

Clara took a deep breath and nodded. "Gena and her siblings were all tested on too. They were at a sister site though, freed at the same time as the one Nicolette and I were in. Landros, from what I've been able to piece together since the asshat is doing his best to stay busy and far away from me, saw to it Gena and her brothers and sisters went to a supernatural couple. He's friends with them like he is my dad. We'd meet with Gena and her family a few times a year growing up, spending a week or two together each time."

Cody registered what Clara was telling him. It felt as if the temperature of the bar had increased exponentially. Suddenly, he was dripping with sweat.

"Cody?" asked Clara. "You don't look so good. What's wrong?"

"Well, he started the night out in search of a mermaid but I'm pretty fucking sure he found his mate instead," said Wheeler.

Clara's eyes widened. "Wow. Um, I guess it would make sense Gena would be Cody's mate. After all, from everything I saw in her files, even quickly, it all indicated she has shark DNA in her too. And a bunch of other things that like the ocean. She can't shift or anything though."

The bar seemed to tilt on an axis as he absorbed what he was hearing. She had shark in her too? Even a little? She was like him?

That meant she was mate material.

His gaze went instantly to his groin. His mouth fell agape. "Holy shit, little shark figured it out before I did."

She's my mate.

"Little shark?" asked Clara, her gaze following his. "Is this some weird new euphemism for penis? If so, I'm going to pass on calling it that. I prefer to call a cock a cock."

"Marry me," said Wheeler quickly.

She snorted. "Passing on that too, but thanks for asking."

Cody would have said more but his shark picked then to try to surface. He cast a desperate look at Wheeler for help.

"Fuck," said Wheeler loudly. "We're gonna need a bigger bar."

"Cody?" asked Clara, worry in her voice. "What's wrong? You don't look thrilled like a guy who just found out he's got a mate should look."

Wheeler laughed. "Honey, he looks exactly like a guy who just found out he has a mate. I'm taking him to the little boy's room. Can you keep Gena busy while I calm him down?"

"Yes, but if you two keep referring to things as little, I'm going to question your alphaness," said Clara, hurrying toward the exit as Wheeler grabbed Cody and yanked him in the direction of the restrooms.

Chapter Fifteen

HELMUTH STOOD JUST OUTSIDE of the holding tank that had been specially created for a wereshark. One specifically.

Cody Livingston.

The large freighter (that he had been told more than once was a renovated mega container ship, but he didn't care what it was termed) let out a loud moan. Had he not been standing in the belly of the beast itself, he'd have thought the sounds had emanated from there. As it was, he knew it was the hull.

One deck below were the engines that kept the massive beast moving. Most of the people working there did so to avoid being used as training dummies for the paranormal underground fight rings. Some had been injured in the fights in ways that left them worthless when it came to the ring. Sure, they'd still fetch a small bit of coin if he was to auction them off to the highest bidder, but forcing them to do manual labor benefited him more.

He'd specifically had bunk rooms that were more like cells than anything else built on the levels staffed mostly with the forced laborers. Those who refused to work found themselves in the starring role of impromptu fights staged at random for the rest of the crew who was paid to be there. The winner of the fights was given the chance to return to work on the ship. The loser's dead body was tossed overboard.

A smile touched Helmuth's lips as he thought of all he'd managed to accomplish even in the face of PSI and their interference in his life as of late.

The ship was a testament to his perseverance. And he intended for it to be not only his ticket back into the good graces of The Corporation but for it to be his legacy as well. He'd already gathered some of the greatest minds in science, giving them full access to any number of the captive laborers they wanted to conduct their experiments on. He didn't judge them when there was a fatality.

You had to break a lot of eggs to make an omelet.

Such was the way of things.

The ship was finally finished with its retrofitting and even he found himself impressed. Pleasing him wasn't exactly easy with as old as he was and all he'd seen in his life.

But there was no denying the ship was a thing of beauty. A floating masterpiece.

There were nine decks in all; the top floor was done with luxury furnishings and more to his liking. After all, it would be where he called home soon enough—at least for the foreseeable future.

There were elevators that ran between the decks. Several elevators were for maintenance and the staff. The others were for the rest of the crew. And then there was his private elevator.

Kahale had caught a crew member using Helmuth's private elevator several days prior and from what Helmuth had been told, what had been left of the crew member after Kahale was finished with him had been tossed overboard to feed whatever marine life was nearest.

Good help was hard to come by.

Kahale had proven himself an asset time and again. He'd been the one to lean on the contractors who had retrofitted the ship to Helmuth's specifications. Any weak links that might talk to anyone about the project they'd been working on had been dealt with by Kahale personally.

Helmuth could only imagine the carnage he'd left in his wake.

He was good about cleaning up his messes, which was another bonus.

There was a loud thumping noise that echoed down the corridor. It came from the direction of one of the many holding cells aboard the ship. Each was designed for a specific type of supernatural.

The ship was a work of art.

While Helmuth wanted to take credit for being the brainchild of the ship, he couldn't. The idea had been in use for decades by The Corporation. As far as Helmuth knew, the research vessels dated back to at least World War I, possibly prior. When Helmuth had gotten his hands on blueprints for one of the other ships, he'd known then he wanted one for himself.

Everything had been going smoothly in the build process right up until the incident in Seattle.

That had put his standing in The Corporation at risk and made them question his judgment briefly. That had resulted in delays with the completion of the ship. But it was finally done.

And it already had a significant number of test subjects, not counting the forced labor, aboard it with room for many more.

The ship would help Helmuth reestablish his position within The Corporation once more, maybe even increase his standing. He wanted to be considered something of a general within the ranks, but he'd hit a ceiling. Then the Seattle incident had yanked the rug out from under him. He was in the process of digging his way out.

And he was so close to solidifying his position among his peers once more.

Victory was at hand, and he planned to seize it fully.

For now, he continued to soak in the sight of his hard work and efforts. Reaching out, he skimmed his fingers on the unbreakable tank glass. He'd be able to watch the tank's inhabitant suffer, kept locked between shifted stages, forever.

Perfect.

It's what the wereshark deserved for daring to think he could stay hidden for so long. Had

Livingston just obeyed like a good little test subject, Helmuth wouldn't have been forced to take such extreme measures. As it stood, he'd been left no choice.

Finding a facility that was located on dry land put it at risk of detection and raids from the Ops. Already a number of his colleagues were dealing with the crackdown from the operatives. Thankfully, enough men from PSI and its offshoots were on the payroll with The Corporation that heads-up were given in most cases.

But not all—as Helmuth had learned while tendering out to the freighter only hours before.

PSI and those it aligned itself with had raided Cal's resort and compound in Colorado. While information was still scarce and hard to come by, all the reports were the same.

Caladrius was dead.

As was The Flock.

He still couldn't wrap his mind around the fact that Cal was gone. It didn't seem real. Cal had always been larger than life and one of the most powerful supernaturals Helmuth had ever crossed paths with. But in the end that hadn't saved him or his followers from death at the hands of PSI.

Those fucking bastards were becoming a serious nuisance.

One he hoped to rid himself of soon enough.

Grieving for Cal wasn't something Helmuth felt compelled to do. Yes, the man had been something of a friend, but those came and went. Death was a part of life. Besides, there would have undoubtedly come a time when Helmuth would have found himself pitted against Cal. And Helmuth wasn't so sure he could have taken the man. It was better that PSI handled the matter for him. Even if it meant the loss of a friend.

For now he just needed to stay the course. Once he had what he wanted—the wereshark and Gena—he'd live aboard the ship, staying on the move to decrease the chance of detection. That arrangement would afford him the time he required to have his teams of experts perfect the serum he'd been using and gather every other sample they could think of from the prime specimens aboard the vessel. Between the lot of them, a cure would be found.

He was sure of it.

Hope was all he had left, and he refused to give it up, even with the news that Cal was no more.

He stared down at his hand and watched as his skin turned a dark gray, only to fade back to normal once more. The beast that lingered just below the surface wanted to be free, and he knew if he dared allow it to get loose, there might very well be no caging it ever again.

From there he'd turn to stone. Maybe not today or tomorrow, but soon, and he'd do so while trapped in the form of a fucking monster.

"Do not lose it now," he said to himself as he stared at the results of all his hard work and money. The freighter was perfect. It was basically a floating city.

Gena would be tested on extensively to start with, of course, and then she'd find herself either bending to his whims or tied to his bed aboard the ship. He didn't care which one she picked.

In the end, he'd fuck her, and he'd find a way to force a claiming. Eventually, she'd come around to his way of thinking. Sure, it might be after he bred her a few times, but that was no matter.

It was hard to temper his excitement.

Kahale approached from one of the side labs. He looked pleased with himself if you counted the pep in his step as happy for him, which Helmuth did.

Helmuth couldn't help but laugh. "Scaring the scientists again?"

"Maybe," returned the orca-shifter as he nodded to the containment tank. "It's to your specs. So is the other tank. It's smaller, though. Much smaller. That for the woman?"

"It is," said Helmuth, downright giddy.

It had been months since he'd felt such a rush. Months since things had gone his way. Everything was lining up perfectly. Meeting Gena earlier had been a highlight for him. It had taken all his self-control to permit her to leave. It would have been so easy to simply take what he'd wanted from her when she'd arrived with her work colleague.

But Cal had been clear in what he'd told Helmuth. He'd stressed that patience was needed and that if he did not rush things, the woman would be the bait required to draw the wereshark back to him.

"Is Roberts back yet?" asked Helmuth, his ire rising as he thought about the conceited human male who thought his brains and scientific knowledge gave him some sort of protection from harm.

He was a bottom feeder.

The fool actually believed Helmuth would see

to it that he was converted into a supernatural himself. That everlasting life was within the man's grasp.

Please.

As if anyone with The Corporation would ever permit a backstabbing leech like Roberts to live forever. No. Roberts would be allowed to continue behaving the way he was so long as his skill set was still useful.

That was fast coming to an end.

He'd already given Helmuth the information he'd needed on Gena, and he'd overseen the specs and creation of the holding tank and testing facility aboard the floating research vessel. All of which he'd been brought on to do.

The ever-moving vessel would make detection from his enemies all the more difficult. If they couldn't find him, they couldn't stop him. The thought process behind it all was simple and all the chips had fallen into place perfectly.

Helmuth made sure the research vessel was kept in international waters. While that meant having to tender out to it via a smaller boat, as well as extra time, it also meant more freedoms.

Not to mention, no one was around for miles

and miles to hear the screams and cries of those held on board.

"Did you check on the other?" asked Helmuth.

"Since there is currently a shit load of test subjects being held and tested on here, I need more to go off than that," stated Kahale.

Helmuth continued to stare at the fruits of his labor. The containment tank for the wereshark was a thing of beauty. The exact one he'd had depicted in the painting in his home. "I forget its name. Vincent or something?"

Kahale nodded. "Vic."

He glanced at the guard. "Yes. That one. Have the tests yielded any new results with him yet?"

"His hybrid state is still stable," said Kahale. "At least that is what the scientists are telling me. Never seen anyone survive that many new threads of DNA being introduced to them. The guy looks like shit though. I won't be shocked if he expires before the week is out."

"See to it he doesn't," warned Helmuth. "I have plans for him."

"The smile on your face says you're thinking of something nefarious," said Kahale.

"It's all working out as planned," returned Helmuth. "Have you managed to find out any more details on Cal and what happened in Colorado?"

Kahale was quiet a moment before giving a curt nod.

"And?"

"And it would appear your wereshark was involved in some manner," said Kahale.

Helmuth's breathing increased, and he clenched his fists, fighting off the pending rage as best he could. "Livingston is in Colorado? Cal led me to believe he would be here."

Kahale quirked a brow. "Did the guy who loved wearing white also tell you the shark dude would also have a hand in his death, or did he leave that bit out?"

Helmuth rounded on Kahale. When he saw an eagerness behind the man's eyes, he remained perfectly still. It was as if Kahale was spoiling for a fight. While Helmuth was fairly certain he could take the orca-shifter, he wasn't willing to bet his future on it. And even if he could take him, he didn't doubt Kahale could and would leave him injured. That was something he couldn't risk, not with as close to making his dreams come true as he was.

"That was not mentioned," said Helmuth, making an attempt at humor, as dark as it may be.

Kahale actually cracked something close to a smile. "Thought not. And I put out some feelers with our contacts at PSI. They're telling me a group from the Denver branch got in earlier today. Said they're poking around in the system for details and information on you. My contacts tried to lock it down, but they've got some weird young guy with them who knows shit he shouldn't. They got the feeling the kid knew they weren't on the level, so they hightailed it out of there rather than risk detection. Want me to send them back in?"

Helmuth considered it but knew he might need to draw on those very moles at some point again. "No. Did they have word on Livingston? Was he with the group who arrived?"

"No. But they said they heard some old crazy human guy who did come with the group mentioning a shark shifter. Something about him being in town too. Safe bet is, they're talking about your wereshark."

Nodding, Helmuth stared at the tank. "Be

ready to move early if we need to. I'd prefer this all go according to plan, but we will do what needs to be done. Understood?"

"Yes," said Kahale. "I'll be sure Ernest has everything ready for your lunch date with the female scientist tomorrow."

"I know he was instructed to drug the food and drink she'll have but be sure there are other means of subduing her without causing her any real harm," said Helmuth. He'd meant what he'd said. He wasn't leaving anything to chance.

"Will do," said Kahale, walking off.

Chapter Sixteen

"EXCUSE US," said Wheeler, cutting in front of a group of guys all lined up to get into the restroom.

Several started to bitch and Cody looked up at them, feeling his eyes burning with the pending shift. Whatever they saw made them back up and lift their hands as if to signal they were no threat.

Smart.

Wheeler shoved Cody at the restroom door.

Cody spun around in the dimly lit hall that smelled heavy of beer and sweat. His shark was already teetering on the edge of breaking free; adding in the stench of drunk humans in tight corridors wasn't helping matters any. "What the fuck?"

Wheeler pointed at the restroom, his expression pinched. "In. Now!"

With a huff, Cody did as Wheeler commanded, more to stop the gathering crowd than because he wanted to listen. He then pivoted on his heels once he was inside the two-stall restroom. "Seriously. What the fuck?"

"Stole my very words," said Wheeler, his Southern drawl shining through, a sure sign the man was pissed. "Did you not notice you were about to turn into a giant fucking fish out there?"

"I noticed," said Cody, the words tasting like vinegar on his tongue.

He really hated admitting Wheeler was right.

Wheeler crossed his arms over his chest. "Yet you gave me shit about removing you from the area."

"Bite me," snapped Cody.

Wheeler flashed fang quickly and winked. "Gladly."

Cody thought about everything he'd learned in a short period of time. He then concentrated on everything he'd said and done since meeting Gena. That left no doubt in his mind.

She *was* his mate.

And she was more than likely what Gus would term a mermaid.

The very one he'd told Cody was in danger and needed him.

In an instant, it felt as though the temperature in the small room had been jacked a good fifty degrees. Sweat dripped down his forehead, and he rushed forward to the sink. He bent, jerked on the cold water, and began splashing it onto his face. When he glanced up into the mirror, he found Wheeler with one hand propped on the door as he leaned partially on it, keeping others from entering.

Wheeler grinned, looking down his nose at Cody. "Dude, you are like so off the market now too. You just joined the mated club. Kiss your freedom good-bye."

Cody used the sink to help balance himself as he stared down as if clarity could be found in the drain. Whatever he'd been hoping for, he didn't find it. All he got was more questions.

Someone tried to enter the restroom. There was a large thud that sounded a lot like someone walked face-first into the door. "Hey. Open up!"

"Out of order," stated Wheeler loudly, never budging from his post. He gave Cody a firm stare.

"You need to get your head on right. No losing your shit out there. You heard Clara. Gena doesn't know about supernaturals. Want her to figure out they're real by way of seeing your ugly ass turn into a big fucking shark?"

"No," said Cody.

"Find a place of zen. And fast. You following me?"

Nodding, Cody let out a shaky breath. "I'm following. Okay, sort of. Mostly, I'm freaking out."

Knocking sounded from the door. It was dainty. "Cody? Wheeler? Is everything okay? Clara said Cody wasn't feeling well."

As Gena's voice found Cody, his shark began to grow restless in him once again.

"Uh, yeah, everything is fine," said Wheeler. "I, um, had to take a leak and wanted Cody to join me?"

Cody's eyes widened. "Dude. What is with you and piss?"

Wheeler shrugged before lowering his voice. "What? I'm not used to thinking under the pressure of a possible mating. You have a better thing to tell her?"

"Pretty sure anything else would have worked," snapped Cody.

Wheeler looked at the door. "Uh, I lied. Clara was right. He had some bad seafood earlier and now has the shits."

Tossing his hands in the air, Cody stepped back from the sink and stared at his best friend in disbelief. "Asshole."

He then glanced at the door, easily imagining what Gena looked like on the other side. For a moment, he could almost feel her anxiety as if it were his own. Her concern washed over him, leaving him swaying for a second. He reached out and caught hold of the sink once more for balance.

"Are you sure everything is okay?" asked Gena, knocking again. "I have a weird feeling. I can't explain it, but it doesn't feel like Cody is fine. Is he sick? Oh no, did his hand start bleeding more? Is he suffering from blood loss? I'll call for an ambulance."

Wheeler rolled his eyes and yanked the door open, pulling her in before shutting the door again and blocking others from entering.

Gena yelped and then closed her eyes quickly, lifting a hand and flailing it about at random. "I didn't see anyone peeing. I swear."

Cody tried but failed to keep from chuckling.

Everything about her made him crave sex. Made him want to do things to her he'd never done to another person in his life, yet there was this certain innocence to her that left him wanting to shelter her from everyone and everything.

Himself included.

"You can open your eyes. No one is peeing or doing anything else," said Cody, suppressing his amusement for the time being.

She didn't open her eyes, but she did ease closer to him. "If someone is having digestive problems, I can go wait out in the hall. I just, well, I can't explain it."

Cody closed the distance between them and came just shy of touching her stomach. "You feel this tugging in your gut? It's telling you to come to me, isn't it?"

"Y-yes," she managed, her voice barely there. "How did you know?"

He took a deep breath in, his gaze flickering to Wheeler. "Because I feel it too. From the second I saw you, Gena."

Wheeler began to hop up and down while using both hands to point at Gena. He mouthed his words. "Kiss your mate."

It was on the tip of his tongue to attempt

denial once more since it seemed hardwired into his programming, but even he knew the signs staring him in the face were all pointing to yes.

Gena was his mate.

Wheeler motioned his head to Gena. *Can I leave you alone with her or are you going to shark out?*

I'll be fine.

Wheeler didn't look so sure, but he did open the door only to find two men standing there about to enter. He stared down at them. "It's occupied, and no one is to bother them. See to it."

The push in Wheeler's voice was hard to miss.

The human males nodded to him in a trance-like state.

Wheeler glanced back at Cody, appearing worried. *I'll make some calls. Don't do anything stupid.*

Once Wheeler was gone, and the door was shut again, Cody touched Gena's arm lightly.

Her eyes opened, and she glanced down the length of him quickly, before appearing relieved.

He chuckled. "The idea of seeing all of me that scary?"

He'd wanted to lighten the mood.

Her hands darted out and to his chest as she shook her head. "No. I've already seen all of you…ignore me. Uh, are you okay? Clara said you weren't feeling well."

Cody dipped his head slightly to get a better look into her eyes. "Seen all of me, how?"

Bonnie's parting words to Gena at the park came back to Cody, and his chest tightened. She really had dreamed of him, too?

"The dreams," he said softly.

She tensed but nodded and averted her gaze.

He touched her chin, directing her attention back to his face. "Don't be embarrassed."

She grunted. "Kind of hard not to be."

He grinned. "Gena?"

"Yes?"

"I'm pretty sure I've dreamed of you too," he confessed.

That caught her attention. "Really?"

"Yes," he said, cupping her face, getting lost in her big brown eyes. Cody wanted to tell her everything, but he found himself kissing her instead, the need to taste her again superseding anything else.

Chapter Seventeen
───────────────

GENA PRESSED on Cody's chest as she ate at his mouth. The man tasted like pure sin and she loved every second of kissing him. The kiss deepened and Gena couldn't stop herself as she grabbed the back of his neck, pulling him down to her level more, as their tongues laced perfectly around one another.

The next she knew, Cody was lifting her. She gasped. "Your hand."

"Is fine," he said, kissing her more.

As if independent of her brain, her legs wrapped around his trim waist. The second she felt the bulge of his pants pressing against her panty-covered mound, her breath caught, but she didn't dare break the kiss.

In her dreams he'd taken her every way imaginable, and she intended to make that a reality. It was past time she stopped living for work and research and take a second to live for herself.

And there was no better way to do so than to take advantage of the opportunity fate seemed to have dropped in her lap.

The man from her dreams.

Cody thumped his hips against her as he moaned into her mouth. What limited control she had shattered into a million pieces.

Gena dug her nails into his shoulders, grinding against him as a torrent of cream flooded her sex, making her panties damp.

With a growl, he walked her toward the sink and deposited her on it, their lips still locked.

Gena yanked at his shirt, tugging it up in the process. She wanted to feel him. All of him. There were far too many articles of clothing between them for her liking.

He eased back, still kissing her, and took hold of his shirt. He broke the kiss only long enough to yank his shirt over his head and toss it aside. The act gifted her a real-life view of his toned chest, rather than merely the dream one she'd had.

Her dreams hadn't come close to doing the man justice.

She skimmed her hands over the rippling contours of his torso and bit at his lower lip. She barely recognized herself as she slid her hands lower, going for the top of his jeans. The minute her fingers grasped the button of his jeans, Cody broke the kiss and caught her wrists.

She whimpered.

He groaned, his forehead finding hers. "If you want to get to the good part, doing that is a bad idea," he said, his voice quivering as he spoke.

"Cody?" she asked, worried she was doing something wrong.

He lifted her hands to his lips and kissed each of them tenderly, his smoldering gaze never leaving hers. "I just need a minute."

"Why?"

The edge of his mouth drew upward. "To keep from finishing before we start."

She nodded, as if totally following his logic. When it dawned on her what he meant, heat stole through her upper chest, flaring up her neck. "Oh!"

He chuckled. "Yes. Oh."

"So, you want to stop?" she asked, hoping

he'd say no. She wanted him to be the man who took what she'd been holding on to for so long—her virginity. But she wasn't about to tell him as much. The last thing she wanted was for him to feel like he was about to have sex with an inexperienced twit.

A shaky breath came from him. "Never really had this issue before. And there was a point in time I was something of an expert when it came to the opposite sex."

Her jaw set at the idea of Cody being with other women. Instantly, it felt as if she'd been doused in a bucket of ice water. Her ardor cooled quickly.

He stiffened. "Shit. I didn't mean to say that out loud."

Gena tried to get down from the sink, but Cody's body left her pinned in place. "I think I'm done now."

Nodding, he began to ease back but stopped and dipped his head. He put his lips to her ear. "I'm an asshole who is so nervous and excited to be this close to you that I'm blowing it. I'm sorry. I don't want this to end but if you do, I'll stop. But you need to understand, when I say I've never had this issue before it's not to toss other women in your face. It's to let you know how fucking much you turn me on. And just how much I want to be inside you."

There was something about the rawness in his voice that left her changing her mind about being done. Her body began to heat once more with the same speed in which it had cooled.

She had no idea what had possessed her since seeing him in the park, but she hadn't been acting like herself in the least. Normal Gena would not have kissed a man she'd only just met. And normal Gena certainly wouldn't have been ready to have sex in a public restroom.

Yet, that's exactly what was happening.

Reason crept in slowly, but it didn't stop the burning urge she had to feel every inch of the man's chiseled form. Her hands returned to his upper chest. "You have a really hard body."

A half-laugh came from him. "Baby, you have no idea how right you are at the moment."

There was no missing the bulge that was still in the front of his pants. Drawing deep, Gena gathered her nerve and locked gazes with Cody. "I want this. I want you. If you want me, I'm yours."

Cody's shoulders heaved a second before he

crowded her body more, leaning, forcing her back a bit. His mouth slanted over hers and he kissed her in a way that told her he *more* than wanted her too.

And she was totally fine with that.

He broke the kiss momentarily.

With a grin, he looked her over and then kissed her again, his hands finding their way to the bottom of her skirt. He inched it up ever so slightly, and she strongly suspected the act was meant to give her time in case she had a change of heart.

There was no chance in hell she was backing out.

Not now.

Not when she was so close to having him.

"Hurry up," she said against his lips, making him laugh. Gena slid her hand down his steely chest and eased the tips of her fingers below the waistline of his jeans. The second her fingers connected with his hot, hard member, his laughter died.

Cody jerked and put his hand over her, holding it there as their gazes collided. She nodded and he went to work undoing his jeans, her hand still partway down his pants. When his long, hard erection sprang free, she jolted like it might bite her or something. And once again, she blushed.

His bad-boy grin helped to soothe away any embarrassment she had. He took her hand in his hand and placed it on his throbbing shaft.

Gena was surprised at how velvety smooth his cock was. She'd never actually held one before and had for some strange reason never realized what it would feel like. It was hot to the touch and the moment she stroked it, a small bit of clear liquid eased forth from the head.

She had the strongest urge to lick his cockhead and managed to resist.

Barely.

Cody began to guide her actions, helping her to find a good rhythm as she continued to stroke his shaft. When he kissed her again, he let her handle his cock while he went to work running his legs up her inner thighs.

Gena felt as though she might burst from both heat and anticipation of what was to come next. She more than understood the basics of sex. But studying them in an academic setting and living them were two very different things.

When the pad of his uninjured hand met her damp panties, Gena gasped into his mouth.

His lips drew into a smile, still pressed to hers. He eased her panties aside and lightly brushed his thumb over her clit, sending shockwaves of pleasure radiating throughout her entire body.

She jerked hard on his cock and was about to apologize when he growled into her mouth and began pumping his hips. It was then she realized he liked how rough she'd been with him. That was a good thing, considering how nervous and excited she was. There was a darn good chance she'd be rough again without meaning to be.

Cody rubbed her body just right once more and pressure started to build deep in her lower half. A tingle began in her toes and eased up her legs, focusing on her inner thighs before reaching her wet core. One second she was there, on the sink, squirming while she stroked his cock, and the next she was clamping her legs to his sides as ecstasy raced over her, stealing her breath, making her legs shake.

He picked that moment to ease his cock from her hands and line up with her pussy. He wasted no time driving home, going balls deep in her. For a second there was pain, but it gave way quickly to pleasure.

He froze, his hands finding the sides of her head. "G-Gena?"

"More," she said, her body starved for all of him. She wanted him driving into her. Not stopping.

Why was he stopping?

"You were a virgin?" he asked from between clenched teeth.

That was why he'd stopped?

Reaching up, she tugged hard on his hair. "I swear on all the research data in the world that if you don't keep going, I will hurt you."

For a second his expression was unreadable. Then he grinned before all out laughing.

Somehow, she didn't think hysterical laughter was a good response while having sex. She whimpered, her body aching for more.

It took him a minute to compose himself before he kissed her lips tenderly and began to ease in and out of her with deliberate slowness at first. Then his pace increased and with it came the building of pleasure once more. Soon he was pumping in and out of her like a piston.

Gena arched her back as he kissed his way to her neck.

Never had she felt anything as amazing as this, and she didn't want it to ever end. It didn't matter to her that she'd handed herself over to a man she'd only just met or that her first sexual experience was happening in a men's restroom. All that mattered was they were now joined—they were one.

It took her a second to realize Cody had started to growl. The sound was low but there, coming from deep within him.

She panted as she ran her hands into his hair, holding his head to her neck. The strangest urge to speak came over her, but her words made little sense to her. "Do it, Cody. Make me yours."

He tensed right before he began fucking her so hard and thoroughly that she began to feel lightheaded. Another orgasm struck and she tried to get away from the overwhelming pleasure. Though she wasn't sure why. All she knew was it was so intense that it left her body automatically trying to break contact with him. Like her body was unsure if it might burst into flames or have a gush of cream burst free from her.

Cody wasn't having any of it.

He held her hips to him and cried out a second before he put his mouth to her neck. "Mine!"

There was a sharp pinching around the base of her neck, near her collarbone, but the pain ebbed away quickly as pure, unadulterated bliss swept through her body. "Yes," she breathed out. "Yours. And you're mine."

She didn't know what had come over her and made her say those words, and she didn't much care. Before she could really put anything close to thought into it all, her stomach began to feel funny. Like someone was there, tugging just behind her navel, attaching a string of sorts there. It felt as if the other end of the string was being fastened to Cody.

He jerked and rooted deep in her, his mouth still on her neck, near her collarbone.

Gena cried out loudly and tried to stop, knowing people in the bar could hear her. But it felt too good. Too right as he came in hot waves in her.

Her breathing was harsh as she clung to him.

He stayed settled balls deep in her but lifted his head, his gaze glassy. He looked high. She could understand why. She felt as if her head was buzzing too.

Cody seemed to come out of a daze as he stayed in her but looked around the restroom. His brows met and he shook his head. "No. I didn't do this here. Tell me I didn't do this here—not like this. No."

"Cody?"

He stiffened and closed his eyes a second. "Shit. Gena, I'm sorry. I didn't mean for it to happen here in a fucking bar lavatory of all places."

"You mean sex?" she asked.

He stayed in her but sighed loudly. "I mean claiming you. I should have made it special, baby."

"Claiming me? That's a really weird way to point out you ejaculated in me, but okay, sure. We can go with that," she said. "Can we also maybe do that again very soon?"

He let out a shaky laugh. "Yes. How about we go somewhere that isn't a public toilet? I have something I need to talk about with you."

She looked around and swallowed hard at her lack of self-control. She wasn't sure what he wanted to discuss, but she didn't want to spend any more time in the restroom than need be. "Yes. That's probably best. My boat isn't far from here. Want to go there?"

"Boat?" he asked.

She bit at her inner cheek. "I live on a boat. Weird. I know."

He grinned. "No, baby. It's perfect. Just like you. And I've lived on a boat once or twice in my life too. I currently live out of a van. It's renovated but still."

Her eyes lit. "Sweet! I want to see it!"

He laughed. "Not the response I get from most people."

"I'm not like most people," she said.

He winked. "I know."

Chapter Eighteen

CODY FINISHED TUCKING himself back into his jeans, which was something of an ordeal because little shark was far from done. His cock was so excited to be working again it apparently didn't require any downtime. As much as he wanted to never leave his mate's body again, there was the matter of needing to explain to her what he'd done.

That he'd lost control and claimed her.

But that would mean having to explain what supernaturals were and that both he and she were one. It was a conversation he wasn't looking forward to. The black cloud that hung over what should be the happiest moment of his life wasn't lost on him.

He was now a married man.

He had a wife.

His shifter side was currently doing its version of a celebratory dance deep within him. It was easy for the shark to be excited. It didn't have to explain itself to anyone.

A slight buzzing in his back pocket caught his attention and he exhaled slowly, debating on ignoring the phone call. It could be important. He retrieved his phone while giving Gena a quick peck on the tip of her nose as she remained seated on the sink, with Cody still standing between her open legs.

He answered the call, assuming it was Armand since it was the man's number.

"Sharkie, Gus tells me congratulations are in order," said Bill, practically shouting into the phone.

Cody pulled back from the phone slightly and double-checked the call had indeed come from Armand's cell.

It had.

"Do I want to know why you're calling me from Armand's phone?" asked Cody.

Bill burped. "Probably best you not know. Plausible deniability and all that shit. Anyway,

Gus wanted me to call to tell you that you done good. You found the mermaid."

His gaze swept to Gena who had taken an interest in the bandage on his hand. She set about straightening it in a tender manner while he continued to talk to Bill. "She is the one then?"

"Yeppers," said Bill before sounding muffled. "No way. I'm not drinking that shit. I want a beer. People drown in water, you know. Sharkie, these shit-for-brains here keep trying to give me healthy crap to eat and drink. It's like they want to kill me or something. My body is a temple. I give it offers of weed and double cheeseburgers. None of that pita chip shit."

"I'm with the crazy man," said Mac in a deep voice that could easily be heard over the phone.

Cody felt slightly better knowing Bill and Gus weren't running amuck alone, but saying they were supervised was something of a stretch, considering the person with them was Mac.

"Anything new develop there?" asked Cody, needing to know if Helmuth had been located.

"No. Other than your dead friend being dickier than normal," said Bill nonchalantly. "Man, what is this Gus tells me about you screwing your woman in the shitter? Ain't you got no sense? Boy, that's what cheap motels are for. You can get them by the hour, you know."

Cody glanced quickly at Gena who was still fiddling with his bandage. "I don't want to know how he knows what happened."

"You sure?" asked Bill, amusement in his voice. "I got the play-by-play. You done good, kid. Real good. Banged her right. Would have been better in a cheap motel though, but whatever."

"I'm hanging up now," said Cody with a shake of his head.

"Okay, I should probably find Count Dick-u-la and slip his phone back in his pocket. He don't even know I got it," said Bill. "Special forces my ass. Bunch of punk-ass worthless…"

Cody had to stifle a laugh.

He hung up and put his phone back into his pocket.

"Everything okay?" asked Gena.

He grinned and kissed her lips quickly once more. "Mmm, yes."

He eased her off the sink and groaned at the feel of her body pressing to his. "Baby, we need to take a few steps back from each other."

A question formed on her brow.

He winked. "Or I'm going to be in you again."

"Oh," she said with a slight smile before glancing around the restroom and curling her lip. "Did it look this dirty and dingy the entire time?"

"Afraid so."

"Huh. I guess I was so worried about you and then caught up with touching your muscles that I didn't notice. Neat distraction trick you have there, Cody."

"Thanks. For the record, you can feel *any* part of me you want, any time you want to," he said, meaning every word of it.

She grinned more. "I swear I just heard a hint of an accent there."

"You did," he confessed. "I was born and raised in Australia."

Guilt gnawed at him. His mate should have known that detail about him before he up and claimed her.

"Cool. I love Australia," she said. "I spent a couple of months there as a child. My parents had a research project there. My favorite spot was Bondi Beach. I've been meaning to go back now that I'm grown."

Cody took her hands in his. "Say the word

and I'll take you there tonight. I'll get us a flight out. We'll be there before you know it."

She grew quiet.

"Gena?" he asked, disliking the way her shoulders seemed to tense at his suggestion of flying her to Australia.

She took a deep breath. "I understand why you might feel the need to make me empty promises, but they aren't necessary. I understood what this was when I decided to do it."

Baffled, he tilted his head, watching her closely. "I'm not following. What do you think this is and why do you think the promise is empty?"

She rolled her eyes. "You're a very attractive man. And you said it yourself, you're popular with the opposite sex. I don't really think you want to fly to another country with me five seconds after meeting me and screwing my brains out. But thank you for the effort to make it appear as if this was something more than it was. I had a lot of fun and I'm hoping we can go back to my place and have more fun, but I don't expect anything to come of it all."

It was Cody's turn to fall silent as he attempted to wrap his mind around the fact his mate just wanted him for sex. He opened his mouth to comment, but rapping on the door cut him off before he even had a chance to start.

"Are you both decent?" asked Wheeler, opening the door. He poked his head in. "Cody, I reached out to Landros."

Gena eased closer to Cody and he put his arm out, permitting her to use him to shield herself. Something he was learning she liked to do in social situations. That was fine by him. He liked holding her.

"Can we talk about this later?" asked Cody as the urge to get Gena somewhere private began to build.

You claimed her, pushed Wheeler down their mental path.

Yes.

Wheeler grinned and then licked it away quickly. *Does your wife know she's your wife?*

Cody ran a hand over the back of his neck as he held Gena with his free arm. *Not exactly.*

That would be a no then, returned Wheeler with a snort.

Asshole.

Hey, don't blame me for your lack of control, said Wheeler. *What now?*

I can't explain it, but I need to have alone time with her. For more than one reason.

Wheeler nodded. *Hope one of those reasons is so you can tell her she's your wife. You might have to back up and start with the whole bit about her being a mermaid.*

Gena's hand came to Cody's chest. "Um, this is really weird."

"What is, baby?" asked Cody.

She glanced between him and Wheeler. "The standing in a men's restroom, while two men just stare at each other, nodding and stuff without saying anything."

Just then, Clara pushed past Wheeler and came into the restroom. It was feeling smaller and smaller by the second. "You'll get used to it. Gena, how about you, Cody, and Wheeler come back to the house with me? It's so empty without Nicolette there and it will give us all a chance to talk."

"I was really hoping to take him home with me to procreate some more. It was so much more fun than I thought it would be," blurted Gena before cringing and turning into him. She buried her face against his chest.

Clara pursed her lips and then proceeded to laugh. Loud. And hard.

Wheeler joined in. "I like your wife, Cody! Good pick."

"Wife?" asked Gena and Clara in unison.

Cody tensed, his gaze whipping to his friend.

Wheeler glanced upward and pretended to be interested in the lights.

Clara pointed at Cody. "You better not have done what I think you did."

Wheeler reached out fast and pulled Clara back a second before she made a move to come at Cody.

Clara's nostrils flared. "You did! Cody, you claimed her?"

"Why does everyone keep calling it claiming?" asked Gena.

"No clue," said Cody quickly, earning him several laughs from Wheeler.

Clara stamped her foot like a child. "Don't ignore me."

Gena launched into action, looping her arm through her friend's. "Someone sounds hangry. Have you eaten tonight? You're always in a mood when you're hungry."

Clara grunted as she glared at Cody. "I came straight here after working late."

Wheeler licked his lips and then stepped

forward, touching Clara's shoulder. "How about you and me go get something to eat and let these two spend a little time together?"

Clara shook her head. "No. We need to explain everything to…"

Gena smiled. "I think that sounds perfect. Clara. Please?"

Clara sighed. "Fine."

"Thank you," said Gena.

Clara lifted her hand and pointed at her eyes and then Cody's. "I'm watching you. We're going to have a long talk very soon. In the meantime, you better be leap in front of a speeding train for her should the need arise. Am I clear?"

"Feisty," said Wheeler, earning him an elbow from Clara. He laughed more. "I like it rough. Come on. Let's get something in you."

She eyed him.

He put his hands up. "Food. Just food. But I'm open to more."

Chapter Nineteen

GENA WALKED hand in hand with Cody on the way to the marina, and she continued to steal peeks at him from the corner of her gaze. Her evening had been a whirlwind and she was half afraid to close her eyes for fear she'd wake up to find that this, like every other time, had only been a dream. That he wasn't real, and he was merely a figment of her imagination.

"How is your hand feeling?" she asked, wanting to fill the long stretch of silence that had been between them since they'd left the bar.

It had been touch and go at Stanley's when she'd announced to Rene and Bonnie that she was cutting the celebration short to head back to the boat. The dual shocked expressions the women had worn were downright comical.

Much to Gena's delight, Clara had come to her aid, assuring Bonnie and Rene that Cody was on the level and that she was totally and completely safe with him. Clara had then followed them out of the bar and threatened Cody's man parts should any harm come to Gena.

Since Gena had known Clara nearly all her life, she believed the threat wholeheartedly.

From the way Cody had paled slightly, so did he.

He lifted his bandaged hand and tipped closer to her as they walked. "Totally fine. I think you have a magic touch."

"Pfft. Hardly. I'm good with marine life. Not people," she said.

He faltered in his step, drawing her to a stop. "W-what?"

Unsure what had prompted the response, she simply stared at him. "I'm not following."

"Did you say you're good with marine life?" he asked.

She nodded.

"I never asked what it is you do for a living,"

said Cody, tugging her closer to him by way of their joined hands.

She didn't mind in the least. Once she was pressed to him, she inhaled deeply. "You smell really good. Kind of reminds me of the open ocean."

He chuckled.

"What's funny?"

He bent his head, putting them closer to eye level with one another. "I was just thinking how good you smell and how much you smell like the ocean. It's my favorite thing, you know."

"The ocean?" she questioned, unable to believe she found not only the man who was from her dream but that he loved the ocean as much as she did.

"Yes. So, going to tell me what it is you do for a living or do I need to guess?"

She bit at her lower lip again and touched his chest, disappointed he had a shirt on once more. "I'm a marine biologist. I specialize in sharks. They're something of a passion of mine."

For a few long moments, he didn't respond. Then he quirked a brow in disbelief. "Did you just say you're a biologist who specializes in sharks?"

She cringed. "Yes. Let me guess. You're scared

of them and think they should all be killed to make the oceans safer for people."

He looked to be fighting a laugh. "Uh, no. It's safe to say I do *not* think all sharks should be killed. I'm pretty big into protecting them."

"Really?" she asked, her eyes widening.

"Yep. It's been a passion of mine for a long time," he said, grinning.

"If you tell me you hate finning, I'm going to think you're my soul mate," she said in an off-the-cuff manner.

Cody took his hand from hers and then cupped her face, much like he'd done in the restroom when they'd had sex. His blue gaze bore into her as he stared down at her with an expression that screamed passion. "What if I told you that I know for a fact that we are soul mates? Would that freak you out?"

Any other time she'd have laughed off something like that, thinking it was nothing more than a joke. But this felt different. And strangely, it felt right. "Yes. No. Maybe."

"I was hoping for something a little more definitive," he said, his accent there but slight.

"The rational side of my brain, which admittedly checked out for most of the evening since I met you, is telling me you're nuts and telling me something most women would want to hear."

"I'm not," said Cody evenly.

She hesitated before biting her lip harder. "The other side of my brain believes what you're saying. Full disclosure: it's the side that let me jump you in the restroom."

He licked his lips. "Oh, *you* jumped *me*? Is that how it went?"

"Yes," she said, trying and failing to keep from laughing.

He kissed the edges of her mouth before grazing his lips over hers in a seductive manner.

She moaned.

He grinned.

She bit at his lip and it was his turn to moan. "Baby, careful or I'll be jumping you here and now."

The constant state of euphoria she seemed to be in since meeting him intensified. It wasn't something she was accustomed to, and his talk of being soul mates for real made her want to keep the subject far from that. "I told you what I do, but you didn't tell me what it is you do for a living."

"I tell you I'm about to jump you and you

want to know what my job is?" he asked, smirking more, clearly finding amusement in her line of thinking. "I should be offended but I think you're adorable. And to answer your questions, I'm something of a fixer."

"A fixer? Like a carpenter or handyman? I'm not very good at fixing anything that is non-boat related. I only know how to keep my boat afloat because if I don't, bad things will happen to her. And it wouldn't be very fun to be stuck in the middle of the ocean on a boat that needs to be repaired and no one around who can fix it."

He swallowed hard. "For now, let's go with yes. I'm something of a handyman."

"Anyone ever tell you that you're very attractive but very odd?"

"Yes. I get that a lot actually," he said with a wink. He then sucked her lower lip into his mouth. The act turned quickly into a kiss that left her falling against him, lifting a foot, feeling as if she were starring in a romantic movie.

One with a hero who was out of this world.

He eased back a touch and gave her a quick hug before taking her hand in his. "I'm going to be a good boy until we're back to your boat. Then I'm going to be very, very bad."

A laugh bubbled up from deep within her. She eyed the small alley off to their right. It was dark and under normal circumstances, she would have stayed far from it at night. But she was feeling wanton and wild.

Daring.

"Or," she said, tugging on his hand. She led him to the alley and went to her tiptoes, kissing him passionately.

He turned her and pressed her back to the wall of the building there before he began kissing his way down her collarbone. He bent and grinned before going to his knees in front of her.

Confused, she ran a hand through his hair. "Cody?"

The sexiest of grins splashed over his handsome face as he began to hike her dress slowly.

She'd wanted to kiss in the alley. This was taking being wild and free to a whole new level.

Strangely, the thought of being so naughty in public, even with the cover of darkness, only served to turn her on more.

Cody put his head under the bottom of her short dress and pressed his lips to her panty-covered mound.

She yelped.

He laughed against her pussy.

"Cody," she breathed out in a harsh whisper.

Ignoring her, he eased her panties to one side and put his mouth to her slit.

Gena nearly climbed the wall, stuck between wanting more of what he was doing and wanting to be away from it because of the overload of pleasure that slammed through her.

His tongue eased between the folds of her slit and she thought for sure she'd come right out of her skin. Her hands found his hair and she grabbed hold of it.

He chuckled against her pussy once more and the act left additional pleasure assailing her.

Gena tipped her head back and bit her lower lip as her hips took on a life of their own, grinding against his face. The moment he added his hand to the mix, and dipped a finger into her wet core, she was unable to stay quiet.

In the softest voice she could manage, considering the circumstances, she moaned and moved her hips more.

He swiped his tongue over her clit and desire pooled in her lower belly. Try as she might to remain semi-silent, she cried out as he added another finger to the mix. The moment he began moving his fingers in and out of her, simulating sex, she lost it and gripped his hair tighter, holding his head to her.

Looking down, she moved her dress bottom to see him there.

He stared up at her with a devilish gleam in his blue gaze.

Everything on her body seemed to explode with tingling energy. A loud moan came from her as she struck her zenith.

Cody stood, his mouth glistening with the proof of his skills and her pleasure. The sultry look he cast her left her pulse racing. With one hand, he undid the front of his jeans and freed himself.

He lifted her quickly and wasted no time entering her. He pushed in with one long, fluid motion that caused another orgasm to strike. She clung to him and rode out the pleasure as he began to ease in and out of her. He took his time, pumping almost lazily into her, his lips capturing hers in the process. She tasted herself on him.

He put his forehead to hers and kept fucking her, thrusting again and again, showing no signs of tiring or that she was too heavy for him. He locked gazes with her and put his palms to the brick wall behind her.

It left her being impaled sweetly on his cock and she loved every single second of it.

"You feel so good," he said, his breaths coming in pants.

Nodding, she kissed at his jawline. "You too."

He grinned and then stopped moving, holding himself firmly to her, his cock filling her completely.

She tried to speak but he put a hand to her lips, silencing her as he tipped his head.

He was quiet a second before he began to move once more. "Sorry, baby. Thought I heard footsteps."

At that exact second in time, she didn't care who happened upon them. He felt too good to stop.

Cody's mouth closed over hers once more as he resumed his pace. He plunged deep into her over and over, leaving her crying out into his mouth. He ate away her audible sounds of pleasure and continued fucking her.

Liquid heat filled her core right before she closed her eyes and tensed on his cock, hitting culmination. Her pussy fluttered around his cock, clenching down on it more with each pulse of pleasure.

He slammed his hands to the brick wall and drilled into her so hard and so fast she feared she might actually break. Somehow, she didn't. But she did come again. This time he joined her, slamming into her and erupting. He began to move slowly once more, continuing to empty himself in her.

He gave a drugging kiss to her before withdrawing from her body.

Instantly, she wanted him back.

He put his mouth to her ear. "I plan to spend weeks in you. No, years. To hell with it, centuries."

Laughing, she wrapped her arms around his neck and then wrinkled her nose at the feel of him leaking out of her. "I'm sticky."

"I could clean that," he said, setting her down and making a move to go to his knees again.

She giggled and touched his cheek. "Mmm, let's get a move on it. We can do all kinds of things I've always been curious about when we get to the boat."

He lifted one brow. "You're saying I'm your research dummy?"

"Yes," she said with a laugh.

"I'm so fine with that," he said, grinning more before tucking himself into his jeans once more.

Gena righted herself and wiggled a bit as cream flooded her panties. It wasn't exactly comfortable, but they weren't far from her boat. She could get out of the panties then.

He gave her a quick kiss before taking her hand in his again. He led her from the alley and to the sidewalk once more.

The street was empty, and she was relieved. Thankful they'd not put on a show for anyone.

They began to walk in the direction of the marina once more. She couldn't believe how late it was or that she didn't feel the least bit tired. She felt invigorated. On a high she might never come down from. And horny. Did her body not get that she'd already had sex? That it should rest? All it seemed to want to do was jump the man's bones again.

Gena understood the how's and why's of the feeling. That it stemmed from a biological reaction in her body and that it would, at some point, wear off. But in the meantime, she intended to enjoy it to its fullest.

Bonnie had been right when she'd pointed out

how much Gena had only been living to work, not working to live. One evening with Cody had turned her perspective on it all upside down, and she didn't want to "right" it anytime soon.

Live in the moment.

"Great motto," said Cody, his hand wrapped around hers.

Unsure what he was talking about, Gena frowned in puzzlement. "What is a great motto?"

"Living in the moment," he replied.

Stiffening, she came to a complete standstill and pried her hand from his. "What made you say that?"

He appeared confused. "You said it first. I was just agreeing with you."

Her mind raced as she thought over what had and had not come out of her mouth in the last few minutes. Certain she'd not said the words out loud, a trickle of fear creep up her spine.

Cody did a blatant sniffing of the air. "I made you nervous. I'm sorry. I didn't mean to. Honestly, I don't know what I did to cause it. Whatever it is, tell me so I can fix it."

Had she been wrong? Had she said the words out loud?

It wasn't possible to read another person's

thoughts. Sure, there were people who were attuned to others' body language and took cues from micro-expressions, but flat out mind reading? No. That wasn't a thing.

Yet her gut said he'd done just that.

Ever the scientist, she found herself wanting to test her theory.

Can you hear what I'm thinking?

Cody's eyes widened for a split second before he schooled his expression. His face was suddenly an even façade. "Are you going to tell me why you're scared of me?"

Despite all her knowledge, and all her training, every ounce of her said he very much had read her mind. Not once, but twice.

She stared harder at him, wondering if she was right or not.

Shit. Shit. Shit. How in the hell do I explain this to her?

Gena managed to avoid an outright scream of shock at the sound of Cody's voice in her head. Instead, she managed to hold it together and just stand there, staring at him more, as if she were having a contest for dominance over an animal in the wild.

That or a seagull. She'd recently read an

article that said if one stared into the eyes of the bird, it would make them back down and go away.

Picture him like a seagull. You got this. Just a bird wanting to steal a fry. Just a bird.

She hoped the rationale would calm her some.

Cody huffed. "I'm a lot of things. A seagull isn't one of them."

She pointed at him and leapt back, shaking her head as she did. "Get out! No way! You…no freaking way. Stop. Hold on. How? Do it again."

He blinked several times before lifting his hands very slowly, as if to keep from making any sudden movements and spooking her. "Which do you want, baby? Me to do it again or to stop? In the interest of no longer lying to you, it should be noted I can't control it right now. It's too new and I'm not sure it's something that can be shut off between a mated pair."

She narrowed her gaze on him.

Gena, baby, I would never ever hurt you.

There was no denying what she'd just heard in her head. Launching into hysterics was an option, but she was too much of a scientist to pass on the moment to learn something new. Instead of backing away from him more, she went at him fast, grabbing his hands in hers. "How can this be? Do it again."

His lips twitched a second before he started to laugh. "I was worried you'd take off running from me and never stop. This is an interesting twist."

Gena released his hands and grabbed his face, pulling downward, making him bend his head as she went to work inspecting him.

He laughed more. "What are you looking for?"

"I don't know," she said, her mind spinning with all the possibilities. Another thought occurred to her. He'd referred to them as being a mated pair. "What does mated mean to you, in the context of us, in relation to what is happening?"

He licked his lower lip. "My woman is super smart and that is wicked hot."

She snapped her fingers in front of his face. "Focus. How is this happening and what do you mean by mated pair?"

He chuckled and kissed her fingers quickly before taking her hands in his and drawing her closer. "Baby, this is what I wanted to talk to you about. In private. It's a conversation best had when we're totally alone. Not standing out here where anyone can see and hear us."

He was right.

"Okay, but if I take you back to my boat and you turn out to be some mind-reading murderer, I'm going to be really mad. And really disappointed I handed you my virginity," she said, a teasing note to her voice.

He grinned and kissed her forehead. "Understood. I have a *lot* I need to tell you. Some of it you may want Clara and Nicolette there for. They might make you feel more at ease near me. I don't want you scared of me. In fact, that is the last thing I want."

"This is something they know about?" she asked.

He nodded. "Nicolette is mated to my friend Garth."

Still attempting to process everything coming at her, she focused on him in an intense manner. "And that means?"

He sighed. "For all intents and purposes, they're married, baby. In the eyes of our kind, they are husband and wife. The bond is unbreakable and for life. No divorce. No out clause. Just forever together."

"Okay," she said as her mind raced. "They're mated and you're saying it's for life. Husband and wife deal. But you said we're mated. That would imply you and I are married in the eyes of… wait…what kind? Who, or what, are we talking about here, Cody?"

For the longest time he said nothing, and she feared that was the end of his open line of communication. He took a deep breath. "It wasn't an implication. It was a fact. When I bit you, after saying 'mine' and while coming in you, I claimed you. You claimed me back. I don't know why it is you didn't need to bite me, but every type of supernatural is different, and your mix of DNA obviously didn't require that step to make the claiming official. And before you ask how I know it was legit, I felt the threads of the bonding weaving between us in that restroom. And the fact we can read each other's thoughts is proof positive it worked."

Her entire body numbed at his words. "I'm sorry, but did you just say supernatural?"

"I did."

"I'm torn between freaking out in a bad way and freaking out in a scientific way," she confessed.

"I vote for option two," he said before tensing and pulling her close to him. It wasn't in a way that left him holding her so much as in a way that was protective. When he outright moved her behind him, she felt it then—his fierce need to keep her safe.

"Cody?"

"Come out," he said toward a darkened corner of the street. "I smell you there. And I know it was you I heard a little bit ago."

Much to Gena's amazement, Ernest stepped out and into the glow of the streetlight.

"Ernest?" she asked, surprised to see him before she wondered how long he'd been there, following them. Had he seen them having sex?

Cody glanced back at her. "You know him?"

"Kind of," she admitted. "He works for Helmuth."

Cody whipped around to face Ernest, bent slightly, put his arms out to each side and snarled. Nothing about the noise sounded human.

Her gaze slid down the length of his arms and she watched with nothing short of wonder as his bandage seemed to tear away on its own. It was then she realized his hand had gotten bigger and long, sharp, dagger-like claws had emerged from his fingertips.

"Your hand isn't hurt anymore," she said, her voice barely there. She knew what she sounded like and that it was from shock. But that didn't make the events process any faster for her.

"Come near her and I'll tear your fucking head off," growled Cody.

Ernest lifted his hands. "Helmuth doesn't know I'm here. I came to warn her and you."

"Keep talking," snapped Cody.

Ernest was sweating profusely, and Gena didn't think it was from the heat. "The second Helmuth got off the phone with Dr. Fowler and found out Gena canceled their lunch date for tomorrow, he lost it. He's moving up his plan. He's going to make a play for her tonight. She's not safe. Neither are you."

"Lunch date for tomorrow?" asked Cody, this time rounding on her. Horror-filled eyes greeted her. "You're fucking dating him? What is this? Are you bait? Is that it? Did he send you to retrieve me? Did he figure out who you are to me and then, what, you two sat around having a good laugh at my expense? Make me see you, instantly fall in love with you, and then watch you turn on me?"

Gena gasped as his eyes began to glow slightly with a vibrant blue in place of his normal already striking blue color. "C-Cody?"

He took a step in her direction and she backed up fast, fear slamming through her as she took it all in. His eyes. His hands. His healed hand. His mind-reading. His comment on being supernatural.

Tears welled in her eyes as fear caused her heart to feel as though it was going to thump clean out of her chest.

"Livingston!" shouted Ernest, sounding much closer than he had been. "Stop. She has no idea who he really is. To her he's simply the man funding the research center she works for. She is not part of the nefarious actions of The Corporation. Neither are her friends. They're simply pawns Helmuth used to get to her, and in turn, to get to you. He wants you for all the reasons you already know. But he wants her for far, far worse. He thinks she's a mermaid. That he can manipulate her DNA to make her mate material for him. He doesn't care how willing she is."

Gena backed up more from Cody, fear still

coursing through her veins. She barely registered what Ernest was saying.

Cody's brows met. "You didn't know?"

"No," said Ernest, even closer than before. "She didn't. Look at her. She's terrified of you, Livingston. This is all new to her. I've heard Helmuth planning this all. I know she's unaware of it all. When I met her today, there was an innocence to her. One I knew I couldn't let be destroyed by the likes of that madman. I've been forced to stand by and watch him and his despicable acts for far too long. I may not be able to stand against him in a fight. But I can warn you both. Go far from here. Quickly. Savannah is not safe for either of you. Especially her."

"Now, Ernest. I thought I knew you better than that," said Helmuth, strolling out from the darkness as well. "Rushing off to tattle on me? Really? How completely cowardly of you."

Cody's eyes widened and she felt his fear as if it were her own. But his fear wasn't for himself. It was for her.

Run, baby!

She nearly did as he said but stopped. Whatever was going on, she understood enough to know Cody was the good guy and Helmuth wasn't. He'd given her bad vibes from the start.

One moment Helmuth was thirty or so feet away and the next he was to Ernest who was only several feet from them. Gena watched in disbelief as Helmuth punched his hand through Ernest's back. It came out the other side of the man and in it was Ernest's heart. It gave three more beats before it stopped completely.

She wanted to scream. But no sound came from her.

It was as if her mind and her mouth had a distinct disconnect.

Cody snarled and went at Helmuth.

Gena stood paralyzed with fear and shock as Helmuth kicked Ernest's dead body from his arm and tossed the heart. He then leapt up and slammed into Cody head-on, the force of which made the ground around them shake.

Strong arms wrapped around her, encasing her fully from behind. Whoever grabbed her lifted her high off the ground. The shock wore off fast and she acted on pure and completely instinct as she lifted a foot and brought it back fast, her heel connecting with a very masculine groin.

The person holding her dropped her at once.

Gena fell to one knee and ignored the bite of pain, pushing up and twisting to see who had grabbed her. She found Kahale there, nursing his groin.

"Bitch," he spat before lunging at her. He struck her with so much force that everything around her went dark a second before she saw nearly twenty men swarming Cody.

Chapter Twenty

WHEELER WALKED down the center of the one-way street, whistling as he did. He had his guitar case in one hand, having just played a bit near one of the many park areas. It was sort of his thing. No one paid any mind to the street performer. Some would toss money into his open guitar case when he played, and Wheeler always gave whatever tips he was given to the homeless folks he'd come to know and care about.

His reasons for performing on street corners in downtown Savannah had nothing to do with earning money. His job, which was questionable ethically, left him taking big risks but for even bigger payouts. He didn't have to take many jobs and in truth he probably could retire, but it kept him busy. Plus, it kept his skills honed.

Still, a gun for hire wasn't something one could put on a resume.

Then again neither was the fact he was something close to a vampire after failed government experiments or that he was immortal. Needless to say, playing it straight with a legitimate profession wasn't in the cards for him and never would be.

The last year or so had seen some positive changes happening in his life.

For one, he wasn't having to look over his shoulder nonstop to see if his own government had managed to find him to finish what they started—ending him. For another, he'd started to reconnect with men he'd known from his Immortal Ops days.

There had been some PSI operatives he'd always remained close to even after the attempted wipeout of the Outcasts. Those were few and far between.

Kaiko had been one, and losing him had been a hard blow to both him and Cody. But they'd managed. They always did.

And he'd had a large number of Outcasts over the years whom he kept in contact with.

None as much as Cody though. The guilt Wheeler held over not looking for Cody after Cost Rica was something he'd never be rid of. Not that he wanted to be. It was important he never make the same mistake again.

The lapse in judgment had cost him Kaiko and nearly cost him Cody as well.

Letting history repeat itself again wasn't an option.

Yet, a sinking feeling had settled over him just before dawn's light. He'd gotten the sense that Cody was in danger. That history, in fact, was going to repeat itself, but he didn't know how or when. All he did know was that the feeling had been strong enough to leave him shaken for the entirety of the day.

Had he not known Cody was out on a boat with Gena, having the time of his life, Wheeler would have sounded the panic alarm and called in every guy he knew. But his friend was technically on his honeymoon.

No alarm needed.

Wheeler kept walking and paused in his step as he glanced across the street. There was a tall, skinny man with brown hair, dressed in full snorkel gear (including flippers on his feet) and a pair of blow-up children's arm floaties. The man was staring out from a face mask, his eyes bulging, while his lips were wrapped around the mouthpiece of the air tube.

Oddly enough, very few people were giving him or the guy next to him a second look.

Which was saying something since the guy next to Snorkel-Guy was in a pair of shorter-than-short swim trunks with the American flag on them —kind of, since a lot of the flag was covered by the man's stomach as it hung over the short top. With the trunks he had on black socks and water shoes. The shirt he wore was one he'd seen before on another operative. However it actually fit that operative. Unlike the way it was pulling hard at the small, older man's stomach, riding up some.

"I don't see no dead wheel," said the short man to Snorkel-Guy. "You sure you got the right spot?"

Snorkel-Guy flapped his arms in the air in a dramatic fashion while he turned to face a brick retaining wall.

Flag-Dude grunted loudly. "I hate it when you get in one of your moods. I swear. Pre-menstrual syndrome ain't got nothing on you, Gus."

Gus?

No.

They couldn't possibly be the two humans Cody had told him of. The ones who were supposed to be with the PSI-Ops.

Wheeler watched the men closely.

As two women walked by, they smiled at the men and Snorkel-Guy practically leapt in the other direction as if he was allergic to hot chicks. Flag-Dude puffed out his stomach of all things, patted it, and lifted one of his bushy brows.

"Why hello, ladies. Can I interest you in a ride on Bill's Love Train? It departs every two hours," he said, holding up three fingers. "Even sooner when I take one of them little blue pill things."

The women laughed and stepped closer to him as if they were actually interested.

Wheeler was so stunned by the fact the women were suddenly very into the guy that he nearly missed what the man had said.

Bill's Love Train?

"Shit," said Wheeler softly.

Bill and Gus were most certainly the names of the humans who belonged to Casey and if they were wandering around unattended, something was up.

Snorkel-Guy took off doing something that

looked slightly like a run, but with the flippers on it was anything but fast or practical. Mostly it was a lot of fast high-stepping.

"Gus, get back here!" shouted the small man.

Groaning, Wheeler took off across the street in the direction of Gus. He was nearly to him when he found himself being tackled from the side by Flag-Dude of all people. The man was small and clearly out of shape, but that didn't stop him from knocking Wheeler off balance enough to send him tumbling to the ground.

Flag-Dude fell on top of him with a harrumph.

"What the hell?" demanded Wheeler.

Flag-Dude, whose face was now planted squarely in Wheeler's lap, stared up at him with something that was supposed to look like a threatening look. "Nobody touches Gus. Got it?"

Wheeler rolled his eyes. "Get off me."

"Och, Wheeler, I dinnae know you were into that kind of sex play," said a voice with a thick Scottish accent.

Looking up, Wheeler found two men standing there, side by side, grinning from ear to ear. The matching pair began to laugh before the one on the left noticed the hot chicks.

"What do we have here? Yer bonnie lasses, are you nae?" asked Car of the women.

The women didn't appear very interested in the shifter-male. They did seem very concerned for Flag-Dude.

They rushed past the twins and bent near Flag-Dude.

One touched his back. "Are you okay? I can't believe he attacked you like that."

"Wait. What?" asked Wheeler, still flat on his back with Flag-Dude's head near his crotch. "He tackled me!"

"You're half his age," snapped the other woman. "Have you no shame?"

The twins rolled their eyes and came in for the assist.

Mac bent and it was then Wheeler realized the man was holding a football helmet in one hand that had a head in it. "Ladies, if you do nae mind, we'll take it from here. He's with us."

The women didn't look so sure, but they did finally back away before leaving.

Mac and Car hoisted Flag-Dude off Wheeler.

"Bill, we told you to wait in the car," said Car. "I know you heard us. You do nae listen for shit."

Mac nodded. "Agreed. I want to know how

yer here. I do nae think Armand would let you roam freely."

Car glanced at his brother. "Want to bet Armand is either tied up or unconscious because of something Bill did?"

Wheeler pushed to his feet, his attention going to Snorkel-Guy, who was still fast high-stepping in the other direction. "Should we get him?"

Mac whistled loudly. "Turn around, Gus, or the head gets it."

Just like that, Gus pivoted and came toward them, high-stepping the entire way.

"I'm sorry I wanted to meet them," said Wheeler partially under his breath.

Bill sized him up. "Gus says you're a dead wheel. Doesn't look like you roll worth a shit though. You got a pulse, or are you like Count Dick-u-la?"

Ignoring him, Wheeler focused on the twins. "Something tells me you're not down here to see the local nightlife."

Car nodded. "We're nae. Gus says Cody and the mermaid are in trouble."

Wheeler snorted. "He's mated now. So, if we're counting him having ball and chain trouble, sure. Other than that, they're fine. They're on

Gena's boat. Have been since last night. I'm guessing he's out cold from having a fuck-ton of sex."

The twins glanced at each other and then Wheeler.

A sinking feeling came over him. "He's not on the boat, is he?"

"Nae according to Gus," said Mac. "Helmuth has them and time is of the essence."

"Shit!" shouted Wheeler.

Chapter Twenty-One

CODY GLARED at Helmuth from within the containment tank as water pressed in around him. Bubbles temporarily masked his ability to see. Had he not been a shark-shifter, he had little doubt the saltwater would have burned his eyes. As it stood, it was just annoying.

But not as fucking annoying as being bound underwater as if he were Houdini.

Thick chains were secured to the back wall of the unit. The chains were hooked to shackles on his wrists, ankles, and to a collar around his neck.

His lungs burned with the need to take a breath as he remained there, chained, underwater in the tank. If he tried to shift forms into a shark, it would end poorly since his neck was bound as was the rest of him. But if he remained in human form much longer, he'd drown. Even as a shark-shifter, he had limitations when it came to being underwater. One of those was, he could hold his breath for a long time, but in the end, he did have to breathe air at the surface. That or shift forms fully.

He'd expelled a good deal of oxygen struggling when he'd first come to and found himself being lowered into the tank, so he was running on empty.

He hated the fact he'd been overpowered to start with. But Helmuth had brought too many men for Cody to take at once. His worry for his mate had also cost him precious reaction time. That, and he'd been sure he'd smelled a scent he shouldn't have.

Kaiko.

But that couldn't be. The man had been dead and gone for seventeen years.

None of that mattered now. All that mattered was Gena. Ernest had warned them. What Helmuth had planned for her was unthinkable, and there was no way in hell Cody was allowing it to happen.

Helmuth was standing on the other side of the

glass with a smug look on his face. Cody wanted to rip the expression off along with the man's face. That actually seemed too nice a punishment for what he wanted to do to the bastard.

When Helmuth winked, Cody thrashed more, the need to slaughter the male breathing new life into the wereshark.

All of Cody's movements and obvious fury only served to make Helmuth laugh more.

Hate was such a mild word to describe what Cody felt for the man.

Helmuth stepped to one side, and horror filled Cody as he saw Gena's limp form being carried in by a man he'd not seen in seventeen years.

A man he'd thought was dead and gone.

Kaiko Kahale.

The scent that Cody had been sure he's caught a second before he'd been overrun had really been the man's.

Where had he been all these years?

And why in the fuck was he helping Helmuth?

Cody yanked against the restraints, a rage the likes of which he'd never felt before growing in him.

Helmuth motioned for Kaiko to bring Gena's motionless form closer.

Kaiko did, and Cody went nuts, thrashing and expending more of his oxygen reserve.

Helmuth tipped his head back and laughed as he reached out and stroked Gena's cheek. When he bent and licked the same spot on Gena's cheek, Cody's brain fogged with a red haze, and he saw nothing more for a second as his inner beast surged upward in him.

Cody assumed that would be his end.

That the second the shark took the lead, forcing a full shift, it would be strangled from the collar.

As his body began to change shape, it did so at a rate of speed he'd never experienced before. The force of it snapped the collar and the shackles from his body, leaving them sinking to the bottom of the tank.

The shark didn't demand a full change, it actually permitted Cody to do a controlled semi-shift. It gifted him the ability to breathe underwater while still having arms and legs.

He charged the glass and struck it with a force that reverberated through the ship. A stress fracture appeared on the glass, and Helmuth's smug expression began to falter. Real worry touched the man's brow as he shouted something at Kaiko.

The man Cody had once thought of as a friend proceeded to carry Gena to a tank that was across the way, still in sight of Cody's holding container. Kaiko climbed a metal staircase with Gena in his arms and then tossed her limp form into the smaller tank, filled to the brim with water.

His next action sent a shiver of shock through Cody.

Kaiko pulled a heavy metal lid down and fastened it over, sealing Gena in with no space to catch her breath if she managed to somehow wake.

Helmuth laughed.

Cody moved to the back of his tank and set his sights on the fractured portion of the glass. He then went at it, like a torpedo. He didn't care if the action left him hurt or worse. All he cared about was getting to Gena.

As he made impact with the glass, it gave way and burst outward, sending Cody and the contents of the tank rushing forward. The force of the water pushing out caused Cody to veer off course, but it also swept Helmuth's feet out from under him.

Cody's hands shifted more, claws emerging as they did. Left between forms, Cody came up, breaking the surface of the water that filled the open area, leaving the water around two meters high.

Darting under the waterline once more, Cody spotted Helmuth scrambling to get to the shut exit door. At that moment Cody knew if he went after the man, he'd not only catch him, but he'd kill him, finally ending the man for good.

He'd spent years hell-bent on getting revenge and ending the bastard. Here was his chance. The perfect opportunity had presented itself.

But revenge was the furthest thing from Cody's mind.

Saving Gena was all he cared about.

He swam for the tank she was in.

A second before he was to the metal stairs that led to the top of the tank, something sliced through the water, striking him with the force of a freight train.

The impact sent Cody slamming into the metal floor.

He stared up at the partially shifted form of a man he'd thought of as a friend, and his brain shut off, striking Kaiko in the face. The two locked in battle, using the water to their advantage.

Cody slammed Kaiko's head into the floor, and the man twisted fast, snapping out with a mouth full of sharp teeth. He tore into Cody's upper arm, taking flesh as he did.

Blood filled the water around them, which was already murky from everything in the open area. Debris floated by, as did glass from the broken containment tank.

Cody rammed into Kaiko and forced them to the surface. They broke through the water, snarling as they did. The men traded blows, each giving as good as he got. During it all, Cody realized Kaiko and he were evenly matched, both having clearly been experimented on by Helmuth and his goons. Whatever they were, it was more than they'd gone into the testing as, that much was clear.

Movement out of the corner of his eye caught Cody's attention, pulling it from Kaiko momentarily as he looked over to see Gena coming to within her holding tank. She roused and then jerked, thrashing for a second before twisting in the water, her long dark hair going up and around her. In an instant, he was taken back mentally to when she'd been a child, and he'd saved her.

Her wide brown eyes held the same curiosity they had all those years ago before they widened.

Something struck Cody in the back of the head, knocking him under the waterline once more. He slammed his head back, cracking it hard against what he could only guess was Kaiko's head. Friend or not, he'd kill the man to get to Gena.

Protecting his mate was all that mattered.

Old friendships be damned.

He elbowed Kaiko in the ribs and spun in the water. He delivered a nasty strike with the pad of his hand to the man's chin, snapping Kaiko's head back. All that seemed to do was piss the other alpha male off more.

Kaiko swiped a clawed hand at Cody, just missing Cody's neck.

None of that mattered.

All Cody could think of was Gena and how much air she had left before she'd drown. Panic welled in him, making him slip up in his fight against Kaiko. The opening left Kaiko ramming his clawed hand through Cody's shoulder. The pain was immense, but he pushed through it, drawing on his strength and resolve to launch himself at Kaiko once more.

He struck the shifter and swam with him at a wall of piping. Cody didn't stop. He increased his speed and body-slammed Kaiko into a large pipe, making it burst. A rush of water came bursting free from it.

Cody drove his claws through Kaiko's lower side.

The man's eyes lit with fury as he lifted both hands above his head, just out of the water and brought them down on Cody's back.

The act knocked Cody under the line of water once more.

From the commotion of the fight, the newly broken pipe, and everything else, the water was murky and rushing in a way that left both men struggling to maintain their positions.

Cody looked back to see Gena pushing at the glass of the tank she was in, having no success getting free.

He wasn't sure how much time had passed. It felt like minutes, but that couldn't be. It had to only be seconds because she didn't look to be running out of air, and her concern seemed to be for him as she stared over at him.

Behind you!

Her voice filled his head, and he turned just in

time to see Helmuth, in partially shifted form, coming at him through the water. The man looked like a mix of a bat and a reptile. Talons that were far longer than Cody's came from Helmuth's fingertips.

The bastard nearly took Cody's head off. Had Gena not warned him, and he not spun when he did, Cody had little doubt that Helmuth would have been successful in beheading him.

Kaiko rushed Cody from below under the water and hit him in the side, tackling him and dragging him under all the way.

Giving in, Cody shifted more, allowing his head to nearly fully form into the shark. He pushed upward and zeroed in on Kaiko's long form. Opening his mouth, Cody took aim and breached the water. His massive jaws clamped down on Kaiko's torso, and Cody thrashed his head back and forth.

Kaiko's blood filled Cody's mouth, driving the shark onward, causing him to bite down more. He could have bitten all the way through, cutting the man in half, but something deep down stopped him. He knew the damage he'd done to Kaiko was significant, possibly life-threatening, and that he'd no longer be a threat. Killing him wasn't something Cody wanted to do if he didn't have to.

Every instinct in him said there was more to the story than Kaiko being a traitor. And if there wasn't, Kaiko would be alive to answer for what he'd done.

Cody released the shifter male and took human form quickly, thrusting Kaiko's bloody, broken body from him. He came up and over the top of the waterline, searching for signs of Helmuth but finding none.

There wasn't time to look more.

Gena needed him.

He swam fast in the direction of her holding tank, fully expecting to find that she'd drowned. What he found caused him to draw up short and stop going forward. She was there, in the tank, fully submerged, her eyes locked on him, her long hair all around her, appearing totally and completely fine and calm. She didn't seem to be struggling to breathe in the least.

It took him a few seconds to snap out of his state of stunned stupor. He made it to the stairs near her tank and climbed them, emerging from the water as he did. The handle to the lid of her tank had been broken off, and he knew that had been Helmuth's doing.

Bastard!

He dropped to his knees and tried to pry the lid open. It didn't give. Blind panic gripped him as he thought of his mate dying. Of how he was so close to saving her only to lose her in the last minute.

No!

An explosion rocked the ship and echoed so loudly through the space that Cody's sensitive hearing left him grabbing his head. He blinked and looked over to find the exit door was no more. In its spot was a giant hole. One that left a large amount of water rushing out of the room.

The most unexpected of people appeared in the opening.

Bill.

He was in a pair of swim trunks with an American flag on them, and he had a rocket launcher over one shoulder while he smoked a cigar with his free hand. He grinned. "Need a hand?"

The twins pushed through the opening next, running as quickly as they could through the rush of water that was flooding out of the area. The two alpha males looked to be struggling to stay upright from the current of it all, yet Bill stood perfectly still at the mouth of where the water was going, never wavering.

Cody twisted, let his hands shift forms, and then he drew one back and punched as hard as he could. His hand went right through the thick metal lid. He repeated the action with his other hand, and once it was through, he let out a roar as he tried to get the top off.

It gave some but not enough to come off.

Mac was the first man to him. He nodded to Cody and punched through the lid as well. "Fuck! That hurt, Aussie."

Cody yanked again as did Mac.

This time, the lid gave and snapped open.

Mac flung it aside and Cody dove into the tank full of water. He was to Gena in seconds. She was there, looking at him, appearing unharmed and fine.

He grabbed her and pulled her to the surface.

When they were up, he twisted her around and cupped her face. He kissed her as if he'd never get to kiss her again, pouring every ounce of love he felt for the woman into the act.

She clung to him, and when the kiss broke,

she lowered her head, and he held her to him in the water, his lips finding her forehead.

"I love you," he said, causing her to stiffen and Mac to suck in a large breath. "I should have told you that already. The second I knew who you were to me. I thought…I thought I was going to lose you and never get to say the words."

"Cody," she whispered.

He shook his head. "Don't say anything. Just let me hold you a second more."

"As touchin' as this is," offered Mac, his voice cutting through the moment. "Yer bleeding something fierce, Aussie."

"Fuck later!" yelled Bill from the exit. "We've got a gargoyle to kill."

Gena's eyes widened.

"Come on, babe," said Cody, easing Gena toward Mac, who was bent at the edge of the tank.

Mac extended his hand to Gena.

She glanced back at Cody.

He winked. "He's good people, babes. I trust him."

She put her hand in Mac's, and he lifted her out of the holding tank with ease. Mac set her behind him and then turned, lifting a hand out for Cody.

"I'm fine," said Cody, making a move to hoist himself out of the tank. Just then, his body decided to let him know how banged up he really was. Pain seemed to radiate from everywhere at once. He winced.

Mac grunted, bent more, and yanked Cody out without waiting for approval. Once they were standing, Mac gave him a good once-over. "Tell me the other guy looks worse."

As the words left the Scotsman's mouth, Kaiko's body floated by. He was still partially shifted, face down, limp, with a massive bite wound nearly cutting him in half. Seeing a man he'd thought of as a brother like that, knowing he was the reason for it, left Cody tearing up slightly.

"Gus says the whale ain't dead," said Bill from the doorway. "Grab him, and let's get this shit show moving. I'm hungry."

Kaiko wasn't dead?

Car was nearly to the stairs, and he reached out quickly, grabbing Kaiko and turning him over. As the man looked down, he stiffened. "That's… no. We thought he was dead. He was being held by these fucks all along?"

"No," said Cody, his jaw tightening. "He wasn't being held. He was fucking working with them."

Gena pressed in close to him, shivering slightly. "No. I don't think he was."

"I watched him carrying you and then I saw him toss you in that tank and seal it shut," said Cody, anger filling him. "He turned on his own people. His brothers."

"Cody," said Gena, running her hands over his chest. "Stop. I don't think he turned on you willingly."

"What are you saying?" asked Cody.

Bill burped loudly. "She's saying the whale got his mind fucked with. He don't know which way is up. Grab him and let's get a move on it. This ship gives me the willies."

Car lifted Kaiko and stared up at Cody and the others. His expression was grim. He was thinking the same thing Cody was. Kaiko probably wouldn't survive his wounds.

They were almost to Bill when his eyes widened and he stepped to the side fast. "Get down!"

Cody shielded Gena with his body as Mac bent. Car did his best to get down but since he was carrying Kaiko's limp body it was easier said than done.

There was a massive roaring noise and Helmuth, still in gargoyle form, came flying past them, but it didn't look to be his own doing.

"What the ever-loving fuck?" Mac came up fast, staring at Helmuth's shifted form. "That is the ugliest fucking thing I've ever seen, and I've been looking at Car all my life."

"Arsehole," grunted Car.

Helmuth came up with a deafening roar. Fangs flashed as he spread his batlike wings.

Gena clung to Cody. "I'm with the Scottish guy. That is ugly."

Cody lifted his mate, his gaze colliding with Mac. "Get her to safety!"

He then tossed Gena as gently as he could in Mac's direction.

The wolf-shifter caught her with ease and went for the exit.

Wheeler was suddenly there, filling the opening, in partially shifted form. It was something Cody had only seen a handful of times in his life. He didn't look like a normal vampire did. No. He looked every bit the hybrid the scientists had made him. And now that Cody had gotten a good view of Helmuth in gargoyle form, he saw the similarities in Wheeler.

He also saw pure hate burning in his friend's eyes.

Mac whistled. "Och, is it me or did the dead wheel throw the giant flying lizard?"

Wheeler paid Mac no mind as he defied gravity and flew above the water level right at Helmuth, who had only just gotten to his feet fully. The two collided and it rocked the ship.

Mac kept hold of Gena, protecting her.

"Cody!" shouted Armand from the exit. He was standing near Bill, who was picking something out of his teeth. "Are you hurt?"

"I'm fine," said Cody fast, nodding to Mac. "Get my mate to safety!"

Armand's gaze went to Kaiko and he raised a brow but didn't comment. Instead, he glanced at Bill. "Escort Mac and Cody's mate topside. Gus is there, waiting for all of you. The rest of the enemies on the ship have been dealt with."

Bill grinned. "Count Dick-u-la, you're more badass than I gave you credit for. Kind of. If we don't take into consideration the whole sparkling in the sun thing."

Armand groaned.

Bill kept smiling as he motioned for Mac to follow him. "Bring the mermaid. Should any of those commie bastards still be kicking, I'll light them the fuck up. Ain't nobody hurting the mermaid on my watch. They try and they'll be picking a rocket out of their ass."

Mac lifted Gena higher and she scaled him, nearly getting free. "Hey now, lass. Do nae go that way. The big ugly thing is that way."

"We can't leave Cody alone," she protested.

Cody's heart swelled. "I'll be fine, Gena. Go. Please. I can't worry about you and fight."

She didn't look happy about his plan, but she nodded and permitted Mac to escort her from the area. Car followed, carrying Kaiko out as well.

Once they were gone, Cody set his sights on Helmuth and Wheeler, who were locked in battle.

Armand moved up alongside Cody and put his hand on Cody's shoulder. "Wheeler will listen to you if you tell him to stop. Do it quickly, I can feel him losing control. If he succumbs fully to that side of himself, I'm not sure we'll get him back."

"Hey, asshole, save some of the big ugly for me," said Cody loudly.

Wheeler ignored him and kept fighting with Helmuth.

"Don't make me piss on you!" yelled Cody.

Wheeler's gaze whipped around and landed on Cody a second before Helmuth took a swing. The punch connected with the side of Wheeler's head and he went down hard.

Cody wasted no time. He surged forward, his sights locked firmly on Helmuth. For the longest time he'd thought he'd want revenge for what had been done to him. As he extended a hand, making sure his claws were out, and let his mouth do a partial shift, he knew deep down he wanted Helmuth dead now to protect his mate.

He jumped up and over Wheeler and came down, slashing out at Helmuth. As he did, Helmuth's skin turned partially to stone, deflecting the blow. Cody landed in the water crouched and came up, tossing his head back, sending water flinging in every direction. He twisted fast and glared at Helmuth.

The man was there, his upper body shifted back to something close to human form while his lower half was all gargoyle. He sneered. "You can't stop me. Others have tried. I always come back. You'll forever have to look over your shoulder, always wondering when I'll strike. When I'll come for her. And I will come for her. After all, this has been seventeen years in the making."

Cody snarled. "You won't fucking touch her."

Helmuth laughed. "Tell me something, Livingston. How does it feel knowing the little girl you saved, and were captured because of, is your mate? How does it feel knowing she's to blame for you being locked away as long as you were?"

The man's words sunk in and Cody gasped.

Gena was the little girl from Costa Rica?

No.

As he thought about her hair, her eyes, and the way he'd noted the similarities instantly upon first seeing Gena at the square, relief swept through him. The little girl had lived. She had grown into an adult. And she was now his wife.

He narrowed his gaze on Helmuth. "Fuck you and your mind games. She was just a kid then. She isn't why I was taken. You are, you sick asshat. And you mark my words. You won't be touching her."

Helmuth laughed wickedly again. "Oh, that is where you're wrong. You see, none of you can stop me. And you all know it. I'm too powerful. I will come for her and for the little brat she'd got taking root inside her now. I'll raise it as my own. It will call me Father. You'll be a distant memory in her and your child's mind."

Gena was pregnant already?

The very idea of Helmuth ever being near Gena again already left Cody unhinged. Thinking of the man near his child was too much. Cody let go and gave in to the blind rage that wanted to control his every move.

He seized hold of Helmuth and lifted the man out of the water with one hand before slashing out with the other. In one fluid motion, he took Helmuth's head clean off his body. He then tossed the headless body aside and stood there, staring at the bloody water, his breathing harsh, his body amped from adrenaline.

"Ohmygod, he beheaded…ohmygod!"

At the sound of Gena's voice, he cringed, afraid to turn around and see fear in her eyes. He shifted fully into human form once more.

"Did you see that?" she asked.

"Aye," said Mac. "Though I'm thinking he's wishing you dinnae."

"That was…holy crap, Cody. That was amazing!" she yelled.

"Ha. She's perfect for you," said Wheeler, sounding banged up but fine.

Slowly, Cody turned to face Gena.

She was there, just inside the doorway with Mac right behind her.

Mac shrugged. "She's a slippery thing."

Gena smiled as she teared up. "You're hurt."

"I'm fine," said Cody. He teared up as well. "I'm so sorry, baby."

She made a move to come for him and stopped as she looked down at the bloody water. "Uh, no offense, but there's a head and a body in there somewhere. I'll wait right here for you."

Armand laughed. "Wheeler is correct. She is perfect for you."

Cody hurried to her and once there she launched herself at him. He caught her and hugged her to him, burying his face in her hair. He squeezed her tight, inhaling her scent. It was then he noticed the slight change in it.

He tensed.

Helmuth had been telling the truth.

Gena was expecting. It was new but there.

She kissed his cheek. "I love you, and I forbid you from death matches with gargoyles again. Am I clear?"

"Crystal," he said with a laugh. He then licked his lower lip and eased her down slowly. "I love you too. But, Gena."

She stared up at him. "I heard what he said. And I can see the worry on your face. I'm fine. And we don't know that he was right. I might not be…"

"You are," said the men who were present.

She looked at him and smiled. "Then we should probably think about our living situation unless you're good with raising a baby on a boat or in a van."

He kissed her forehead. "Pick a house. Any house. It's yours. Just say the word. But first, I want you checked over thoroughly. I want to know you and the little one are okay."

"If we're with you, we're fine, but I'm so quitting my job. I work for assholes," she said with a wink.

Cody laughed. "One of the assholes is missing a head so there is room to climb the corporate ladder. Kidding. I do not want you anywhere near The Corporation."

She tensed. "Bonnie and Rene. They don't know…"

Armand smiled. "Your friends are safe and

with Clara and Ruby. They are filling your friends in on everything. It's important they know the truth about The Corporation."

"Ruby is back in town?" asked Cody, surprised to hear the Para-Reg was back so soon from her assignment in Virginia.

Gena stared at him. "You know Ruby?"

"Yes. Do you?" he asked.

Wheeler laughed. "She is or was Bonnie's significant other. From the way they hugged and then kissed when they saw each other, I would say things are back on for them. Is it wrong to admit seeing them making out turned me on?"

Cody groaned.

Armand laughed.

Wrapping an arm around his wife, Cody looked at his friends and then back at the room to see Helmuth's decapitated body floating in the back corner. "It's over?"

"Yes," said Armand. "It is. He'll never hurt anyone again. Now, what do you say we get you and your mate back to shore and then get all the captives on board set free?"

Cody exhaled slowly. "I say hell yes."

Chapter Twenty-Two

GENA STARED at the testing results on the screen before her, trying to wrap her mind around everything she'd been told. Had she not seen for herself, firsthand, that supernaturals were real, she'd have thought this was a cruel trick. But now that she knew the truth, that there was more out there in the world than met the eye, there was no turning back.

The genie wasn't going back in the bottle without a fight.

And her life would never be the same again.

Gargoyles were a thing, and one had tried to keep her and kill Cody. Not only that, she was apparently far more than human herself. Then there was the fact she was married in the eyes of the paranormal world. And the man she was married to could turn into a shark.

Yes.

It had certainly been an interesting couple of days.

The icing on the cake was that she was expecting. Try as she might to deny as much, pointing out how long it would normally take to figure out a woman was expecting, the men surrounding her had been adamant. She was pregnant.

They'd also been quick to point out they were anything but normal so why was she expecting pregnancy to follow the rules?

She'd spent the last few hours in an infirmary that looked like something out of a science fiction movie. It had equipment she'd never heard of before. Not to mention it was staffed by nothing but built hunks. They'd given her a good once-over, despite her protests and reassurances that she was fine. They weren't taking her word for it.

Not that she could exactly blame them.

Cody had basically lost his damn mind over her safety and his concern left them all scrambling to prove just how fine she was.

He'd spent the first hour hovering nonstop to

the point she wanted to throttle him herself. Wheeler had come and pulled Cody away, insisting they debrief the others. She strongly suspected that was code for giving her a break from her overprotective husband.

Which was very much welcome.

The infirmary had only just begun to calm since her arrival. It had been packed with people who had been freed from the ship. From what Gena had been able to overhear, a lot of them weren't in good shape at all.

Her hate of Helmuth only grew.

She was glad he was dead.

She glanced up from the test results on the handheld tablet and spotted one of the men from the infirmary there. She knew he was a doctor, but she couldn't recall his name.

His long dark hair hung to his mid-back and when he turned partially, his profile screamed male model. He'd been watching her quietly, giving her time to process everything before her.

"Overwhelmed?" he asked.

"And then some."

"Want some coffee or anything?" he questioned.

She nodded. "I would love something stronger

if you have it, but I know that isn't an option now."

He paused before pressing a smile to his face. "I make a mean cup of tea."

She smiled. "That sounds perfect."

He hurried away.

Wheeler entered and came right for her.

Gena stood quickly. "Oh no. Tell me he didn't really tear anyone's head off—again. I know he was threatening to do it to everyone if they didn't check me over all the way."

Wheeler laughed. "No. He got his fill of head tearing in for the night. But he is currently occupied so I thought I'd check in on you. How are you holding up?"

A tiny choked laugh came from her. She was so far out of her depth that all she could do was tear up.

Wheeler hugged her. "None of that now. He'll kick my ass eight ways from Sunday for making you cry."

Gena did her best to wipe away her tears. "What about the other man? Kahale?"

"Kaiko is still in surgery," said Wheeler, a grim expression coming over him. "From what I was able to gather, his outlook isn't as good. There is a pretty big chance he won't survive."

She lowered her head, filled with grief over a man she barely knew. "I'm sorry. I'm guessing he was your friend too. I heard the others mention he's one of you guys."

"*Was* one of us," said Wheeler, his jaw setting. "I don't know what he is now. Far as I can tell, he was willingly doing that madman's bidding."

"The little hairy guy says that isn't so," corrected Gena. "He said Kaiko had his mind tampered with. Is that possible? I mean, to have your mind bent to that extreme?"

Wheeler was quiet for a moment before nodding. "Yes. It's possible. Takes some doing though."

"Then you can hardly blame Kaiko for what he did and how he was," she said, her chest aching for both Kaiko and Cody. "It doesn't seem to me that he had as much choice in the matter as everyone wants to think he did."

Wheeler eased back slightly. "If you're right, it means I left two of my friends to be taken, tortured, and experimented on. That I failed not only Cody all those years ago, but Kaiko too."

"What do you mean?" she asked.

He closed his eyes. "When they went off the grid, I thought it was on purpose. They both like to do that—vanish for periods without telling anyone where they'll be. I assumed they were doing that. That they were off in shifted form swimming in the ocean or something. I didn't know they were being held captive."

"Don't make me kick your ass," said Cody, entering the room swiftly. "I already told you that you can't blame yourself. The one to blame is dead. End of story."

As Gena stared at Wheeler, she got the impression it was far from over for him.

THE END

NOTE TO READERS: Author recommends reading **Bound to Midnight** next for max reading enjoyment of the overall Immortal Ops Series World. Be sure to sign up for Mandy's newsletter at her website for details about **Bound to Midnight.**

Link to entire Ops World:

The Immortal Ops Series World Webpage

Sources

Roelcke, Volker. "Nazi Medicine and Research on Human Beings." *The Lancet*, vol. 364, 1 Dec. 2004, doi:https://doi.org/10.1016/S0140-6736(04)17619-8.

Black, Edwin. *War against the Weak: Eugenics and America's Campaign to Create a Master Race*. Dialog Press, 2012.

Boussarie, Germain, et al. "Environmental DNA Illuminates the Dark Diversity of Sharks." *Science Advances*, vol. 4, no. 5, 2018, doi:10.1126/sciadv.aap9661.

"Chapter XII – The Landing at Gaba Tepe." *The Australian War Memorial*, www.awm.gov.au/collection/C1416980.

Egeberg, Channing A., et al. "Not All Electric

Shark Deterrents Are Made Equal: Effects of a Commercial Electric Anklet Deterrent on White Shark Behaviour." *Plos One*, vol. 14, no. 3, 2019, doi:10.1371/journal.pone.0212851.

"Gallipoli Part III: ANZAC Landing on 25th April 1915." *British Battles*, www.britishbattles.com/first-world-war/the-gallipoli-campaign-part-iii-the-anzac-landing-on-25th-april-1915/.

"Great White Shark Genome Decoded." *ScienceDaily*, Nova Southeastern University, 18 Feb. 2019, www.sciencedaily.com/releases/2019/02/190218153238.htm.

Hobbs, Catherine A. D., et al. "Using DNA Barcoding to Investigate Patterns of Species Utilisation in UK Shark Products Reveals Threatened Species on Sale." *Nature News*, Nature Publishing Group, 31 Jan. 2019, www.nature.com/articles/s41598-018-38270-3.

Knighton, Andrew. "The Gallipoli Landings: A New Kind of War." *WAR HISTORY ONLINE*, 23 July 2017, www.warhistoryonline.com/world-war-i/gallipoli-landings-new-kind-war.html.

Koch, H W. *Aspects Of The Third Reich*. Macmillan Education Ltd, 1985.

Kuhl, Stefan. *Nazi Connection Eugenics, American*

Racism, and German National Socialism. Oxford University Press, USA, 2014.

Laboratory Animal: Welfare-Ethics and Practice. Kendall Hall Special Education Unit, 1987.

Leckie, Robert. *Delivered from Evil: the Saga of World War II*. HarperPerennial, 1988.

Leckie, Robert. *Helmet for My Pillow*. Bantam Books, 1979.

Lifton, Robert Jay. *Nazi Doctors*. 2000.

Lukes, Igor, and Erik Goldstein. *The Munich Crisis, 1938: Prelude to World War II*. Frank Cass, 1999.

McPherson, Charles. *Laboratory Animal Medicine: What It Is and How It Relates to Veterinary Medicine*. Animal Resources Branch, National Institutes of Health, 1974.

"NAZI MEDICAL EXPERIMENTS." *United States Holocaust Memorial Museum*, United States Holocaust Memorial Museum, 2019, encyclopedia.ushmm.org/content/en/article/nazi-medical-experiments.

"Nurnberg Military Tribunals: Indictments." *Nurnberg Indictments*, 1945, www.loc.gov/rr/frd/Military_Law/Nuremberg_Indictments.html.

Nuwer, Rachel. "Respect: Sharks Are Older

than Trees." *Smithsonian.com*, Smithsonian Institution, 27 June 2012, www.smithsonianmag.com/smart-news/respect-sharks-are-older-than-trees-3818/.

Posner, Gerald L., and John jt. au. Ware. *Mengele: the Complete Story*. McGraw-Hill Book Co., 1986.

Rothwell, Victor. *Origins of the Second World War*. Manchester University Press, 2001.

"Savannah State University Hiring Postdoctoral Fellow Marine Sciences in Savannah, GA, US." *LinkedIn*, www.linkedin.com/jobs/view/postdoctoral-fellow-marine-sciences-at-savannah-state-university-1228294945/.

Seaburn, Paul. "The Mysterious Shark Attack in Lake Michigan." *Mysterious Universe*, 23 June 2018, mysteriousuniverse.org/2018/06/the-mysterious-shark-attack-in-lake-michigan/.

Shah, Bina. *Animal Medicine*. Oxford University Press, 2001.

"Sharks! Global Biodiversity, Biology, and Conservation." *UQx CornellX*, 3 Apr. 2019, www.edx.org/course/sharks-global-biodiversity-biology-cornellx-uqx-bioee101x-1.

Thomas, Skyler, director. *Great White Lies*. *Great White Lies*, 2015, www.greenplanetfilms.org.

Winfrey, Michael R., et al. *Unraveling DNA: Molecular Biology for the Laboratory*. Pearson Education, 1997.

YourDictionary. "Homologous Structure Examples." *YourDictionary*, 27 June 2019, examples.yourdictionary.com/homologous-structure-examples.html.

About the Author

Dear Reader

Did you enjoy this title and want to know more about Mandy M. Roth, her pen names and all the titles she has available for purchase (over 100)?

About Mandy:

New York Times & *USA TODAY* Bestselling Author Mandy M. Roth loves 80s music and movies and wishes leg warmers would come back into fashion. She also thinks the movie The Breakfast Club should be mandatory viewing for...okay, everyone. When she's not dancing around her office to the sounds of the 80s or writing books, she can be found designing book covers for New York publishers, small presses, and indie authors.

Learn More:

To learn more about Mandy and her pen names, please visit www.MandyRoth.com

For latest news about Mandy's newest releases and sales subscribe to her newsletter: Sign Up For Mandy's Newsletter

Want to see all Mandy's books? Click here.

Printable PDF list of all Mandy's titles: Click here.

To join Mandy's Facebook Reader Group: The Roth Heads.

Review this title:

Please let others know if you enjoyed this title. Consider leaving an honest review on the vendor site in which you purchased this title. Reviews help to spread the word and boost overall sales. This means more books in the series you love.

Thank you!

- facebook.com/AuthorMandyRoth
- twitter.com/mandymroth
- instagram.com/mandymroth
- goodreads.com/mandymroth
- pinterest.com/mandymroth
- bookbub.com/authors/mandy-m-roth
- youtube.com/mandyroth
- amazon.com/author/mandyroth

Printed in Great Britain
by Amazon